"WARNING this book is ex[?] addictive and cannot be put [?] suggest you make sure you h[?] time on your hands."

"I love this book series, so much suspense and mystery!"

JENNA

"I liked this because it was full of action and it had a great twist at the end. It was awesome."

JAMES

"OMG, it was like my eyes were glued to the pages. This book is too good to be true. I recommend it!!!!!!!!"

ISIS

"Expect lots of page turning moments and surprises. A book I couldn't put down!"

CARLA

WELCOME TO THE SHAPESHIFTER UNIVERSE

- - -

A NOTE FROM THE AUTHOR

When Dax Jones first showed up in my head, skinny, dark-eyed and restless, I had no idea how much he was going to mean to me. As a journalist I interviewed a lot of celebrities. They were fun—but the best stories I ever got were not from celebs. They came from normal people whose lives had been suddenly changed in some unexpected way. They were the *real* deal.

So Dax showed up kind of ordinary. And yet not. His name is a clue. Half ordinary, half extraordinary. I wanted to write about supernatural stuff but not in a wifty-wafty way. I wanted to imagine it as I believe it really would be. So I played the 'what if' game. What if you changed shape one day? Just shifted into something else? In this world—here, today. *Right now* while you're reading this. Look around you. How would people react if you were suddenly holding this page open with the claws and snout of a fox?

Ready to find out? Just sit back and enjoy the ride . . .

For my boys

OXFORD
UNIVERSITY PRESS

Great Clarendon Street, Oxford OX2 6DP
Oxford University Press is a department of the University of Oxford.
It furthers the University's objective of excellence in research, scholarship,
and education by publishing worldwide. Oxford is a registered trade mark of
Oxford University Press in the UK and in certain other countries

British Library Cataloguing in Publication Data
Data available
ISBN: 978-0-19-274610-8

1 3 5 7 9 10 8 6 4 2
Printed in Great Britain
Paper used in the production of this book is a natural,
recyclable product made from wood grown in sustainable forests.
The manufacturing process conforms to the environmental
regulations of the country of origin.

THE SHAPESHIFTER

DOWSING THE DEAD

ALI SPARKES

OXFORD

UNIVERSITY PRESS

The full moon was the hardest time. He could see its light shafting through the gap in the grey box which was now his world and his heart would begin to pound harder and faster.

This time it was worse than ever. The light—the air—the scent of the cooling sky. He was desperate—*desperate*—so that his head buzzed and a voice he could hardly recognize as his own began to cry.

He flew up into the corner of his box and battered and clawed at the gap, trying to push his head outside it, frantic to draw the clean night air into his starved lungs. And then there was a tearing sound—a giving of the box. It *was* giving—and he might be able to get out! His heartbeat began to skitter around in a skirmish of hope against fear. The gap was widening. He was going to get out!

A feral scream of joy erupted from his throat.

And then it was cut quiet by the clench of one strong hand. He was seized and pulled back and folded down into the grey again.

The man's eyes were blue and cold.

'You can't go out,' said Owen Hind. 'Get over it.'

1

'Oi!!! Wake up!'

Dax shot up in bed with a grunt. 'What?! What?!'

Gideon scratched his messy fair hair and stared at his best friend. 'You were doing it again!'

'What?!'

'That screechy thing. I'm telling you, mate—it gives me the heebies!'

Dax felt his throat. It stung. He shuddered.

'I think you should go to Owen—you're still getting that dream, aren't you?' Gideon padded across the bedside mat and peered hard at Dax. 'You don't look good, mate. I mean—you know—you're a bit pasty and all that. Go to Owen—or Janey.'

Dax sighed and shook his head. He'd already been to Janey, the college doctor, but there was nothing she could do. For weeks now, he'd been getting worse; finding it hard to eat, to concentrate in class, to laugh at Gideon's daft jokes. He couldn't even get excited about the tree house they were building in the grounds of Fenton Lodge—and he had *always* wanted a tree house. He kept hoping that this strange weariness, which was weighing him down like a coat made of sandbags, would just go away. Every day he pushed food in and took the multivitamins that Janey gave him, but nothing made any difference.

He stared through the tall Georgian window of their bedroom to the beautiful Cumbrian valley which was now their home, and felt like crying. He got up. 'Sorry, mate,' he said to Gideon, who was still hovering and staring at him with concern. 'Maybe I should go into another room—one of the spare ones—for a while.'

'Don't be stupid,' said Gideon. 'It wouldn't be the same in here without all that rank fox fur on the window seat and the feathers dropping in my bedside water. Hey!' Gideon dropped onto his bed again, his green eyes wide with a sudden possibility. 'What if you're going to shift into something new? Eh? Maybe all this tired and wobbly stuff is because you're going to shift into . . . I dunno . . . a—a dragon or something? You could be doing a meta-metamorphic thing. You could be crystallizing! You know . . . in a crystal.'

'Metamor*phosing*? In a *chrysalis*?' Dax grinned, in spite of everything, and Gideon nodded eagerly.

'Yeah—about to transform into . . . ' Gideon's voice dropped deep and dramatic, ' . . . something from the PIT OF HELL . . . ' He raised one eyebrow and held out his palms, inviting Dax to join in with his mad suggestion.

Dax laughed but a wave of weariness stole over him as he went out of the room and down the softly lit corridor to the boys' bathroom. It was early and nobody else was up. He stared at his reflection in the mirror above the sinks. Gideon was right. The gloss was fading in his thick dark hair and his brown eyes seemed to be sinking back into his face. Lines of tiredness curved beneath them, shading grey into his skin. His lips were thin and pale. He ran the water hot and scrubbed his face hard with a flannel, pummelling some temporary colour into his cheeks. Almost as bad as how he felt was the constant querying from Gideon or Lisa or Mia. You'd think they would have got used to it by now. He looked awful and felt awful, and none of the tests the scientists had done so far could explain why.

The medical room which Janey ran upstairs looked much like a medical room in any boarding school or college. It wasn't. Although Janey was a qualified doctor and seemed to genuinely care for them all, she was also one of the scientists who lived with them at Fenton Lodge. The scientists were here to study ten extraordinary children with powers so phenomenal that the government chose to hide them in the loneliest range of Cumbrian hills it could find.

Gideon, for example, might look like an ordinary thirteen-year-old and most of the time he behaved like one too—but Gideon could lift a television three metres into the air now. With just his mind. He was a telekinetic. Next door was Barry, who could make himself invisible. Jennifer, down the girls' end of the dormitory wing, could do the same.

Dax's own power was to live his life as a boy part-time. He was also a part-time fox and a part-time peregrine falcon. This meant everything to him. It had released him from a sad, grey existence and brought him into one of the most exclusive gangs in the world. The Cola Club. It had nearly killed him—and it had brought him the time of his life.

'Maybe your time is up though,' he said to himself as he pulled the plug out and the water gurgled away. Through the steam across the mirror the boy gazing back looked like a ghost. Perhaps it was a premonition.

'Take your seats, *please*! And get ready for the geography lesson of a lifetime!'

Mrs Dann beamed at the class and one or two of them chuckled. After breakfast, the Children Of Limitless Ability (Colas) began their day with Mrs Dann in Geography. It didn't matter that they were the most amazing living beings on the planet—they still had to keep up with the national curriculum. Later they would go into Development sessions in the basement of the lodge, where it was considered safe to run their *other* classes.

Dax slid into the chair behind his desk and tried not to notice Mia glancing back at him as she did so often now, and sending him a wave of healing which felt lovely for about three seconds and then faded as fast as a retreating wave.

It was a sign of how worried the authorities were that Owen had even asked Mia to help. That went against *all* his rules. At fourteen, Mia was getting tall and her dark hair had grown to her shoulders since Dax had first met her. She had lovely, violet-blue eyes and a kind smile.

She was not breathtakingly beautiful, but she always took the breath away from anyone who first met her. This was because of the Mia Effect. That's what all the Colas called it. Mia's power to heal was so incredibly strong that just being in her company could make you feel fantastic. Everyone—male, female, young or old—fell for Mia. The feeling, until you were exposed to it for long enough to get used to it, was quite unsettling.

She came over to him now, while Mrs Dann was clearing the whiteboard and writing out some headings about the Netherlands. She rested her hands on his desk and said: 'Dax—did you manage to get any sleep last night?' Her words buffeted against him, warm and caring, but he wished she wouldn't. He couldn't give her the answer she wanted. He didn't meet her eyes, but rubbed his hair and coughed.

'Come on, Mia—back to your seat,' said Mrs Dann, chucking her whiteboard marker pen from hand to hand. 'I'm going to dazzle you all with the history of Holland's sea defences! Maybe even keep Mr Jones awake!' She gave a wry, but sympathetic grin.

It was in February that Dax had started finding it hard to sleep. At first he drifted off with everyone else, around 9.30 p.m., but he began to wake up very early. It didn't trouble him to begin with; he thought his nocturnal instincts as a fox probably had something to do with it. Then his 5 a.m. wake-up became 4 a.m., and then 3 a.m., 2 a.m. . . . eventually he was falling into bed, shattered, at 8.30 p.m., while the other Colas relaxed and chatted and played games in the common room—only to wake at midnight.

By day he grew vague and unable to concentrate in class—his class test results were appalling in March and that was when they started doing blood tests and checking his eyes, and trying out tonics and iron pills and vitamins on him. They remained cheerful and upbeat in the medical room, but Dax could still smell the anxiety on Janey and Owen and their principal, Paulina Sartre. Despite his exhaustion, his fox senses remained as sharp as ever.

Today Dax wondered if it was possible to feel any worse and still be walking about looking almost normal. At his desk, as he got out his books, he felt as though he had shrunk away inside himself. As if he was a tiny, tiny creature, trying to operate a huge, cumbersome body with levers and wires from within a cramped, dark control room somewhere inside his head.

He was dimly aware of Clive standing up and turning to stare at him—asking him something. His mouth said something back, but Dax, working the wires and levers in the cramped dark control room in his head, had no idea what. Clive was his good friend from the world of non-Colas. Although he was quite definitely a genius in science and engineering, Clive had no supernatural powers. He was here at Fenton Lodge with them because he had shared in some of their adventures and the government was happier to have him on the inside, rather than wandering around in public. He was also a useful boy to have around. A good comparison.

And it was Clive who stood it no longer. He dropped his Geography textbook with a thud and announced, 'All right! Enough's enough. You're killing him!' Mrs Dann turned round from the whiteboard in surprise.

'What *do* you mean, Clive?'

'Look at him!' said Clive, pushing his spectacles up his nose and then folding his arms across his chest (which always signalled that he meant business). 'He looks like a bowl of cold porridge—his eyes are always going funny and now he can't even speak properly! You've got to let him out! If you don't, I'm going to have to make an official complaint.'

The rest of the class stared at him, mouths open. Clive bumbled about, planning clever projects and frequently talking to himself. He was the school boffin in all the ways you would expect of a child genius—he even had the glasses, the bad hair, and the awful fashion sense to go with it. He was allowed almost free reign in the lab and the school workshops—but he was not given to ordering teachers around. Now he leaned on his desk and peered across at his classmate. 'Talk again, Dax! Let them listen properly.'

Dax gaped at his old friend, and then squinted at him. He was back out of the little wires and levers room now, but his right side was weak and achey and his throat was dry. His tongue felt thick and too big for his mouth. He had only slept two hours in the last twenty-four.

'Say *"The quick brown fox jumps over the lazy dog!"*—in your own time,' prompted Clive.

Dax furrowed his brow and gave up after 'The quick'—which came out 'Fwe—kweh . . .'

'All right—how about *"Mary had a little lamb; its fleece as white as snow"*,' insisted Clive, his voice shrill with anxiety. Dax sighed heavily and now Mrs Dann sat down in a chair near his desk and nodded at him.

'Go on, Dax,' she said. She looked grave.

Dax rolled his pencil along with a shaky hand and said, 'Maaee ha . . . a lil la . . . herflee awaya sneh.' The sound of his voice terrified him. The weight of his right arm was tremendous.

'Oh my God,' said Mrs Dann, and it was the intense quietness of her voice that scared him more than her words. 'I think he's having a stroke.'

2

Dax put his head down on the desk and the classroom grew tall and dark, like a chimney. He lay with his head in the fireplace and above him, Owen, Paulina Sartre, and Janey called down in hollow, echoey voices. Owen grew very, very long arms and reached down the chimney (or maybe it was a well, because Dax felt very wet—drenched in fact) and pulled him up through it. 'God alive,' he heard Owen say. 'God alive, Dax. Stay with us . . . stay with us.'

In the medical wing, Dax drifted in and out of consciousness. When he opened his eyes, there was always someone looking at him—Janey, checking his pulse, her shiny dark hair folding around her concerned face; Owen, weather-beaten skin creased with concern; or Paulina Sartre, her soft features strained and her warm grey eyes moist with tears behind her gold-rimmed glasses. 'We will sort you out, Dax Jones,' she said, her French accent thickening with her worry. 'You will be fine again, *chéri* . . . '

'It could be some kind of post-traumatic reaction,' said Janey, behind the principal. Their voices all sounded strange—as if he were listening to them under water. 'After all, in the last year he has seen two of his classmates swept away by a tidal wave and his best friend almost skewered on a giant metal kebab; nearly been electrocuted or shot himself—oh, and let's not forget the bit where he was seconds away from being ripped to pieces by foxhounds. I mean—that would certainly make *me* go into shutdown!'

'No,' said a male voice, through the sea in his ears, and Dax realized Owen was back in the medical room too.

'No—it's not that. Dax is incredibly resilient. I've seen it. Something else is going on here.'

'Could it be—maybe—the same entity that was hunting Gideon last year?' tried Janey.

'Impossible,' said Paulina Sartre. 'This place is *safe*. There is black tourmaline lining every wall and ceiling. No psychic attack could get through that.'

'But *outside* . . . ?' persisted Janey. 'You can't line the entire valley. Maybe it's trying again . . . '

'No,' said Owen. 'The Colas have only done Development indoors since they came here. Dax has not shifted outside for months. And even if one of them did let some talent slip out occasionally, there are no power lines or pylons or any electrical conductors to help bring in that—well—*whatever* it was. Remember, it only got to them last time by travelling the power grid. It couldn't reach us here.' He sighed and said again, 'It's something else.'

They did many more tests on him, he heard later. He was put through the MRI scanner for the third time since becoming a Cola, happily while he was completely unconscious. If he'd been awake the confines of the metal tube with its crashes and thuds might well have brought on a panic attack. He drifted and drifted for what seemed like weeks, but was in fact only two days, while all the test results came back and explained nothing. The world continued to be watery, echoey, and the only real thing in it was a boy, aged about eight, with pale blond hair and sad grey eyes, who wandered past his bed several times. He seemed to be wearing an old-fashioned white nightgown, and as he went by, he pointed to the wall over Dax's head and then nodded at him, frowning urgently and willing him to understand, but he didn't speak. Dax hadn't a clue who the boy was or what he wanted and he was too tired to ask Janey, whenever she came by his bed.

Suddenly Clive was at the foot of the bed with Owen and Gideon—and he was shouting. 'You've got to let him out! Don't you see? Watch his eyes! He needs to get out—shapeshifted and out.'

Gideon came to Dax's pillow, leaned over him and said, 'Look at me, mate.' Dax opened his eyes and Gideon's freckled face, tense with worry, swam into view. 'What do you need, eh?' asked Gideon. 'What is it you need to be well? Nobody knows.'

Dax felt a push in his chest, below his heart—like a small feathery thing trapped and beating to escape. He saw the gap in the box from his recurring dream and could smell the air curling through it. He blinked and Gideon nodded, as if suddenly understanding.

'You're right, Clive—he's just done his funny eye business—the alien thing. Why didn't we notice that before?'

Had he been doing the 'alien thing' without even realizing it? For nearly a year, since his powers had grown from shifting not just into a fox, but also into a falcon, he had sometimes done the 'alien thing' as his friends called it. When he *thought* of flying, but resisted the urge to shift, his eyes would flicker for a second into the yellow-rimmed shape of a peregrine falcon's eyes. It was scary to see. He looked like an alien when he did it (which had been quite useful in the past). Maybe he did the same odd thing when he resisted shifting to the fox too, but his own eyes were as dark as the fox's and it would not be so noticeable.

'Well, he hasn't been making much eye contact, so we might not have seen it—but I bet he's been doing it all the time!' said Clive. He sounded snippy and accusing as he turned to Owen. 'He's not just a boy! He's a fox and he's a bird. And he's wild. You can't shut up wild animals. They pine. They fade away. You've got to let him fly and hunt and . . . be wild.'

Dax felt the feathery thing in his ribcage beat faster. Owen reached to touch his forehead and Dax amazed himself by suddenly shooting his hand up and gripping the man's wrist. 'Yes,' he croaked. 'Yes.'

'It may not be safe,' said Owen, glancing across at the window, 'but it's got to be better than this.' He strode to the window and threw it open and Dax shot up in his bed, heart racing. Before he could even think about it, he had cleared the mattress, raced across the room, regardless of his weak legs, and thrown himself through the open window. He was airborne instantly, soaring high above the slate-tiled roof of the college and turning joyfully in the breeze. In seconds, though, his weakness assailed him and he had to glide back down, riding the warm rising air down to the ground. Another burst of energy from nowhere shifted him into DaxFox and he simply stood, brush bristling and snout to the wind, breathing in the scent of the earth and its wildness and feeling the planet's pulse under his paws. Then he turned three times in the grass, shuddered with relief, curled his tail to his snout and went to sleep.

When he woke up another twenty-four hours had passed. He was back in his bed, a boy, ravenously hungry and talking normally.

Nobody tried to stop him shapeshifting outside again.

3

'Oh, flippin' earoles!' gasped Gideon. Dax laughed out loud as his friend hopped up and down on the wooden platform, sucking the air in through his teeth and cradling his left thumb in his right palm. It wasn't that he was enjoying Gideon's pain—it was the weird curses the boy came out with.

'Ooof! Bleedin' *eeegies*!' Gideon squeaked, furthermore, as the hammer that had done the damage to his thumb slipped out of the crook of his elbow and dropped onto his toe.

'Do I take it, from that eloquent outburst, that you've injured yourself *again*, Gideon?' came a dry voice from below them. Two large tanned hands grasped the edge of the wooden platform, and the shaggy head of a man in his early thirties followed, blue eyes squinting up at Gideon in frustrated amusement. 'I like a wooden tree house to have a natural look—your bloodstains are messing it up,' said Owen.

Dax and Gideon glanced around the softwood platform that enclosed the thick trunk of the elderly oak, three metres above the peaty wood floor. It formed a roughly hexagonal shape as it embraced the girth of the great tree, resting across four broad boughs. It was stained in at least five places with little splodges of Gideon's blood. Every splodge represented another misfire with hammer and nail, or hacksaw or chisel. Gideon's hands were a patchwork of sticking plasters of varying age. Carpentry was not one of his gifts.

'It's not fair!' grumped Gideon, sitting down heavily on the platform, which creaked in protest. 'I keep trying to do it properly and keep my head out of it—and it just goes wrong! Let me do it the tele way, Owen! I get it right every time like that.'

Owen shook his head.

'Oh go on!' said Dax, sitting down next to Gideon and letting his legs dangle over the edge of the platform. 'Who's going to know? We could get this done much quicker if you let him—and there'd be a lot less bleeding. It's starting to look like a murder scene up here.'

Owen stepped up a rung on the ladder below, hoisted himself up and sat with them. 'Two reasons,' he said. 'One—making a tree house is a thing of reverence; of respect. You are creating a thing of beauty here.'

Gideon snorted and pointed to some of his handiwork. A cluster of misshapen nails pinned some planking to a branch like a mangled iron tarantula. When they'd refused to be driven in fully, he'd had to hammer them sideways so they flattened into the wood. Higher up the branch were some nasty puncture wounds from earlier efforts. Oak sap oozed around them in a woeful attempt to heal.

'It *is* a thing of beauty,' insisted Owen, smoothing

one hand along the plank which he had planed himself in the lodge's wood and metal workshop. 'It's something which shouldn't be rushed. I mean—yes—we *could* take shortcuts. I *could* get a carpenter in to work with me and have a tree house up for you this time tomorrow, but where would be the satisfaction in that?'

'*I'd* be well satisfied!' said Gideon. 'If I carry on like this I'll lose a finger! But not if I do it *this* way.' The hammer shot up two feet from the platform and before Owen could stop him, Gideon had sent it into a swift and accurate double act with a nail. The hammer hung in the air, positioned at a perfect swinging angle, while its partner stood, point down, like a tiny iron ballerina, over the corner of the plank. With three swift sharp taps, the nail was perfectly inlaid and the hammer reclined back on the wood with a discreet clunk. It was as elegant as it was supernatural.

Owen shot Gideon a *look*. 'The second reason you already know.' He glanced around him, beyond the budding green branches of the oak to the verdant pastures that surrounded them and up to the steep brown fells that encircled their basin valley. Fenton Lodge, a three-storey Georgian house, built of golden sandstone from the west of the county, stood gracefully beside a peaceful lake. A small river plunged into the lake from the north; calmed itself in currents deep below the surface, and wound away from it to the south. Sheep grazed near its banks. Insects hummed and a soft spring wind murmured in the small copse. The mildest of May Saturdays, heady with the scent of blossom—*nothing* about it spoke of threat or darkness.

'It's not going to happen again,' said Gideon, quietly. Owen looked back at him, raising an eyebrow. 'It's *not*!' said Gideon. 'You know it. Nothing bad has happened here—nothing has happened since last autumn. And we know that Dax's illness was nothing to do with—with *that*. We're safe here.'

'Inside the house, maybe,' said Owen and there was warning in his voice.

'So what about *Dax*?' said Gideon, sounding sulky. He flicked sawdust off his jeans and slid towards the ladder. 'You never stop *him,* do you? He gets to use his Cola powers outside whenever he wants and you never say a word. What's the difference?!'

Dax pressed his lips together. He felt bad. Gideon clambered down the ladder, huffing with annoyance. 'I'll see you back in the house, Dax,' he said, shortly, and Dax understood that he was trying to let him know that it was Owen he was angry with, not his best friend. Owen let him go. He and Dax waited in silence until Gideon had left the wood and could be seen winding his way up towards the house, kicking at tufts of grass.

'He's got a point,' said Dax, swinging his legs and watching a beetle scurry through the leaf litter and over a green knuckle of the tree's roots. 'If I can shift outside and go around the valley, why can't he do telekinesis? If we're sending out any kind of supernatural signal, wouldn't it be the same?'

'I don't think so—not exactly the same. And anyway, you really *have* to get outside to exercise your powers. We don't want you getting ill again.' Owen sighed heavily. 'You want to keep going?' They looked around them at their progress. They had been working on the tree house for several days now, after classes in the late afternoon and all this morning. Dax was thrilled at the idea of a tree house. Gideon had come up with the notion to build one after reading *The Swiss Family Robinson*, where an entire family lived in a fantastic tree house complex, made from the wreckage of their ship, on a desert island.

The other Colas were excited about it too—except perhaps Lisa and Jennifer, who didn't much like the idea of getting mucky lichen stains on their clothes. Clive had helped to design it. He might not be a Cola, but he was still a genius at engineering and science. He had impressed Owen no end with his swift and accurate calculations and drawings, working precision into the shape of the platform, around the natural wonkiness of the oak.

Other Colas had come up to lend a hand: Barry, the glamourists, Jacob and Alex Teller—brothers who were astonishing mimics as well as telepathic between each other; and Darren, one of the college's two illusionists. Jacob was as good with his hands as Dax and together they had made the ladder which led up to the platform. Alex had collected a large pile of hazel twigs which they planned to weave into a canopy for the roof of the tree house, as soon as they'd built a framework to rest it on.

Once up, the canopy would be topped with earth and moss and evergreen leaves to make it waterproof.

Owen thought it was an excellent thing for them all to be doing and Dax thought he might even sleep in the tree house some nights—when the wild thing really got to him. Like Owen said, he mustn't get sick again.

'I think that's enough for today, really,' he said, and Owen nodded readily. 'I need to spread my wings a bit,' added Dax.

Owen nodded again. 'Remember the boundaries,' he said, needlessly. He trusted Dax. He had to.

Dax climbed down from the platform, ran to the edge of the wood and leaped high into the air. He shifted as soon as his feet had left the earth and soared up high in a wide and lazy corkscrew. In the grass below, voles shrank beneath the green blades as the peregrine falcon turned, a deadly black arrow across the sun.

Dax coasted over the upstretched branches of trees in the small copse and watched sparrows wheel away below him in panic. He was a matchless predator and could seize any one of them, mid-air, and be feasting within twenty seconds if he chose. He tried not to give in to this urge to hunt—it didn't seem fair when there was a perfectly good lasagne on the menu in the dining hall a couple of hours from now. Instead he turned tightly in the air and soared higher, the peaks of the Lake District easing into his field of vision as he rode on the warm rising air. He wondered if the joy that rode with him would ever ebb away; if he'd ever totally get used to it. To fly was still an incredible thrill.

He wished Gideon and the others could be allowed more freedom too. Maybe Gid was right and they *were* all quite safe to be Colas outside now. It was, after all, months and months since the road attack.

Dax stooped in the air, curling up and over, and angled the killer curve of his beak to the meadow below. Dropping through the air so fast that his vision seemed to turn pink, Dax saw tiny rodents scattering among the grass in all directions. He pulled up and turned his talons to the ground with inches to spare before landing. He rested for three seconds and then shifted again—to his most instinctive form. Any idle observer (and there never would be, with Owen in charge) would have seen an extraordinary thing in the grass. One moment a bird of prey with lustrous grey and white plumage and yellow pools around its glittering eyes—the next a blur of red and the emergence of a handsome young fox, standing still and poised among the wild flowers. The fox lifted its snout, white beneath, rust red above, darkening to the black of a nose with a spray of fine black whiskers. The fox took in the scent of the day, lifted its tail, and ran into the copse.

Dax felt elated as a falcon, but totally at one with the world as a fox. He would do one circuit of the copse and then head back to the college to talk to Gideon. Maybe everyone felt the same way as Gideon did and thought it was unfair that Dax was allowed to be a Cola outside when they weren't. They hadn't complained too much to begin with. Not even Spook, the other illusionist, who *never* held back on *his* thoughts and opinions. But this was probably because Spook had been there, and witnessed some of the final attack when it came on a rainy road last autumn.

'I was there—I saw it,' he had said dramatically, when all the Colas had been gathered around in their new common room, a week after that terrible day, wanting to know what had happened.

'It was a great big electrical sort of squid thing, made out of a pylon, which smashed through the roof,' he had declared. 'It grabbed Gideon like he was a bag of chocolate drops . . . which he is, anyway.'

Gideon and Dax had sighed, sitting on the couch by the fire, and let him get on with it.

'Anyway—it threw him down on the road and started smacking him about, and then Dax got scared and flew off and it nearly fried him in the air and then it picked up the coach and tried to drop it on all of us!'

Dax had stood up. He'd walked up beside Spook and leaned one elbow on the sparkly material of the boy's sharp shoulder. (Spook liked to dress up as a magician in his own time.) 'So . . . um . . . where were *you* while all this was going on, Spook? While I was flapping about in a panic attack and Gideon was getting beaten up?'

Spook shrugged him off and sneered. 'I would, of course, have been throwing an illusion to distract it. That's what I was *about* to do!'

Lisa snorted with laughter from the couch opposite Gideon and Mia shook her head in amazement.

'But I got knocked out—as you know!' said the would-be hero.

'So you never actually *saw* the bit when I got scared and flew away and Gideon got beaten up, then? You just—sort of—worked it all out for yourself? And ... um ... remind me, how come you *didn't* get crunched up by that falling coach?' prompted Dax, with relish.

Spook studied his fingers and muttered: 'Because Gideon came to his senses at the last minute and decided to stop it. Not before time.'

'So—what you're saying is ... er ... Gideon saved your life?'

Spook got up and flounced away. 'We've all saved lives,' he said and slammed the door behind him.

'For the record,' said Gideon, to the gripped Cola audience, 'Dax was *not* flying away—he came to help me. Not that any of you ever believed that glittery git anyway, I'm sure.'

However it was told, the story was terrifying enough. Dax still had nightmares about the electrical entity which had possessed pylons and chased them across the country and he knew Gideon did too. There was also the stark fact that so few of the Colas were now left. Nearly a hundred others had lost their powers after an earlier attack. Those few left could never feel totally safe any more.

So fear had held all the Colas obediently inside Fenton Lodge whenever they were using their powers. Even indoors, they were meant to only exercise Cola talents under strict supervision, in Development classes.

These classes were held in a network of rooms below ground. The large house had been refurbished with the Colas in mind and the subterranean Development chambers were considered the safest place of all to study their amazing talents.

Nobody knew why these children had suddenly developed their unlimited abilities—or why only ten of more than one hundred such children had held on to their powers over the past year. Every student knew, though, that to be a Cola was a dangerous thing. The past eighteen months had proved that. The Colas were at Fenton Lodge for their own safety. And, quite possibly, everyone else's.

Dax finished his circuit of the wood and ran lightly back across the stream, his paws deftly finding the higher pebbles amid the tumbling water, and leaped up the far bank. He followed Gideon's trail inside by scent and found him getting a fresh-from-the-oven bun from Mrs P.

'Mr Jones! No animals in my kitchen!' said Mrs P. Dax shifted to a boy and said sorry, and she gave his head a friendly pat.

'You all right?' Dax asked and Gideon beamed, his mouth full and his mood lifted.

'Nothing that a visit to my kitchen can't cure,' said Mrs P and put a warm, spicy gift into Dax's palm too. 'Now off you go, you two. I've got tea to get!'

They sat on the steps of the lodge, munching, and watched the clouds scud across the afternoon sky.

'We *are* safe here,' said Gideon. 'I'm sure of it. She's way too scared to come after us.'

Dax said nothing. He really hoped Gideon was right.

4

Spook Williams walked languidly through the common room early that evening.

'Oh dear—not again, Jones,' he said, his face puckering with theatrical distaste. 'I'm going to have to ask for a litter tray for you, I can see that.' Darren was with Spook and although he quite liked Dax he wasn't above guffawing out loud at the curled brown dog poo which sat beside Dax's usual end of the sofa. He was Spook's friend, and his sidekick. It was his job.

Even Lisa—who was definitely *not* Spook's friend—had to smother a giggle as she painted her nails at the other end of the sofa. Dax wasn't fooled for a second that the dog poo was *real*. He would've smelt a real one from the other end of the college, but he felt a surge of weary annoyance at Spook.

'Did you make it yourself?' he asked. 'You should eat more roughage. Shame you can't do any better tricks on me, isn't it?'

Spook smirked at him, preened his dark red hair and flopped into the sofa on the opposite side of the fireplace, where a low log fire glowed. It had been a fine May day, but here in the Lakes it could still get cold. 'You wait,' he said. 'Just because you're resistant now doesn't mean you always will be. I'm getting stronger and stronger—and even if I can't throw an illusion at you, I'm still learning all the other tricks of the business. I'll be in the Magic Circle soon, and then you won't know what's hit you, dingo.'

'You keep telling yourself that,' sighed Dax, flicking through his book on wildlife. 'Whatever makes you feel better.'

Spook loathed Dax because, unlike everyone else he had met in the past two years, Dax could not be fooled by his illusionist glamour. As far as everyone else was concerned, Spook had incredible talent; he really did. He could make them see anything from a disembodied head floating around at Halloween to a garden full of waltzing snails. His power was astonishing and only Darren could come close to copying it. Darren's illusions tended to be insubstantial and a bit see-through, though, according to Gideon. Like the holograms in *Star Wars*.

It seemed Dax, perhaps because he was a part-time fox and falcon, could not be glamoured. He did not see the mirages that Spook or Darren performed. He knew *when* they were throwing an illusion because the air around them became wavy and distorted, like the air above a bonfire—but he did not see what they wanted him to see. Only what was really there. Sometimes it seemed a shame—a whole group of illusionists (including twelve others who had lost their powers a year ago) had once put on a fantastic firework display—and Dax hadn't seen a twinkle of it.

'Oh, do get rid of it, Spencer,' snapped Lisa, holding up her newly lacquered nails and examining them for perfection. 'It's disgusting.'

'*Don't* call me that!' said Spook. 'Only my parents call me that. It's Spook to you.'

'Oh really, Spencer?' said Lisa, blowing on her pale violet fingertips. 'It's all your grandmother ever calls you. She hates "Spook"—thinks it's really . . . what did she say? Pretentious. That was it. But then, she says you always were that way. Apparently, you used to wear a tiara when you were five. Do you remember that, Spencer? Nothing's changed much, eh? Still mad about the glitter . . . '

Spook opened his mouth to snarl at Cola Club's only psychic medium, sweeping back one side of his favourite black and silver cloak. He shut his mouth again though, when she wagged a pearly finger at him and said, 'Behave, Spencer . . . or I'll have to tell everyone about the jelly incident.' Her pretty face wore a rather cruel smile and she flicked back her long blonde hair with a shake of her head, daring him to push her further.

Spook ground his teeth and got up from the seat. He glared hard at Lisa's fingers and she gulped and blinked. 'Put them *back,* you idiot!' Her mocking smile vanished. 'Or everyone hears the jelly story.'

'Tell her from *me,*' said Spook, flouncing towards the door, 'that she's well out of order for a dead woman! And so are *you*! I've a good mind to report you to Mr Eades!'

'Pick up your poo as you go,' said Lisa. Spook

kicked the dummy dropping angrily across the room and everyone was relieved that it clunked rather than squelched. Darren picked it up and trailed after his friend and they could hear him trying to talk Spook out of his fury all the way down the corridor.

'You really shouldn't do that, you know, Lisa,' reproved Mia wandering across from the window, where she had been watching the sun set. 'You know it's not on. And why would you want to be talking to Spook's grandmother anyway?'

'I *don't*,' said Lisa, with feeling. 'She just pops up and tells me things from time to time. Like all your dear departed rellies. Mostly I ignore them, as you know, but the stuff on Spook is too good not to use.'

'What *is* the jelly story?' asked Dax.

'Not telling . . . yet!' said Lisa, her cruel smile back.

'You would tell us . . . wouldn't you . . . if something important came through for us?' Mia sat down next to Lisa and looked her in the eyes.

'Of course,' said Lisa, flapping her almost dry nails at Mia. Nobody was entirely convinced. Lisa had overlooked important messages for them in the past. Mia glanced at Dax and they both knew they shared this thought. Lisa knew it too. She heard it as clearly as if they'd said it out loud. She was, after all, psychic.

'Look,' she said, shooting them both a haughty look, 'I know I've been a bit patchy in the past, but I do think you could have *some* faith in me! Who tried to tell you about the falling down the hole thing, eh, Dax? And the not being able to breathe thing? And who knew that Gideon was in trouble and who went and got everyone to rescue Mia from ... from the drink thing?' she concluded, awkwardly, as Mia's face fell. Last autumn Lisa had insisted they all went to Mia's council estate tower block. There they had found Mia in a desperate state. Her father, whom she loved dearly, had been drinking too much and Mia could not resist taking his hangover pains from him for days on end. She had suffered badly and once her father realized what was happening he had willingly sent her away with her friends, appalled and ashamed.

'How is your dad?' asked Dax and Mia looked away from them both.

'He's fine. Better,' she said, quietly. 'He's coming up to see me next week. My turn for the cottage.'

'Good,' said Dax. Although the Colas were allowed home, on request, to see their families, the government department that ran the college had set up an alternative family break location. It was a quite beautiful cottage, nestled up in the fells above the lodge next to a tumbling waterfall. The views across the peaks of the Lake District were stunning and the cottage had every luxury imaginable. It was a clever way of encouraging Cola families to come to *them*. As delightful as it was, the cottage was just another secure unit. So far, though, none of the families seemed to see it this way. The safety measures were discreet—invisible laser boundaries and cleverly masked security cameras.

Gideon came into the room on the end of their

conversation. He flopped down next to Dax, grinning at Mia. 'Good for you, healer girl!' he said. 'It's brilliant up there! Me and Dad had a great time last month—you can get DVDs and computer games and stuff and the telly is surround sound. And they've put a hot tub in now. It's cool! Well . . . it's hot . . . obviously. And bubbly and when you turn it up full blast it's like someone's beating you up underwater. In a good way. You know.'

Mia smiled more happily now and the wave of warmth from her washed over them all, buffeting them with wellbeing. 'I know—I saw the brochure that they send out to our dads. I can't wait! A whole week with just us two!'

'Well—just you two and the entire surveillance team,' muttered Lisa, but Mia chose not to notice.

'It'll be lovely,' she said.

'You'll be next, Dax!' said Gideon. 'Everyone else has been to the cottage.'

'Yeah, right,' said Dax. He could certainly *ask* for his dad to come, but he was fairly sure Robert Jones would find some excuse not to.

'No, look—I think it's already in the book,' said Gideon and he got up and went to the wide oak desk at the other end of the room and opened one of its shallow drawers. Out of it he drew a leather-bound book, opened it and flicked through it. It was a desk diary and in it there was a column for cottage or leave bookings. Uneasily, Dax got up and went across to Gideon. Gideon ran his finger down the paper. 'Here you go,' he said.

'Dax Jones—cottage—May 23 to 26. A long weekend for you—there it is.'

Dax stared at the entry, written in Mr Eades's neat black ink. He saw 'Jones' marked down and initials under it—not R for Robert, but a G and an A.

'Oh no,' he murmured, a dismal trickle of foreboding inside him. 'It's not Dad. It's Alice . . . and Gina!'

Lisa spluttered with horrified amusement. 'You are *joking*! No! Oh—I *have* to meet them! I have to meet Gina the Meaner and Alice the Malice . . . and her dolly-packed chalice!' Dax gave her a *look*—she'd come up with the names after several brief phone conversations with his stepmother and half-sister, before the receiver was handed to Dax. She'd never actually met them but Dax's stories about them, together with her psychic insights, had helped her to create a fairly accurate sketch of them. 'Sorry!' she said but a gurgle of mirth wasn't far behind. 'Do you think Alice will put all her Barbies in the hot tub? You might go in there early in the morning and find them all floating face down with their nylon hair all fanned around them—a sort of fashion doll mass drowning scene.'

'Actually, Alice isn't really malicious,' he sighed.

'Sorry—annoying doesn't rhyme,' said Lisa.

'She *is* incredibly annoying—all girls are at that age. I expect you were a total brat at nine.'

'She's still a brat—arch-brat of all bratesses,' said Gideon. Lisa threw her bottle of nail varnish accurately at his head, and he stopped it in mid-air without even

32

looking, closing the desk diary and turning to face Dax. 'You mean you really had no idea that they were coming?'

'No!' said Dax. 'I never invited them! Why on earth would I? It's bad enough having to go home for holidays with them. One week is more than enough. At Christmas there were so many dolls in my old room I couldn't walk without a plastic leg jamming between my toes or something going "ma-ma" under my feet. It was . . . eaurrrgggh.' He shuddered. 'She's even got one that munches up food now. You're supposed to put this mushy stuff in its mouth on a spoon and then its mouth sort of squishes about and it makes these disgusting noises. I don't even want to *think* about what happens at the other end. I wanted to shift to the fox and bite its head off.'

Alice's doll obsession wasn't the only reason Dax dreaded having to go home. Gina was another reason. Before he'd become a Cola he had lived a narrow, dull, sour kind of life with a woman who was called his mum, but really didn't fit the description. Gina couldn't stand him—she made that really clear. Everything he did annoyed her and she had been given to shutting him out in the back garden for hours on end while she went shopping with Alice—whom she adored and spoilt rotten. It would have been easier to bear if his dad had been there to talk to, but Robert Jones was almost always not there. He worked on the oil rigs in the North Sea and came home infrequently. Before Cola Club, Dax had lived for his visits, short as they were. But since he had become a

Cola his father had become more and more distant from his only son. Sometimes it seemed he didn't even want to look him in the eyes—as if he was ashamed of him, or even afraid of him. Dax ached to tell his father about what had been happening to him over the past two years but somehow the moment never came. And, increasingly, Dax suspected Robert Jones wanted to keep it that way. This was the worst thing about going home.

He had so much to *ask* as well as tell. Now that he was a Cola he was part of a group of children who had all lost their mothers before they reached the age of four. The scientists were certain that this had some meaning, but had yet to uncover anything that could explain it. The Colas who could speak to the spirit world (now, sadly, only Lisa) had all tried to contact the Cola mums. Not one ever spoke back to them.

Dax's mother had been called Anita. He knew this much. There was only one photograph of her that Dax knew of. It was hidden in the bottom of a tea chest in the garden shed. He had found it by accident when he was about nine. In it was his father, still young, with nut-brown hair, grey eyes, and a warm grin, his arm around the shoulders of a pretty, dark-haired woman with milky-gold skin and large dark eyes, identical to Dax's. On her hip the woman held a baby with dark fluffy hair, almost like fur. The baby was staring, with great concentration, at whoever was taking the photo. Dax kept the photo safely in the tea chest after he'd found it. Gina would never tolerate it in the house. She probably didn't even know it existed, in exile, in the shed. He suspected that his father unearthed it to look at sometimes—and that he knew Dax did too. It was just another thing they didn't talk about.

How would he have felt, if the entry in the cottage booking list had read R. Jones, instead of G. and A. Jones? Amazed. That's what.

'Gina must have opened your dad's post and found the brochure,' said Gideon as Lisa stalked across the room and collected her nail polish bottle out of the air with a sigh. 'She obviously fancies a luxury holiday. Or maybe—you know—maybe she wants to see you.'

They both grinned and shook their heads.

'Go on!' poked Gideon. 'Give her a treat! You can always spray in the hot tub!'

Dax squawked with indignation. 'I do *not* spray, you knucklehead! I'm not *that* foxy!'

'But you *could*!' snorted Gideon, getting into full swing now, especially as Lisa and Mia were making revolted faces at them both. 'You could mark your territory all over the place! You could shift into a falcon too and do your toilets from a great height on Alice's dolls . . . or . . . wait till you're all sitting down to tea and then just cough politely and chuck up some pellets full of mouse bones at dinner—right into the clotted cream—and say "Oops. Pardon me!"'

'I don't *do* that!' said Dax, but he was laughing, in spite of the horrific thought of a long weekend with Gina and Alice. 'You're disgusting, Gideon! You know that?'

'But you wouldn't have me any other way,' beamed

his friend, pulling some chocolate out of his pocket and breaking off a chunk. He floated it over to Dax, who collected it from mid-air and ate it, still shaking his head. Gideon floated a couple more chunks across to Lisa and Mia. Mia took hers with a smile and Lisa shot him a disdainful look.

'Yum *yum*,' she said. 'Semi-melted brown stuff from your nice sweaty jeans pocket. If only I *could* . . . '

'Suit yourself,' said Gideon, and dropped it on her head.

A bell rang before Lisa could do physical damage to Gideon, reminding them to get to bed.

'Maybe your dad's coming too,' said Gideon, later, flopping back onto his pillow. Dax eased open one of the leaded panes in the tall stone window arch as he knelt on the velvet-covered window seat. The late evening sky was peppermint blue in the west and almost indigo in the east, and stars freckled the heavens, lit by a crescent moon which was only just up above the fells.

'He might,' he said, getting into bed and switching off the lamp, so he could see better outside. He never closed the curtains, and Gideon had got used to this a long time ago. 'But I'll be amazed if he ever comes here. He doesn't want to know.'

'Do you think he's, kind of, guessed?'

'What—that his son grows fur or feathers whenever he feels like it?' said Dax. 'What do *you* think?' He felt guilty. Gideon didn't deserve his snippiness.

'Do you ever think,' said Gideon, obviously not offended, 'about what our mums might have *told* our dads—before they died?'

Dax shifted onto his back and looked up at the ceiling. 'Yes. I think about it a lot. But I don't see how they could have told them *anything*. I mean—with all the government stuff—tests and inquiries and stuff—it would've come out by now, surely. Wouldn't it? Our dads would've said something if they *knew* anything, wouldn't they?'

'I don't know.' Gideon yawned and pulled the quilt up tight around his neck against the cool breeze that Dax demanded every night. 'I've asked my dad loads of stuff, but he never tells me anything useful. Just that she was a total babe and she only had eyes for him, a computer nerd—yeah right! She was good-looking though. How else would you explain me, eh?'

Dax snorted and opened his mouth to say more, but Gideon had already fallen asleep, abruptly, as if he'd been hit with a tranquilizer dart. It was a talent of his; one that Dax had learned to envy greatly during his wakeful winter. He lay for an hour, trying to clear his mind and get to sleep, but an awful image of Gina and Alice, greeting him at the cottage, kept rising before his mind's eye. Gina was leaning across to embrace him, offering a tensely bunched-up cheek to be kissed, in the way she did every Christmas for the benefit of guests, and Alice was waving the little chubby plastic hand of the munching doll at him.

Eeeuuugh. He shivered again and sat up in bed.

There was nothing else for it. He needed to get out for a while. The open window was beckoning.

A night flight wasn't really possible—peregrines hunt and fly by day, relying on the warm rising air and their extraordinary vision. Dax went to the wing only to allow himself to fly down to the sweeping driveway at the front of the lodge, and then shifted to a fox for some proper exercise.

The small copse at night was very different from its character by day. Alive with a bustling community of insects, mammals, birds, and even tiny reptiles, it sang in Dax's ears and curled into his nose in the way that hot garlic flows out on the breeze from a good pizza restaurant—tickling the senses and beguiling the hungry. Or even just the peckish. Dax was not hungry, but always peckish. It was a fox thing. He had hunted as a fox several times—through necessity—and eaten meals of rabbit or pigeon, still warm and only minutes out of life. The boy part of him felt guilty, even when it was a matter of survival. The fox part of him revelled in it.

The hunt made the blood pound harder through his veins and his sinews hum with excited tension as he prepared to kill. The fox in him never thought to hurt or toy with the hapless rabbit or bird it chose—the killing was over so fast the creatures rarely even struggled. The feast that followed was swift and efficient. Dax had learned to clean himself up, too, after the occasion when he had shifted back to a boy and there had been rabbit blood in his hair. What would Alice think of *that*? She had a passion for fluffy things but not in the way that DaxFox did.

Dax paused under the half-built tree house, watching a tawny owl coast low over the lake, seeking water voles. A large spider wandered across the planking that Owen had stacked nearby and Dax snatched it up in his teeth before he could stop himself—a habit he was always vowing to stop. The spider wriggled briefly, and tried to bite, but was dead and swallowed before Dax could even start telling himself off again. Beetles, worms, spiders . . . it really *was* disgusting what he would snack on when he was a fox. He decided to get in a run around the meadow and then head back to the lodge and find some cold meat in the kitchen before he got the munchies for moths too. The run was wonderful—exhilarating. Sometimes Dax ran with Lisa, who was a keen long-distance runner. She still occasionally went out on night runs, when the spirit voices in her head got too loud and annoying. She wasn't out tonight though. She seemed to be better able to cope since coming to Fenton Lodge. As he ran fast through the cool grass and leaped over the narrow part of the river back towards the lodge, he noticed a light on in an upstairs window. There were several lights on, in fact. The teaching and household staff had rooms on the top storey, and might not be in bed yet—although it was a Sunday night and they'd have to be up first thing. But the light Dax saw he recognized as the medical room. It was a soft blueish light, not the usual golden yellow kind. He wondered who was there, this late.

Even as he thought this he found himself flying up to the ledge. The window was closed, but, as his sharp talons gripped the stone sill, he could see inside quite easily. Lisa was there. She had a cup of water and looked as if she was swallowing some pills. She spun around almost instantly and frowned at him, before coming over and opening the window, carefully, so he could edge around it and get inside. He shifted quickly back to a boy in his pyjamas.

'What are you spying on me for?' said Lisa, but quite mildly. She was wearing an expensive white silk robe and soft suede slippers, her long blonde hair thoroughly brushed and gleaming over her shoulders. She always looked like a model in an expensive fashion catalogue.

'Just wondered who was in here,' he said. 'You OK?'

'Yeah—just a bit of a headache. I think it's the nail polish remover,' she said.

'What is it with you and shiny nails?' said Dax, curling his lip.

'Dax—I have a duty to myself, to be as girly as I can be. When the inside of your head is one freak show after another, you have to hang on to these little things, or go totally bonkers.'

He chuckled. 'They giving you grief tonight then?'

She shrugged. 'When don't they? Sylv's holding them off a bit for me now, though. I asked her to.' Sylv was Lisa's spirit guide. Lisa had only recently admitted to even *having* a spirit guide. She found the whole thing embarrassing. Lisa's old life had been charmed; her father was very rich. They lived in a beautiful manor house in Somerset, with a pool and horses and servants. Dax had stayed there for holidays with Mia and Gideon and could well understand why Lisa had been reluctant to leave it to go to the first college in Cornwall.

She'd lost all her posh friends, too, when she first started 'finding things'. Her Cola powers began with dowsing. Suddenly, she could instinctively tell her friends where to look for mislaid scarves, purses, glasses . . . until her friends stopped being impressed and intrigued and instead became suspicious and hostile. Lisa's first 'gift' earned her the title of thief. The next gift sent her into desperation. Clairvoyance arrived. She accurately foresaw the death of a classmate. Then messages began to come from the dead, needing to make contact with the living. A trickle of visions and requests soon became a sea of tangled images and cries for help—unmanageable, terrifying, and overwhelming. Ignoring her powers just made it worse, although that was what Lisa was intent on doing when Dax first met her. Now she was better at blocking out the clamour from the next world and was much less angry about it. Most of the time. Sylv, who apparently had a wicked sense of humour and a very bawdy laugh for a spirit, helped a lot.

'You're being a bit nicer to Sylv these days, then?' asked Dax. 'Keeping in her good books.'

'She knows what I'm like,' muttered Lisa, putting the cup down on the draining board of the medical room sink unit. 'She knows I never asked for this. She tells me

I'm a spoilt madam and she'd give me a good slap if she could ever manifest herself solidly enough to do it. We get on fine.'

Dax laughed and they both turned to leave, but a flicker caught his eye and he turned back, looking across towards the bed which he had spent time in back in February, lost in his illness. For a moment, he thought he saw that boy again. That small boy—about eight or nine—pointing at the wall above the pillow. He felt the hairs on the back of his neck stand up.

'Who's that then, Lees?' he asked, quietly. She turned back and shrugged.

'Which one?' she said. 'There are three here right now.'

Dax gaped at her. 'You're joking!'

'No.' She flipped her hair over her shoulder. 'There's tonnes of them in this house. It's an old place. A maid over there—using one of those three-legged washy things in a wooden tub.' She indicated the space next to the glass fronted cabinets. 'An old man sitting halfway through the wall there—in a sort of robe thing. And . . . a . . . oh, I don't know, a sort of wispy thing by the window. Doing . . . wispy stuff. Wispily.'

'Who are they?' whispered Dax, looking around him, wide-eyed. He saw nothing of the boy now—or any other presence.

'Dunno. Haven't introduced themselves,' said Lisa, and walked out.

Dax scurried out after her as she walked along the

thick carpet runner of the upstairs corridor, lit by soft wall lights on either side.

'You're telling me that this building is haunted right up to its back teeth and you never *ask*? You never talk to them at all? Don't you want to know why they're here?'

Lisa descended the wide curving staircase, her fingers running lightly along the glossily polished wooden balustrade. 'Dax, this isn't exciting for *me*. It's like work. If one of them needs me to know something, you can bet they'll tell me. Then it'll be all I can do to shut them up again.'

'You don't have much respect for the spirit world, do you?' said Dax.

She sighed and folded her arms as she reached the door to the bedroom she shared with Mia and Jennifer. 'Just because they've passed on doesn't make them all saints or incredibly wise or—or any less irritating than they might have been on earth. There's one that likes to perform "Land of Hope and Glory" with his armpits. At least I *hope* it's with his armpits.' She shuddered. 'Some though . . . some are . . . well, they can get to you sometimes. And some . . . some don't want to be found,' she added, strangely.

'You mean you actually *try* to find them sometimes?' said Dax. 'I thought you only ever had them finding you.'

'No, I dowse the dead too. If I'm asked. And I have been asked.'

'Who by? And who are you dowsing for?'

'By Owen and Mrs Sartre of course! And who do

you *think*?' She shook her head as if he was a total idiot and went into her room, closing the door without saying goodnight.

Dax wandered along to his and Gideon's room and found his friend still deeply asleep. He wondered if Gideon knew.

'Mate,' he murmured, knowing Gideon would sleep on regardless. 'Do you know they believe you? Do you know they're looking for Luke?'

5

'Ssso. No yearnings, yet, to become anything *else*? No . . . er . . . stirrings?' Mr Eades spoke in a voice which always made Dax think of dry leaves scraping tiredly against each other in a winter breeze.

He shot Owen a *look* and shook his head. 'No, sir, no other stirrings at all.' He wanted to add: 'Sorr-eee! Fox and falcon not enough for you, eh? Hoping for an elephant or a blue whale today, were you?' But he bit his lip. Mr Eades had no known sense of humour and probably wouldn't even look up from his small desk and his ever-present sheaf of papers, against which the nib of his fountain pen seemed to scratch ceaselessly.

Development 4 was a calming room. Its walls were covered in a kind of soft green felt; there was thick seagrass carpeting on the floor. Shaded lamps spilled gold light at each of its four corners, reflected back in the smoky mirror which took up the whole of one wall. It needed only a wooden bar at hip height across the glass to look like an expensive dance studio, but the mirror wasn't there for ballet dancers to check their poise. None of the Colas was in any doubt about that. It was a two-way mirror and there would almost certainly be scientists behind it, making their own notes, or possibly recording through the suspended microphones which hung discreetly in the darkness overhead. Dax had been troubled by this for the first year or so of being a Cola, but now he just accepted it. He and the others were the subject of intense scrutiny. The world waited.

'So—no more insomnia,' Owen checked, as he still did roughly once a week since Dax had got better. Dax suspected his teacher, mentor, and protector had been badly shaken by his collapse. It was Owen Hind's job to see to the safety of his charges and the mortal threat to his only shapeshifter had come from a totally unexpected place—*inside* the boy.

'No, I'm fine,' said Dax. 'As long as I can get out and be fox and falcon, I'm fine.'

'No urge to be a fish then?' grinned Owen.

'Not so far!'

'I think we're done here,' said Owen, getting to his feet. They had both been sitting cross-legged on the carpet as they usually did in Development classes. In the other three Development rooms other Colas were undoubtedly sitting with other tutors—Lisa and Mia and the Teller brothers with Mrs Sartre; Jennifer, Barry, Darren, and Spook would be with Mr Tucker, an older man who had been brought to Fenton Lodge only that year. He was a psychologist who also, entertainingly, had been a cabaret illusionist in his younger years. He was dry and clever and seemed unshockable; Dax liked him.

Gideon though, had a Development tutor all to himself, like Dax. Oddly, it was a young man of not more than twenty, called Tyrone. Tyrone was tall and gangly, with a kind of geeky, narrow face, but perfect teeth. He kept himself to himself but Gideon said he was fantastic. Furthermore, he was also telekinetic.

'He's not a Cola—he can't be,' Gideon had told Dax breathlessly last term when he'd first met Tyrone. 'But he's got the same powers as me! He's brilliant! And he knows bushcraft stuff, too, like Owen! I've got my own Owen, like you!'

Tyrone had done a lot for Gideon. He had taught him some excellent control techniques and also, Dax felt, in some way filled the gap that lay in Gideon's heart since losing his brother and sister a year ago.

Dax thought about the brother and sister again, for the millionth time, as he and Owen ascended the stairs from the underground network of Development rooms. Away from Mr Eades, he put his question to Owen. 'Is Lisa really dowsing for Luke?'

Owen paused on the stairs and then moved on up again. 'When did she tell you that?'

'Last night. We met in the medical room. She was ignoring ghosts.'

'Right,' said Owen. 'And she told you that, did she?' He seemed mildly annoyed.

'Well—not exactly, but . . . '

'OK, fine. She was bound to, sooner or later. Yes, Dax, she is dowsing for Luke. And Catherine. Without much success, it has to be said—in the living *or* the dead realm. I know Gideon firmly believes they're alive somewhere, but I'm not so sure. OK, I'm prepared to believe their *spirits* may be bobbing about. I can believe that it may well have been Catherine's spirit attacking us through the pylon back in Devon. She was a Cola, after all, so anything is possible. But still alive? You were there. What do *you* think?' He shook his head as they crossed the shining pale stone floor of the lodge's large entrance hall. He walked out through the open front door, across the sweep of gravel drive, and sat down on the grassy lawn beyond. Dax joined him. They both gazed around at the mild late spring day, but neither was seeing it.

A vivid film was playing right in front of Dax's eyes. One that had played so many times that it ought to be jumping and scratched and faded. It wasn't though. It was perfect in every cruel detail. Dax *had* been there. Oh yes. A year ago in Cornwall. A lovely evening, when more than a hundred talented children had gathered for a party on the grassy field above the sea at Tregarren College. Among those children, Gideon, Mia, and himself, along with Gideon's identical triplet brother, Luke—and their sister, very similar with the same green eyes, but dark shining hair: Catherine.

The triplets had not even known about each other the previous winter. They had been found and brought together by the government agency which oversaw the Cola project. Luke, quiet and bookish, wore spectacles. That was the only way of knowing him from Gideon, at a glance. Luke had been living happily with adoptive parents on the Isle of Wight, and had no Cola power at all. He scored zero points in the tests the college worked him through. He was a good bloke, thought Dax, with a familiar twinge of guilt. He had been horribly jealous of Luke. Gideon, amazed at discovering a brother, had spent a lot of time with Luke and Dax had felt left out. When Catherine arrived it had got even worse. Catherine, pretty and winning and fresh from a children's home in America, charmed everyone.

'I should never have given Catherine a second chance,' said Dax with a bitter wrench of a dandelion in the grass in front of him. Owen patted him on the shoulder.

'I would have done the same, Dax. You didn't want to hurt Gideon.'

Catherine had seemed to have little chunks of Cola talent of all kinds. One minute she was floating pencils in the air as a telekinetic, the next she was trying out illusions, and once she even healed her own wound—something none of them had ever seen happen. Even Mia, talented as she was, could not heal *her own* wounds or pain. Everyone seemed to warm to Catherine. She was, like many Americans, affectionate and tactile; always ready to hug and squeeze.

But the hugging and squeezing was not what it seemed. Dax and Lisa found out Catherine's secret— that she had only to touch another Cola to be able to help herself to their talents, draining them as she did so. Within days of her arrival, nearly everyone at Tregarren had become lethargic and dull—Gideon most of all.

'I should have acted sooner too, Dax, if it's any comfort,' said Owen, whose thoughts seemed to be rolling sadly along the same path as his pupil's. He lay back on the grass, folding his hands behind his head and sighed up into the sky. 'I should never have let it go on so long, with everyone so tired. It was tremendously stupid.'

When Dax had challenged Catherine she at once owned up and agreed to stop if he and Lisa promised not to tell anyone. It did seem that she had stuck to her end of the bargain—remarkably cheerfully. She even became a party organizer for everyone and got the whole college together for an American-style barbecue beside the sea.

Then she sucked everyone's talent out of them in a few horrific seconds—and brought the sea thundering down onto the college to drown them all.

'You OK, Dax?' He realized he had let out a shivery breath. Owen had sat up again and was looking at him keenly.

'Yeah—just remembering,' he sighed.

'Me too,' said Owen. 'I can't forget how close she came to washing us all out to sea. But don't forget, if it hadn't been for you and Luke, she would have done.'

Dax's film flickered and then swept on. Yes, he had helped, by warning Owen and the others—but it was Luke who had really saved them all. The boy with no powers had stared up at the titanic funnel of water about to plunge down on them all—and frozen it in its path.

Luke, it turned out, had fooled everybody and proved

to be the most powerful Cola of all of them. He had literally held back the sea as the teachers and students scrambled to safety. Even when Catherine attacked him he held it off for as long as possible—so that when several thousand tonnes of seawater finally fell, there were just two Tregarren students left under it.

Catherine and Luke.

Owen patted his shoulder again. 'You know you did everything you could, don't you? You couldn't save him. Nor could Gideon—or any of us.'

Dax nodded. Luke's last expression swam before his eyes. Despite his sister clawing at his face, the boy had smiled up at the falcon above him, and simply said, 'Go on now, Dax.' Then the ocean fell.

'And you do see,' Owen insisted, gently, 'that he couldn't possibly be alive, don't you? Neither could she. The *force* of that water! It's just not possible. No matter what Gideon thinks or feels.'

'But you're getting Lisa to dowse for them?'

'Yes, we are. But she's dowsing the *dead*. That's where we expect to find them, if at all.'

'Not much you can do about it if you do,' observed Dax.

'It would just help to know. Then at least we can settle things for Gideon. Trouble is, we're not really getting anywhere. Either Lisa's being awkward—and there's every chance of *that*—or there's nothing there to find. Like the Cola mothers.'

'Have you tried bringing Gideon into it?' Dax said,

wrapping the dandelion stem tightly around his fingers, its milky blood smearing his knuckles.

Owen said nothing for a while, thinking. 'Yes. We probably will. Mrs Sartre has an idea that might help him to work with Lisa. She and Mia have been researching it. We don't want to set Gideon back though. He's been much happier these last few weeks—since you got better and since Tyrone came. Do you think he could handle it, if we brought him in with Lisa?'

'Would they have to hold hands?' asked Dax.

'Undoubtedly.'

'Oh yeah! You *have* to do it!'

Owen cuffed him lightly on the head. 'You're a nasty boy, Dax Jones. But I guess that means you think he'll be OK.'

Dax laughed, picturing Gideon's embarrassment at having to sit in a darkened room, holding Lisa's hand and being all 'wifty-wafty'.

'Oh, please say I can watch!'

6

'I have something for you all,' said Mia, running into the lab after lunch. Mr Tucker, who took all science subjects as well as art, hadn't yet arrived, but all the other students were there. Mia looked flushed and pleased as she rattled a rather scruffy looking paper package. 'They've just come!' she beamed. 'They've taken ages!'

'What?' Lisa got to her feet, stepped around the high wooden benches where rows of Bunsen burners sat waiting to be lit, and hurried across to peer into Mia's package. Jennifer followed.

'I've got one for everyone!' beamed Mia, rattling the parcel again. The top was undone and she upended it onto the nearest bench. There was a crackle and a series of sharp thuds and everyone stared at the strange bundle of things settling on the wooden surface.

'They're . . . they're *bracelets*?' said Lisa, picking one up.

Mia nodded and took it out of her hands. 'Yes—but that's not for you. This is yours.'

She handed Lisa an alternative. The bracelets were made of fine strips of dark woven leather, like thin watch straps. But where the small clock dial would have been was something entirely different. A single stone was set there instead. Each strap held a highly polished lump of stone, anchored to it with the fine strands of leather looped through carefully bored holes.

By now everyone was crowding around, making interested noises. Lisa peered at the oval stone on the bracelet Mia had given her. It was a strange, luminous kind of white with a blue tinge. 'It's lovely,' she said. 'What is it?'

'Moonstone,' said Mia.

'I quite liked the green one though,' added Lisa, eyeing up the bracelet Mia had taken back from her. The stone on it was cut into a rough square with facets which caught the light and glinted. It was the colour of spring grass.

'Sorry,' said Mia, firmly. 'But that's for Spook.'

Spook elbowed his way through the intrigued crowd and held out his hand to Mia. 'Why is this one for me?' he asked, tilting his head to one side and eyeing Mia suspiciously.

'It just *is*,' said Mia, but she flushed and didn't meet his eye as she placed it in his palm. The Colas looked around at each other. Mia was rarely this assertive.

'It's peridot,' Mia went on, after a deep breath. 'You can look it up later. I have a book. But for now, just take it. Darren, here's yours.' She handed him a bracelet with a vibrantly yellow polished stone. 'It's jasper,' she added. 'Barry and Jennifer—opal for both of you.' Their stones were both a milky white oval with tiny chips of luminous blue and green and yellow glittering softly in the light from the window.

'Oh, Mia—it's beautiful!' sighed Jennifer. She put her bracelet on and immediately disappeared, but they could still hear her murmurs of appreciation.

'Isn't it a bit ... you know ... girly?' said Barry, fumbling uncomfortably with his own.

'Not when you understand what it's for,' said Mia, smiling at him. 'And if you like, you can turn it inwards to your wrist, so it can't be seen.' Barry immediately did so, leaving his bracelet to look like just a weave of leather, which was in no way girly.

'You can all do that,' said Mia, smiling at them all now. 'If you want. It doesn't matter—in fact it may be better if you do, sometimes. Put the crystal right next to your skin.'

Clive grinned at her. 'I know what you're doing!' he said, as she passed him a silver-grey blob of stone that shone like a dark mirror from its leather setting. 'Hematite for me, yes?' Mia nodded, surprised. 'Mental discipline!' said Clive, peering intently at his gift. 'Helps with the study of maths and mechanics and technical stuff.' He looked up at her and raised an eyebrow. 'You think *I* need help with that stuff?'

Mia shook her head. 'It's not just for that. You'll see. It'll also help you to stop beating yourself up whenever your experiments go wrong.'

Clive made a 'who, me?' expression and they all laughed.

'Mate, you were sulking for hours after you blew up the lab last week!' guffawed Barry, nudging Clive so hard he nearly fell over.

'I did *not* blow up the lab. It was just a little pop of gas.' Barry nudged him again and looked up. The ceiling was stained with starry spatters of purple. 'It'll come off eventually,' mumbled Clive. He concentrated hard on doing up his bracelet as his ears went pink.

Jacob and Alex Teller were strapping on theirs too, and clearly communicating with telepathy because they both glanced up at each other at the same time and laughed out loud with delight. 'It does!' said Alex, looking around as if everyone else had heard their thoughts too. 'It looks like the world!' They both wore matching blue and white and gold stones, which did indeed look like the surface of Earth as seen from space.

'Lapis lazuli,' beamed Mia, touching them both lightly on the head.

'What's yours?' asked Jacob, turning her wrist over to reveal a stone of complete blackness which shone like glass in a roughly triangle shape.

'Black obsidian,' said Mia, quietly, and turned her wrist back over.

'What have you got, Gid?' said Dax.

Gideon was staring into his palm at a strange, uneven polished stone with many colours—red and brown and mossy green. 'Looks like little Stone Age cave paintings,' he murmured.

'It's serpentine,' said Mia.

Dax touched the stone. It felt warmer than it looked. He liked it. He liked his own even more. It was spectacular. Like Gideon's it was uneven but polished to a fine gleam.

It was astonishing to look at. One end was riven with vivid swirls and circles of green and black, like a furiously bubbling swamp, and the other end revealed a sweep of fine lines, like dragon's hair, also in glowing green and black.

'Looks like it came straight out of Merlin's cooking pot, doesn't it?' said Gideon and Dax nodded and ran his fingertip across the stone. The hairs on his arms and neck immediately rose.

'Malachite,' said Mia, who was standing next to him. 'The stone of transformation. Be careful with it, Dax. It'll show you things as they really are. Things you might not want to see.'

Dax stared at her and saw something odd in her expression—if this hadn't been Mia he would have said it was a kind of hardness. But with Mia, that just couldn't be.

'Well—thanks . . . I think,' he said.

'You need it,' she replied. 'You'll see.'

'Uh-oh! Wifty-wafty alert!' said Gideon loudly and Mia stepped back, shaking her head and laughing, and anything odd about her was gone.

Mr Tucker arrived as they were all putting their bracelets on, securing them firmly with leather knots; Jennifer was helping Barry and Spook was holding his wrist high and turning it so the light sparkled through his peridot.

'Aah! I see Mia and Mrs Sartre have got their project under way,' Mr Tucker said, with a benevolent smile.

'Project! What project?' demanded Lisa. She looked at Mia accusingly. 'What's this about? You never told me about any project!'

'She's not telling you now, either, Miss Hardman,' said Mr Tucker, giving Lisa a firm look over his half-moon spectacles. 'You can find out all about it just as soon as you've grasped the details of velocity, gravity, and resistance.'

Lisa gritted her teeth and opened her textbook. She knew better than to argue with Mr Tucker. White haired and kindly though he looked, he took no nonsense from anyone.

The malachite fascinated Dax. After lunch he and Gideon sat by the river and examined their wrists. 'Yours is brilliant,' said Gideon, lying back in the grass and staring at his own stone. 'But I like mine even more. It's cool. What did she say it was? Something to do with snakes . . . ?'

'Serpentine. Don't you remember?' said Dax. 'It comes from Cornwall. We saw it all over the place at Tregarren.'

'Oh yeah!' Gideon rolled over and stared, again, at Dax's stone.

'Malachite,' said Dax, as much to himself as to his friend. The word rolled off his tongue in a pleasing way. 'Transformation stone.'

'What's all this about then?' Gideon sat up again and resumed staring at his serpentine. 'What's this project Mia's doing with Mrs Sartre? She's going all New Age on us again, isn't she? She's probably going to want us all to start chanting and keeping fresh herbs tied to our curtains or something. Or standing on one leg at full moon or snogging apple trees or something. Or—'

'Shaddup,' said Dax. 'This is cool.'

'I know what she's doing!' came a piping, brisk voice, and Clive sat down next to them, holding a large hardback book. 'I just went and got this. Nobody else seemed to notice that Mia said we could look them all up—but I was paying attention.'

'Swot,' said Gideon and Clive smiled tightly. He knew he was.

'Look—it's all in here,' he said, wiping his neatly parted hair back from his forehead and flicking open the book. Dax leaned across to look. The book was called *The Crystal Directory* and promised that it was the 'Ultimate Guide to Crystals'. Clive was sliding his finger down a page with what looked like Gideon's stone on it.

'Serpentine!' he said. 'From Cornwall, in Britain, also from Russia, Norway, Italy, America, and parts of Africa. It's a stone which will aid meditation and spiritual exploration.'

'Oh, retching rabbits!' moaned Gideon and rolled over onto his stomach, burying his face in the grass. 'I knew it. Bags I snog the apple tree before Spook does.'

'Sssh! Listen!' reproved Clive, pushing his spectacles further up his nose and scanning through the rest of the words on the serpentine page. 'Helps balance and detoxification . . . promotes forgiveness . . . blah blah . . .

guidance from angels . . . Oh, good grief. I grant you it's wifty . . . and very probably wafty too.'

Dax chuckled. Clive sounded more like an elderly teacher than a schoolboy.

'Ah—here's the bit!' Clive raised one finger triumphantly. 'Serpentine eliminates parasites.'

There was a silence so heavy it seemed to flatten the air. Gideon lay motionless, his face still in the grass. After a few seconds he sat up. Clive looked at Dax, his eyes large and worried behind his glasses, and mouthed 'What did I say?'

'Well,' said Gideon, getting to his feet. 'Thanks, Clive, for . . . for that.' He walked away.

'What did I say?' repeated Clive, this time out loud. 'It eliminates parasites! And that's what his sister was, wasn't it? And he thinks she's still alive somehow, so it's got to help—hasn't it? If there's any truth in this stuff at all, of course! Some people think there is . . . and they do use crystals at NASA after all . . . so—'

'Clive,' Dax sighed. 'Sometimes you can be a bit . . . well . . . '

'Tactless. Blunt. Obtuse,' stated Clive with a rueful expression. 'I know. But I never know at the right time. Shall I go and say sorry to him?'

'No—leave him alone for a while. Let's look up some of the other stones.'

Clive grinned, instantly forgetting the problem with Gideon and hefting the book across for Dax to look at with him. They leafed through to find malachite.

'Important protection stone,' said Clive. 'Has to be handled with caution—can be toxic! Heavens! You sure Mia really likes you? Um . . . yep—stone of transformation—that's you, all right. Used as an access stone to other worlds . . . blah blah . . . amplifies energies—both positive and negative.'

Dax flipped the pages over to peridot. He grinned at Clive. 'What's she lined up for dear Spook?' There was more protection stuff, a bit about toxin cleansing and releasing negativity. Dax gave a shout of laughter when he read *Peridot encourages its wearer to move away from jealousy, spite, and anger—to admit mistakes and stop blaming others.*

They were just looking up moonstone when Lisa arrived. Clive was squawking with amusement: 'Look! Look! Moonstone can be worn to encourage acceptance of psychic gifts—and calm overreactions in the overly aggressive female!' Dax kicked his ankle as Lisa stood over them, arms folded and lips pursed, but Clive was too caught up to notice. 'Helps with flatulence too!' he concluded with glee.

'*Clive!*' Dax belted his old friend in the chest and then grinned up at Lisa. 'Opal!' he said shutting the book on Clive's fingers. 'That was opal.'

'Dax,' said Lisa. 'I am *standing* here and *listening* to your little Vulcan friend.'

Clive went beetroot red. He got up and tucked the book under one arm. 'I'll see you later,' he squeaked and scuttled away.

'Have you seen Gideon?' she said, shortly. 'He's needed in D3.'

'D3? That's the psychics' room. Gideon and Tyrone work in D1.'

'Not today,' she said. She looked annoyed and tired.

'You're going to get him to help, aren't you?' She said nothing, but looked at her feet in their expensive golden suede boots. 'You're getting him in to dowse for Luke and Catherine.'

'It's none of your business what happens in D3,' she snapped. 'Just tell me where he is.'

Dax tried to get into her head, but he didn't really need to. He knew she was angry that Mrs Sartre felt she needed *help* to dowse for Luke and Catherine.

'Stop that!' she said, and her mind closed to him like a steel shutter across a shop window. 'It's all pointless anyway,' she said. 'They're not there. It's like the Cola mums—you can't reach them once they're dead.'

'Maybe they're not dead,' said Dax.

'Oh, *right*!' she snorted, flouncing away. 'Just tell Gideon I'm looking for him, will you?'

'Yep. He went back towards the lodge.'

'And Dax . . .' she turned back towards him, 'I *don't* overreact!'

'Don't you?'

'No, I DON'T, you idiot!'

7

Lisa was in a bad mood for days and Gideon wasn't much better. Dax found his friend hiding behind the gym one afternoon and signalling wildly at him to not give him away.

'What *are* you doing?' He slid into the narrow passageway between the back of the low brick building and some hedging.

'Wishing I was Barry!' hissed Gideon, darting his head around the corner and then pulling it back in with a puff of relief. 'She's gone!'

Dax chortled. 'Is that why you want to be invisible? Lisa on the rampage again?'

Lisa had been regularly coming out of her Development sessions over the past few days, sent by Mrs Sartre to get Gideon to help with dowsing for his brother and sister.

'She doesn't like it much, either, mate!' said Dax. He picked up the sound of someone approaching and lifted his chin, drawing the scent in to find out who it was. Gideon's eyes widened in panic.

'It's all right—it's only Tyrone!' said Dax, and sure enough, a few seconds later the tall young man appeared, grinning, at the end of the passageway.

'All clear then? Managed to give your girlfriend the slip?' Gideon narrowed his eyes at his teacher who guffawed with amusement.

'If we go quickly we'll get into the woods before she finds me,' said Gideon.

Poor Gideon was definitely suffering. Several of his Development sessions with Tyrone, in which the two of them got to have mind-moving contests or go outside for wildlife walks, had been hijacked now. Instead Gideon had been forced to sit in a darkened room with the increasingly irritable Lisa. Holding her hand.

Dax offered to help. He shifted and quickly flew around the lodge. He spotted Lisa stalking up the steps back into the building, swinging her ponytail defiantly at Mrs Sartre. 'I can't find him!' she was huffing. 'Let's not bother!' He flew quickly back to Gideon and Tyrone to tell them the coast was clear.

'You need to remember this,' Tyrone was saying. 'You are not obliged.'

'Not obliged to do what?' said Dax, as soon as he'd shifted, and Tyrone blinked and shook his head. He was still amazed about Dax.

'I was just saying,' he said, quietly, with a glance around them, 'that none of you here should feel you *have* to demonstrate all your power. Not necessarily. In fact—sometimes—particularly when you're a telekinetic—it's wiser not to.'

Dax was surprised. It was Tyrone's job, after all, to 'develop' Gideon.

'I know—I know what you're thinking. That it's my job to bring on Gideon's powers—but you're wrong,' said Tyrone. 'I only agreed to come here and work with Gideon on condition that it was to teach him *control*. That's the most important thing. If I hadn't been able to keep control for the past few years, since my powers arrived, I would probably be in a concrete-clad prison by now. Or six feet under.'

Dax walked towards the woods with them. Tyrone loped along with a small backpack on, and took out a wildlife tracking book. 'How did you get your powers, Ty?' Dax asked.

Tyrone smiled. 'Not the same way as you. It was something to do with—a substance—that I came into contact with.'

Gideon grinned. 'You know—like gamma rays or a radioactive spider or something! That's all you'll get out of him though.'

'Official Secrets Act,' said Ty, with a shy smile. 'I play by the rules and the Cola project protects me. That's how it works and that's why I agreed to come here. The one thing I've learned is this—*not showing off* your powers is one of the brightest things you can do. I know it's hard in a place like this—but keep it controlled. Always. Gideon—RUN!'

The boy and the man suddenly hared off through the woods as Lisa's impatient bellow echoed across the valley. Obviously Mrs Sartre wasn't willing to let her off her session with Gideon. Dax grinned to himself and walked back to the lodge. He liked Tyrone and he knew he was right—especially when it came to Gideon. What his friend could do was astonishing. It would be awful to find it in an enemy.

Mia and Mrs Sartre were in the hallway as he walked in, talking about the bracelets. It didn't seem to be a secret conversation, so he found himself listening in without guilt.

'It will be interesting to see if there are any changes—any improvements,' said Mrs Sartre. 'Are you sure you have selected the best stones for everyone? Did you manage to get the stones you wanted?'

'Yes,' said Mia, with a smile. 'That's why it took quite a while. The malachite and the peridot took ages to get, but I wanted to hand them all out together. I chose them for protection and to bring out what's best for us all.'

'And serpentine . . . you chose that with Gideon's task in mind?'

'To help him dowse with Lisa? Yes, of course. Serpentine is the best one for Gideon. It will help him search, but it will protect him in case . . . well, you know.'

Dax felt his eyebrows go up. So their bracelets really *were* a project. He knew Mia was fascinated by all kinds of New Age ideas, from flower remedies to aromatherapy, but these stone bracelets were obviously something that the Cola project saw as useful. He wandered on past the principal and the healer and as he did so, Mrs Sartre took Mia's wrist.

'So—amethyst for you, *chérie*, yes?' she said, but Mia

eased her wrist away again and mumbled, 'Um . . . no . . . no. In fact, not amethyst. Obsidian.'

There was a pause. Then Mrs Sartre let out a breath. 'Oh. I see. Obsidian. Snowflake obsidian?'

'No. Black,' said Mia.

'And this is what you need?'

'Yes,' said Mia, firmly. 'It's what I need.'

'It's a nightmare!' said Gideon, at breakfast the next day. 'She found us in the woods and I had to go back into stinky D3 with her. It's like holding hands with a killer crab. She's so pinchy.'

Dax and Barry patted Gideon on the back in a comforting way. 'I'd *freak* if you sat *me* in a darkened room with Hardman,' said Barry, his horrified face fading away slightly, so that Dax could see Jacob Teller eating a sausage through it.

'Then, sometimes, when she sees something a bit nasty, she's just about to snap my blimmin' fingers off! And I wouldn't mind, but it's nothing to do with Luke. Someone else's old geezer or dead dog or something.'

'Aren't you getting anywhere at all?' asked Dax, loading his toast with butter.

'Oh yeah! Auntie Pam's in and out all the time. Full of interesting and useful stuff, like—oh—I should really get my hair cut—and why don't I try harder in French?' Barry snorted and popped fully back into view again. 'She's worried that now I'm a teenager I'm going to get a piercing and keeps going on about the dangers of going septic. Oh—and I should practise my over-arm throw. Apparently.'

Dax laughed. Gideon's Auntie Pam had been a kindly old lady in life, whom Gideon only vaguely remembered, as she'd died when he was seven. She'd been much more in touch *since* her death.

Gideon sighed and dragged his fork through a small lake of baked beans, without any obvious plans to eat them. Not stuffing every last bit of his breakfast at the speed of light was a sign that he was out of sorts. Dax patted his back again.

'Sorry, mate,' he said. 'It must be murder.'

'Murder, yeah,' muttered Gideon.

'But nothing . . . else.'

'No. They're not dead.'

'But they don't need to be dead for Lisa to dowse for them, do they?'

Gideon shook his head, lifted half a dozen beans onto his fork and then allowed them to slip off again and land with the tiniest of plops back in the tomato sauce. 'She's tried using some stuff of theirs that Mrs Sartre got hold of. Some stuff sent up from Luke's Isle of Wight mum, and over from the children's home Catherine was at. She holds it and shuts her eyes and lets her fingers move around a map—or sometimes she uses a needle on a bit of string. So she goes around the map, first the world, then a country, then a bit of the country. That's how it should work. I've watched her do it with other stuff, for other people, and I'm telling you—it's way weird. She really does it! I mean—not just like finding Barry's favourite pants when he asks—'

'Oi!' said Barry.

'Not just the little stuff, but I mean—missing persons! Dead or alive. She can tell. She does loads of them every week. Just sits there with maps and bits of people's stuff and just churns out SCN slips with all the information on. I mean—she's *working* for the government already. It's—well, *cool* I suppose,' he concluded, reluctantly.

'But nothing for you,' said Dax. Gideon shook his head.

'Maybe it's the LOB.'

Gideon shrugged. 'I dunno. I just wish she'd tell them she can't do it—but you know her. She *hates* to admit she can't do something—LOB or not.'

Lisa had told them that although her medium and dowsing skills were probably the best in the world, she always had a problem with the people closest to her. It was what she called the Loved Ones Buffer and apparently it was common with all kinds of people who had special gifts. Healers often said the same, according to Mia. The more you cared about someone, the harder it was for them to get the best out of your power. The emotion just seemed to mess it up and make it less reliable. It *could* be done—certainly Mia had helped them all, and so had Lisa—but Lisa's messages for Dax, Gideon, and Mia were often more confused and strange than for complete strangers. And when Mia healed anything serious in someone she cared about, it would always be more costly to her—would take far more energy than for other people. And, as in the case of her father, any pain she took from someone she cared about was always much harder for her to release from herself. That was the curse of the Loved Ones Buffer. The LOB.

'Can *I* hold your hand, Gideon?' came a sweet voice and they spun around to see that Alex Teller had come in and was beaming madly at the back of Gideon's head, doing an exact copy of—no—it *couldn't* be, thought Dax.

'Oh, go *on*!' pleaded Alex, dancing about like a nine-year-old girl. '*Let's* hold hands! I'll let you play with my dollies!'

Gideon sent his fork high into the air and compelled it to make stabbing actions at Alex's head. He was just about to physically whack the genius mimic, too, when Dax yanked the smaller boy out of harm's way, by the elbow.

'Alex! Stop larking about, you little doofus! This is important! *Where* did you get that voice?'

Alex had ducked down away from the possessed fork, which had shot a single baked bean onto his ear, but he was still giggling. 'Some girl in the reception centre. I was out on my bike before breakfast—she was down there with her mum. Why—do you know her?'

'Oh no,' groaned Dax. 'Was she wearing pink?'

'Pink? Oh yeah. Really scarily pink. So were all the dolls.'

'Oh no,' groaned Dax, again. 'They're early.'

'Alice and Gina? Here already? But it's only Friday!' gasped Gideon.

Jacob now wandered over to the small party around Alex, who was getting up again and collecting the baked bean from his left ear. He and Alex exchanged glances and Jacob looked solemnly at Dax. 'There's something else you should know,' he said. 'He says the mother was holding something . . . something *bad*.'

Dax looked wildly back at Alex. 'What? What?'

Alex patted his shoulder gravely. 'A home-made jumper, mate. A home-made jumper.'

The reception centre was a lodge house close to the main gate into the Fenton Lodge estate. A single storey, yellow-brick building, it had been converted by the Cola Club project to act as a stopping off point for any visitor to the college. Most of the family members of the Colas knew about their abilities, and, over time, had been told a certain amount about the other children's powers. Some, like Lisa's father, Maurice, had even had other Colas home to stay with them in the holidays. But this was before Maurice had helped Lisa, Dax, Gideon, and Mia to escape the government agents who were tracking them last year. Dax doubted that they'd all be allowed back to Lisa's manor house again.

He walked slowly through the college grounds towards the reception centre. Soon after Alex's warning, Mrs Dann had arrived in the dining room with a slip of paper from Mrs Sartre, requesting his presence there. He was to be let off the first hour of morning lessons to greet his family. Then they were to be settled into the luxury cottage and he would rejoin them after lessons that afternoon. Oh, joy.

Dax shuddered and resisted the urge to shift and fly away. The next few days were going to be appalling. When he could have been finishing off the tree house with Owen and his friends, he'd be stuck in a cottage with *Gina*! Alice, he reckoned he could just about cope with—but three days of *Gina* and no excuse to get away from her. She would expect him to show her around and introduce her to his friends and he'd have to keep the lie up all weekend about why he was here and what was special about them all. Lost as he was in his miserable thoughts, Dax knew Owen was following him. He could hear and smell him. He turned around, grateful for the chance to delay getting to the reception centre.

Owen wore a rueful smile as he caught up with him. He knew all about Gina. He fell into step with Dax and spoke gently.

'You do realize that you're now the only Cola whose family doesn't know, Dax?'

Dax sighed and nodded.

'Sooner or later, you're going to have to tell them. Show them.'

Dax nodded again.

'You wanted it to be your dad, first, didn't you?'

'Yes. But he's not here, is he? Big surprise.'

'Have you ever thought, Dax, that maybe he does know something?'

Dax stopped and turned to Owen. 'What do you mean? Has he said anything?'

'No. Nothing to me. But sometimes people have a kind of instinct—a subconscious knowledge—about the people they love. You might find when you finally tell him that he's not as shocked as you might think.'

'Well, that'll be fine, if I ever get a *chance* to tell him,' muttered Dax.

'We could get him here for you. We could . . .'

'I know what you can do,' said Dax, and his words came out hard. 'No, thank you.'

Owen sighed and rubbed his hands through his shaggy hair. 'That still leaves us with the problem of Gina and Alice. I will make sure that everyone at Fenton Lodge understands your situation and must be extra careful when you show them around, but, Dax, letting them know while they're *here* might be the best way. It's safer here. We have a trained counsellor ready for them. We have security. If your stepmum freaks out, we can . . . *contain* her.'

Dax had a momentary vision of Gina, screaming and boss-eyed with shock, *contained* in a large see-through canister. He grinned, in spite of his doleful mood.

'I suppose, once she knows, you'll have to keep a watch on her and Alice—and do the phone tapping thing and all that. Once they know . . .'

'Dax—we already do.'

Dax kicked the heads off a few innocent dandelion clocks as they walked on. The reception centre loomed yards ahead of them. 'I can't tell you what's going to happen. I don't know if I'll tell them,' he said. 'But I'll think about it.'

Owen reached the door first, punched in a code, nodded to the security guard behind the window to his left and then led Dax inside. In the white-painted hall, seated on a blue suede couch was Alice, her arms bulging with ten or so of her favourite dolls and Gina, her eyes bulging with fake delight at seeing her stepson.

'Dax—*love*!' cooed Gina, leaping to her feet and walking around two suitcases on the floor. She was wearing one of her poshest dresses, a red and white number which made her pasty skin look like uncooked dough, and her orangey-brown hair was knotted into a bun. Large gold hoop earrings swung against her fleshy face as she bore down upon him and hugged him. Dax did his best to return the hug politely. It would help if he didn't have to smell, below the heavy violet perfume, the anxiety and distaste she was feeling towards him. No change there, then.

'Hi, Mum,' he said. 'How are you?'

'Fine! All the better for seeing you, my love. You look really well.' She worked up a sickly smile and fluttered her eyelashes over his shoulder at Owen. She fancied Owen, Dax remembered, and tried not to wince. Alice stood up and dropped her dolls on the couch. She wandered over and peered up at him with interest.

'You look bigger,' she observed. Dax felt relieved. With Alice there was no under-smell of anything bad or sinister. She was still the same straightforward, selfish little girl, but she was genuinely quite happy to see him. He felt oddly pleased about this. Her light brown hair was in plaits and she was wearing pink lip gloss—pungently strawberry flavoured—probably a free gift with one of her doll-related magazines. Her pink T-shirt had glittery stars on it and her pink jeans were fashionable and new. Even her little leather boots were pink. He reckoned she'd adore Lisa once she'd had a look in her wardrobe.

Gina led him to the chair beside the couch. Owen drew up another, and they all sat down. Alice gathered her dolls back on to her lap, but her large grey eyes rested curiously on Dax. Gina picked up a clipboard from the arm of the couch. On it was a form which she had been filling in. 'This is all very formal,' she said, breathily, fluttering at Owen again. 'Like the Official Secrets Act! Anyone would think this was the Ministry of Defence.'

Dax and Owen laughed lightly and exchanged a quick glance. The form Gina was filling out *was*, in fact, issued as part of the Official Secrets Act. It informed parents that because of the exceptional nature of their children's gifts, new teaching and development techniques were in practice at this college, which must not be discussed with any other party. Of course, by now, everyone understood what this meant. Everyone except the Jones family.

'Well—we have to safeguard our country's brightest,' said Owen. 'It's a competitive world, and I'm sure you wouldn't want Dax poached by France or Sweden as soon as he comes of age!'

Gina giggled. 'No, of course not!' She would probably

be delighted to see him leave the country, Dax thought, but she was hardly likely to say so.

Gina finished the form and signed it. She handed it over to Owen, who scanned it quickly. 'Excellent,' he said. 'Dax will be able to show you around the college after classes today—but for now we can take you up to the cottage and settle you in, and then, I'm afraid, we have to steal him back for his lessons. We must ask you to stay within the cottage gardens until he comes back for you. If you don't know the layout of the grounds you can easily set off the security alarms by mistake.'

'That will be fine,' said Gina as Owen picked up their cases. She and Alice followed him back outside into the gentle May sunshine and Dax wandered after them. Gina shivered elaborately. 'It's quite chilly for this time of year, Dax,' she said, in a syrupy voice. 'You might want to put this on, my love.' She began to rummage in her large shoulder bag and brought out something yellow and blue and woolly, which stretched alarmingly as she tugged it.

'I made it myself!'

8

Dax slumped into his desk seat beside Gideon and everyone gave him a sympathetic look—even Mrs Dann. Dax realized that they must have been talking about him—in class! He glanced around and saw Spook smirking. Now he was sure of it.

'Settled your family in, Dax?' asked Mrs Dann, with a kind smile.

'Yeah,' mumbled Dax, opening the lid of his desk and fishing out his geography books, hoping she wouldn't prod further. Mrs Dann was quite sensitive. She didn't.

Dax clung to lessons that day. He focused his attention as hard as he could on the polar ice caps. He poured himself into the sparking of World War One by the assassination of Archduke Franz Ferdinand. He lost himself in mathematical matrices and buried himself in still life drawing, but nothing could stop 3.15 p.m. coming around.

Gideon slapped him on the back. 'Good luck, mate. Just smile and nod and before you know it, it'll all be over. They'll be gone again on Monday. Hey—you'd probably better put this back on.' He handed Dax the awful blue and yellow jumper which Gina had knitted (she *said*—in fact Dax suspected she'd just bought it at a jumble sale somewhere—it had that musty smell about it). He sighed and pulled it on over his T-shirt. The sleeves were way too long and he had to roll them up. The woolly blue and yellow striped hem hung almost to his knees.

Dax trudged up the gentle slope of the school grounds, punched in the code at the inner perimeter, passed through the wrought-iron gate in the old wall and then walked up through the steep meadow towards the fells that surrounded the Fenton Lodge estate. Normally he would simply fly up, in seconds, but today he was as anchored to the ground as a man in concrete boots. It took him ten minutes to reach Gina and Alice.

The cottage was a typical Cumbrian building of grey stone with a roof of bluish-grey slate. Set in a lovely garden filled with bright late spring blooms, it nestled into the crags of the lower fell next to a small but spectacular stream which gurgled and plummeted and cascaded in small, energetic torrents down between the rocks. Stone seats had been placed beside the stream at a number of pretty viewpoints and the vista across the valley was breathtaking. In every direction the peaks folded up and down along the horizon, some still capped with snow. If it weren't for the college and the pale ribbon of the road that wound in from the east, it could have been something almost prehistoric. There weren't even any electricity pylons and wires in view. They had been removed and the cables buried underground, Dax knew. For safety reasons.

Dax heard Alice laughing and splashing and realized

she must be in the hot tub. The round pool was deep enough to sit in up to your chest, and, at the press of a button, would erupt with plumes of bubbles. It was built into the wooden decking that jutted out from the lower end of the cottage. Dax smiled, in spite of himself. Alice must be knocked out by the place.

He found Alice accompanied by—he did a quick count—twenty-two dolls. Most were sitting upright around the edge of the tub; a pink, plastic audience with fixed smiles and staring eyes. Two favoured dolls, though, were in the water with Alice, wearing little swimsuits. Barbies, he reckoned, although he didn't claim to be an expert. Alice was wearing a lilac swimsuit with pink sequins on and her hair was bunched up on top, making her head look like a pineapple. 'Hi, Dax,' she said, without even glancing at him. This was the best thing about Alice. She really didn't care that much whether he was there or not. It was relaxing.

'What do you think of the place, then?' he asked, sitting on the edge of the hot tub, which rose up from the wooden decking like a very wide wooden barrel.

'It's wick!' she purred.

'Wick?'

'Ye-es! Wick! Don't you know what that means? You are *so* OAP, Dax!'

'So OAP?' He shook his head at her.

Alice rolled her eyes. 'Old! Out of touch! Everyone says wick!'

'But what does it mean?'

'*I* don't know! Just everyone says it.'

He laughed and she looked slightly cross, but soon reabsorbed herself in getting her Barbies to do synchronized swimming. 'I need more than two really,' she murmured. 'To make a proper pattern. Dax, would you—?'

'Not a chance!' He shuddered. Not just at the thought of joining Alice in a watery Barbie ballet, but because Gina had now arrived in a towel and a lurid orange swimsuit.

'Dax! The colour really brings out your eyes!' she said, eyeing the jumper with another treacly smile. 'We were beginning to think you weren't coming! Get in with us.'

'Um . . . I haven't brought trunks,' he said.

'Ah well, never mind.' She climbed in beside Alice, dropping the towel to reveal a wide orange bottom, which caused a tidal wave as it hit the water, knocking half of the pink plastic audience onto the floor.

'Mum!' scowled Alice and then Dax had to help her set them all up again while Gina settled back in the cauldron of bubbles and closed her eyes. Once the dolls were back in place and Alice was back in the water, Dax couldn't think what to do. Or say. He sat down on the decking and looked across the valley. What now?

Gina continued to bob up and down gently, her eyes closed and her face getting pink with the heat. After a while she opened her eyes again and seemed surprised to see Dax still there. 'Oh,' she said. And then closed her eyes again. Dax got up and went into the cottage to try out the TV.

At the college there was only a very basic TV set up. Just the terrestrial channels, One to Five. There were no computers. None of them were able to access the internet. The supernatural charge that endlessly flickered around the building between the Colas messed up the screens and, of course, talking to the outside world through the internet could be dangerous. This meant that the Colas, despite being the most extraordinary children on the planet, were embarrassingly behind normal kids when it came to technology. Dax would know what 'wick' meant, otherwise, he guessed. Adverts on some of the grainy channels they did watch were full of gamestations and playcubes and other astonishing gadgets. Clive, the last to join them all, was still quite up to speed on these things, which he fiddled around with when he went home on holiday—but even there he had been forbidden to use the internet. It was very easy to trace, so there was no getting around it.

They didn't really miss it. The college facilities—the pool, the gym, a library full of beautiful books, puzzles, and games, the outdoor adventure playground, Owen's occasional bushcraft treks and the tree house building—were more than enough to keep them occupied in their spare time. Even so, after months and months without gadgets, the widescreen plasma TV, with its endless satellite channels and surround sound, was thrilling. Dax closed the sliding patio door to the deck and the hot tub, and settled down with the remote control. With any luck, he and Gina would just slip back into doing what they used to do at home. Staying out of each other's way. If so, he could make it through the weekend. He flicked through channel after channel of loud, mad, intense TV; stuff they just never got to see any more. He paused several times through the music channels, but then found himself drawn to *Storm Warning* and then *Raging Planet*, and was just settling in to a brilliant programme about living in the wild, with a man called Ray something who reminded him of Owen, when Gina stepped in front of the screen, and snapped the TV off with a damp finger.

'Enough of that!' she grinned. 'We can watch TV any time!'

Well, no, actually, thought Dax, but he summoned up a weak smile. 'What do you want to do, then, G—Mum?'

'Meet all your friends, of course! Just as soon as I'm dried off!'

Dax twitched, and he knew she saw it, but he kept his smile in place. 'Fine,' he said. 'Whenever you're ready.'

He had been given a word to use as a signal when he punched the code in again on the other side of the inner perimeter gate. The word was 'Colony' and it was to tip off security and pass on the message to the teachers and Colas that family were being shown around and everyone was to behave. Of course, they *knew* exactly where Alice and Gina were at all times anyway. As soon as they arrived they had been given a little elastic band to wear on their wrist with a metal tag which read 'VIP' and then a number. They were asked to wear it at all times, for security, of course. What they didn't know was that each metal bracelet held a tracker chip. Wherever they went, the surveillance team were always with them. Dax wasn't sure that any of the other Colas knew about this, but he could hear the particular pitch of the radio frequency which connected with the bracelets. His fox senses told him a huge amount about the world around him that normal people could not know.

It didn't bother him. It would only bother him, he realized, if he started to hear that pitch on Gideon or Mia or Lisa. He had been tracked himself, once, by Clive, but hadn't recognized the sound. Now he knew it well.

'Colony,' said Dax and then pushed open the gate. Here was where his two worlds would *really* collide. He felt faintly sick as he led them around the corner of the lodge's west wing and across the lawn towards the steps to the huge oak front door, which stood open, as it often did on warm days. Dax saw Gideon spring up from the front steps and bound across to them. Just behind him was Mia.

'Hi!' shouted Gideon. 'You must be Mrs Jones and Alice! Dax has told us so much about you!' Mercifully, Gideon, who was now shaking hands politely with Gina, had kept his voice straight. Dax felt a warm rush of relief. Gina was *really* smiling at Gideon, who was giving back his most charming beam and widening his green eyes at her. 'Hi, Alice!' he said. 'Love the pink jeans! Where are the dolls?' Alice giggled and pulled two miniature teenage figures out of both jeans pockets and Gideon even took them from her and examined them without making retching noises.

Now Mia arrived, and sent a pulse of wellbeing across the party. Gina stared at her as if she were her long lost sister. 'You must be Mia!' she said, and Dax had absolutely no idea how she could know.

'Yes—we've come to help show you around,' said Mia. Dax could have hugged her. This is what friends were for. Mia and Gideon just took over, leading the Jones family away around the grounds, with their gently sculpted lawns and shrubs, ponds and streams, through the adventure play area, where Alice whooped and climbed all over everything with Gideon while Mia had polite conversation with Gina about how their lessons were going.

Spook walked by with Darren and he couldn't resist coming over to gloat about the jumper. 'Hello, Dax—this must be your mum!' he said, his smile like an oil slick across his face.

'Oh—and who might you be?' simpered Gina, mistaking him for another friend.

'I'm Spook Williams—how do you do?' And he actually took her hand and *kissed it*! Gideon and Dax exchanged looks of revulsion and Dax had to struggle not to boot Spook's behind as he bowed.

Gina giggled and patted her hair. 'Very well, thank you! How polite you all are here!'

'And is this vision of knitwear *your* handiwork?' said

Spook, with an expression of wonder and joy as he turned to Dax, ignoring his enemy's hostile stare. 'Why, Dax—it really brings out the colour of your eyes. You should wear electric blue and,' he sniggered, 'daffodil yellow, more often! Oops—bit of fur!' He picked an imaginary speck off Dax's shoulder and Dax could do nothing but stand there, gritting his teeth, with Gina watching.

'I'm sure Mrs Jones would make you one too, Spook,' said Gideon, 'if you asked really nicely. Maybe with sequins on. You know how much you love twinkly things!'

'Of course, you've only to ask,' breathed Gina and Spook said he couldn't possibly put her to so much trouble and made a quick exit. Dax noticed a holly branch abruptly twist itself around and poke Spook in the eye as he strode off through the trees. Gideon grinned and bit his lip.

Then they went inside the house and Owen came along to show them around the classrooms and labs and workshops. Mia and Gideon continued to trail along with them, supporting Dax, while Gina fluttered and giggled girlishly around Owen. 'Oh, what lovely surfaces!' she trilled in the lab, and he and Gideon bit their lips and tried not to collapse into honks of laughter as Owen nodded and agreed, patting the workbenches as Gina stared up at him like a besotted poodle and Alice clamped a small, fashionably dressed figure onto a retort stand.

At one point they rounded a corner into the dining room and Gina gave a startled cry. 'Ooh! I just . . . I thought I bumped into something . . . but . . . ' She glanced around her, confused, and Mia leaped across the dining room carpet and touched her shoulder.

'I'm always tripping over myself around here!' she gasped, sending a strong wave of distracting healing and glancing uneasily at Dax and Gideon. Gina walked on with Owen and Alice and as soon as they went through the door into the kitchens, Barry swam into view, beetroot red, and sniffing with embarrassment.

'You *idiot*!' hissed Gideon. 'What did you want to be doing a glamour for? You nearly blew it for Dax! They don't *know*!'

'Sorry, Dax,' mumbled Barry. 'I was, like, having a go at the cake tin, and I thought Mrs P was coming to tell me off, so I, like, disappeared . . . ' The cake tin lid was, indeed, askew, and there were telltale crumbs down Barry's stout chest.

Clive emerged from the other doorway. 'Shall I get him out of the way, Dax?' he asked, earnestly. Dax nodded, feeling pinpricks of sweat down his back. This was too weird. Clive dragged Barry, a head taller than him and twice the weight, out of the room, tutting and telling him off. Dax took a deep breath and walked on after his family.

Owen did not make any attempt to show Gina and Alice into the basement level. The Development rooms were out of bounds to visitors—with good reason. Anything might be happening down there, even outside school hours. If Colas felt the need to work through their special talents, they were allowed to go down to the basement, punch in their personal code, and spend time in the rooms. There would always be an observer present, but it was the closest thing to privacy they could have and it was surprising how many of them seemed to forget the scientists behind the mirror. Dax never forgot, but then, he was the only one allowed to exercise his powers outside.

Owen walked right on past the door to the basement stairs, heading towards the library, but before they'd got very far down the corridor there was a crash and everyone spun round to see the basement door fly open and Lisa stamp out of it. She was clearly in a terrible mood, her face glowering and her eyes fixed hard onto the thin air a few feet in front of her. Dax knew she wasn't sharing the same world as the rest of them—he could smell her distraction and annoyance even more than he could see it.

'No!' shouted Lisa. 'Absolutely not! Get out of my head, you witch! How many times do I have to say it—I *don't care*! Watch and learn! Just *see* how much I *don't care*! I'm OFF DUTY!'

'LISA!' bellowed Owen and they all jumped. Lisa snapped her head round and her eyes fell on the party in the corridor, but Dax's insides cringed, because he could see that she wasn't taking them in. She had transferred her anger to Owen, but she couldn't even *see* the rest of them, he was sure of it.

'What do *you* want?!' she snarled, her dark blue eyes

large and glittery. 'More of these?' She shook a bunched-up wodge of pink SCN slips at him. 'I'm telling you—I'm *done* for the day and if you start on about those stupid triplets again I'm going to scream!'

'Lisa! Meet Dax's *mum* and *sister*!' said Owen, heavily, glowering right back at her.

Lisa caught her breath and stared around at all of them now. She seemed to take in, at last, what was happening. But her expression still wasn't right. She still hadn't properly got back from the spirit realm that was so aggravating her.

'You!' she said, blinking and peering curiously at Gina. 'You! Here! Come for the hot tub and the scenery, have you?'

'I—I beg your pardon?' spluttered Gina, glancing from Lisa to Owen.

'Nice of you,' snapped Lisa, her eyes still glittering—still half in the otherworld. Dax pulled a face at her and tried to get into her head. *Lisa! Stop it! This is GINA!*

'Wondering what else you'll get out of Dax, are you? Oooh—you don't know the half of it yet,' Lisa babbled on and Owen actually groaned out loud and stepped across to take her by the shoulders.

'I'm sorry, Mrs Jones,' he said. 'Lisa's not quite herself.'

'No! No!' agreed Lisa. 'I'm about fifteen other people right now, Mr Hind! About fifteen!'

'Get Sylv to help,' said Owen, his voice very low, giving her a small shake. 'And stop this *now*!'

Lisa gave a hard laugh and said one more thing, staring over Owen's shoulder at Gina. 'You burnt them, didn't you? Burnt them all! You selfish cow!' Then Owen slapped her across the face.

9

'Nasty little madam! I don't care if she was hysterical or not—she had that slap coming.' Gina speared a slice of sautéed potato violently and stared across the table at Dax.

'Well?' she snapped, and it was as if the last two years hadn't happened at all. Just like old times. Alice hummed to herself, totally ignoring the nasty atmosphere around the table and tucking into the steak medallions in peppercorn sauce, sautéed potatoes, and finely steamed vegetables that Mrs P had had delivered to the cottage.

'Well, what?' muttered Dax, staring at his plate and willing himself to start eating before everything went cold.

'Well—are you just going to sit there or are you going to agree with me that your spoilt little brat of a friend insulted me and deserved a good slap? Several of them, if I'd had my way. She's the one who kept phoning you up last year, wasn't she? Snotty little madam—I didn't like the sound of her voice then. Thinks she's too good for us!'

'She does *not*,' sighed Dax, although he suspected Lisa almost certainly *did* think that. 'She was just . . . stressed out. She gets like that sometimes.'

'Oh does she, indeed? And I suppose everyone lets her get away with it! I know what kind of school this is. It's one of those hippy places where nobody ever gets told what to do and all the children just slop about behaving any way they want to. You don't even wear uniform any more! You all need more discipline, that's what I say!'

Dax snorted. He'd never been anywhere as strict and disciplined as Cola Club. 'It's fine here! It's not a hippy place. And you didn't think that about Gideon and Mia and . . . and *Spook*, did you?'

'Hmm,' grunted Gina, gnawing on steak now. 'That was before I *knew*! Before I met that little she-devil.'

'Oh, this is ridiculous!' burst out Dax, shocking even himself. 'You can't judge everybody here by what Lisa was like! She *is* a brat sometimes, I admit! But she's also brilliant and clever and brave and you can just *stop* talking about her like that!'

'Oh, *really*?' Gina narrowed her eyes at him and he could smell the sharpness of her dislike again, stronger than any peppercorn sauce.

Dax put down his knife and fork and looked at her levelly. 'What did she mean?'

'About *what*?' Gina started sawing at her steak, with far more vigour than necessary.

'You know what. She said you burnt them all. What did she mean?'

'I've no idea! The girl's clearly insane.' But she didn't lift her eyes from her plate and he could see that she had paled a little. The scent of fear crept in with the dislike.

'Fine. I'll ask *her*.' He was up from the table and out of the cottage before she could protest. As soon as he was out of sight he shifted to the fox, ran swiftly down from the fell cottage in the twilight and leaped lightly across the inner perimeter. In less than a minute he found the open common room window and jumped through it. Lisa and Mia and Jennifer were sitting by the fire looking at magazines and talking quietly. Lisa looked up as his claws clipped across the floor. She looked guilty, but bit her lip and lifted her chin.

Dax didn't bother to shift. In fox form his telepathy with Lisa was most effective. *What did you mean about her burning things?* he demanded. Lisa dropped her eyes and fiddled with the magazine. 'I'm sorry, Dax,' she said, out loud. 'I was confused, I didn't know what I was saying.' Then she looked up, startled, as a low growl filled the room. *You knew exactly what you were saying!* he sent again. *Don't mess me about. What did she burn?*

Lisa sighed and hugged her knees towards her, resting her forehead on them. *Your photos, Dax,* she sent. *The photos you should have had. Of your mum and dad. And you. All the stuff before she came along. She couldn't stand your dad having them. She burnt them all one day—when you were about five, I think—while you were at school. She was jealous. She still is. She made a bonfire behind the shed and used your dad's silver lighter.*

'Dax! Don't—' she began, out loud, but he was back out of the window before she could finish.

They were no longer eating when he got back. He suspected Gina had lost her appetite, because he'd only been gone four minutes. He strode back in and stood in front of her.

'Why did you do that?'

She widened her eyes, at first with indignation and then with a kind of panic.

'Do what?'

'Oh come *off* it, Gina! You *know* what you did!'

'I don't know what that girl has been telling you, but I—'

'My photos! You burned them all! You did, didn't you?'

Alice came into the room from the kitchen, wide-eyed. Gina was now so pale her lips were turning white. She murmured weakly, 'I don't . . . I mean . . . how could she have known? It's a trick . . . '

'Oh don't you *get* it?' said Dax, his voice dripping with contempt. 'She's a psychic! And a medium! She *knows* this stuff.'

'A—a psychic? Dax, there's no such thing.'

'Yeah, right—there's no such things as psychics, or illusionists, or telekinetics, or healers! What do you think we *do* here?'

She stared at him, open mouthed.

'You set fire to them behind the shed, didn't you? With Dad's silver lighter—the one he got from Mum— my *real* mum! If there's no such thing as psychics, how do I know that, eh?'

Gina gulped. 'You—you don't understand how hard it was for me. I could never replace her . . . '

'Got *that* right!' His voice sounded clamped and twisted; his throat swelling with anger.

Gina hit the table, making the cutlery and plates clink violently. 'It's all right for *you*! You never had to keep it all together as soon as your dad sloped off, did you? That was *my* job! To become his glorified housekeeper and nanny to an ungrateful little brat like you! *And* I was pregnant! It was all right for *you*!'

Dax gaped at her in astonishment. 'All *right*? You think it was *all right* for me? Why do you think I was SO GLAD to get away from you? You hate me! Did you think I didn't notice?'

She opened her mouth to speak, and then snapped it shut and closed her eyes. 'I didn't come here to listen to *this*!'

'No—no, you came for a free holiday, so let's do each other a favour and just be honest about it! I mean—sorry, Alice,' he flicked his sister a glance and saw that she was pale too, 'it's been nice to see you, but . . . ' he looked back at Gina who was now glaring at him with undisguised venom, ' . . . you can't stand me, Gina—and I can't stand you.'

Gina dropped her voice low. 'You'd better remember, young man, who signed the forms for you to come here. I can stop you coming here if I want—I'm your legal guardian. Don't you cheek me! As it happens, yes—I *am* glad you're here. You're where you belong, with the rest of the freaks like *her*! What she does is the work of the devil.'

Dax felt his fists clench and realized how close he had come to shifting and attacking her. Too close. The look of fear now on his stepmother's face made him realize he must have done the alien thing.

'What did you just do with your eyes?' breathed Alice, staring at him.

'Nothing.'

'You did! You did something funny with your eyes!'

Gina curled her lip. 'You *are* one of them. You're a freak. I always knew it. There was always something bad about you and I always knew it!'

Dax leaned forward, resting his hands on the table and staring into her face.

'How bad do you *want*?' he snarled.

Then the screaming started.

10

'Well, *that* went well,' said Owen, sliding the patio door shut on the busy scene inside the cottage. Alice and Gina were sitting on the sofa and Janey and a counsellor called Rosalind had been brought in to attend to them. Two security guards were posted front and back of the cottage. A smell of lavender wafted around the place—a soothing spray scent to calm hysteria which Rosalind had brought.

Dax rested his head in his hands. 'I knew this was a bad idea.'

Owen grimaced. 'Fair enough. I'm sorry—I didn't think it would be as bad as this. I reckoned without Lisa's little show, of course. What *was* that about, by the way?'

Dax explained to him about the photos. 'She missed one, though,' he said. 'There's one my dad keeps hidden in the shed. I've seen it. So she failed. I do know what my mum looks like and how I looked and how my dad looked before she died. I do know . . . '

'What did she see? Fox or falcon?'

'Both,' admitted Dax, shaking his head. 'Fox first—bit of growling—then falcon—bit of screeching. Seemed like a good idea at the time.'

The patio door slid open and Alice stepped out.

She looked dazed but much better than Gina, who was currently sitting with her head between her knees, breathing into a paper bag.

Alice sat next to him. 'You should have told me sooner,' she said, in a voice that was squeakier than usual. 'You should have told me last time and not pretended.'

Dax blinked in surprise. She remembered, then.

'What do you mean, "last time", Alice?' said Owen, sitting next to her. She leaned towards him, away from Dax.

'I saw him being a fox one night—but he told me I was dreaming. I believed him then, but now I know I was right.'

'I couldn't tell you then,' sighed Dax. 'You'd've freaked out.'

'I wouldn't.'

'You *would*!'

'I wouldn't!'

'You *would*!'

'Enough!' Owen raised his hands. 'Look, Alice, there's really nothing to be afraid of. Dax is just a bit—different—from other kids.'

'You're not kidding!' said Alice. She got up and wandered across the decking, looking down across the garden to the college beyond. 'I *know* what this place is!' she suddenly whispered, turning to them with a look of awe. 'It's the place for the X-Men, isn't it? Dax is a—a—X-Boy!' She sat down again with a bump.

Owen laughed. 'Actually, it *is* a bit like that, but not so dramatic. It's quite ordinary in lots of ways. Everyone has to do lessons just like you.'

'What are their powers?' asked Alice. 'Have you got a wolverine? Or the one who sets fire to things?'

'No,' said Owen. 'I'm glad to say. Just some very talented kids with extra special abilities. Dax is probably about as X-Men as it gets. And he's still your big brother. And he still loves you.'

Alice pulled a face but Dax was glad Owen had said it. He'd never be able to say it himself.

'The thing is, Alice,' Owen went on, 'we need people in the outside world that we can trust. Will you be one of them?' She nodded, eyes huge, feeling important. 'You can't tell anyone about this, do you realize that?' She nodded again. 'Because we have to keep everyone here safe—and if people got to know about them, they wouldn't be safe. Do you understand?'

'Yes.' Alice looked grave. 'But I don't know if Mum will.'

Owen glanced back into the cottage and nodded. 'Come on,' he said, and led them back in.

Gina was calmer and ready to pack their bags but Owen moved smoothly across to her, touched her shoulder and urged her to wait a day or two. 'I know it's come as a shock to you, Gina,' he said, losing the formality of 'Mrs Jones'. 'It's a terribly shocking thing. But I would be worried about you driving tonight, after having such a trauma. Come and sit down and have some tea with me.'

Trauma or not, Gina liked the attention. She sat down with Owen, casting a dark look at Dax as he leaned in the doorway. 'Can I go now?' said Dax and Owen nodded, taking Gina's hands in his.

'Shouldn't he be . . . you know . . . locked away?' he heard Gina ask as he left. Even now, as he walked back down the fell, he was surprised that these words slightly hurt him. *Truth isn't always beautiful*, he thought, remembering the words of some of the old junior school hymns he used to sing.

Dax found Gideon in their bedroom, sitting in the window seat, waiting for him. 'Everyone's talking about it!' he said, as soon as Dax opened the door. 'What happened?'

Dax flopped down on the bed and told him. 'Oh, how cool was *that*?' said Gideon when he came to the bit where he'd said 'How *bad* do you want?'

'Not very, really. It was stupid.'

'Nah. She had it coming. Eat this.' Gideon gave him four chunks of chocolate from his bedside stash. Dax didn't think he'd ever swallow it, but it went down quite easily and he did feel a bit revived.

'But what if she tries to stop me being here? Like she said she might?'

'Why would she? She doesn't want you at home, does she? She was just trying to scare you, like you were scaring her. Don't worry. They won't let her mess things up for you. And there's still your dad, isn't there?'

His dad. Dax realized, with a thud of misery, that now

his dad would find out about him. And he'd find out from Gina. The worst possible way. The prickly, clammy mantle of his own stupidity settled around his neck and shoulders, making him want to shrug his very skin off. 'I've been really dumb, Gid,' he mumbled.

'Yeah. But we like you anyway. Have a shower and go to sleep. It'll be better in the morning.'

Gina and Alice spent Saturday and most of Sunday at the cottage on their own or in the company of the counsellor, who was trained not only to help ease the shock to newly informed Cola relatives, but also to spot signs that they might prove to be trouble once they returned to the outside world.

Rosalind came to see Dax late on Saturday, nearly twenty-four hours after it had all happened. She was a kind woman, older than Gina, but much prettier, with curly dark hair. She tended to wear lilac and amethyst pendants and could have been quite wifty-wafty, but she wasn't. Her laugh was way too normal and nothing seemed to shock her.

'Are they going to be—you know—a problem?' Dax asked her, when they sat down alone together in Paulina Sartre's book-lined study.

'I think Alice will be absolutely fine,' said Rosalind. 'Gina—well, we may need to work with her a bit more. Although the shock hasn't put her off the hot tub, the food, or the indoor cinema, I noticed. What about you, though, Dax? How are you feeling?'

He thought for a bit. 'I feel . . . stupid. Shaky. I shouldn't have done it. It should have felt brilliant—getting back at her. And it did, for a little while, but when she wouldn't stop screaming, I realized it was just stupid. I should have waited.'

'Perhaps there was never going to be a good time,' said Rosalind.

'No, maybe not. I just wish . . . '

'What do you wish?'

'That my dad had been there. He's the one who really needs to know, and now he'll find out from *her.*'

'We can bring him here, you know,' she said, but Dax shook his head. He'd blown it now. Getting Robert Jones down here by force wasn't going to help.

'So, what will you do—to—to *contain* Gina?'

'Oh, we're coming to an arrangement,' said Rosalind, with a tight smile and all at once Dax knew.

'You're paying her off, aren't you? You're going to give her money to keep quiet.'

Rosalind put her palm against his cheek, like a mother. 'Can you think of a better way?'

'No,' he said. 'I can't.'

Owen said he should see them both again before they went. Clear the air a bit. Dax couldn't imagine a time when the air between him and Gina had ever *been* clearer. Telling each other the truth about things was never going to be nice. But he could see that maybe Alice might need reassuring, so he followed Owen back up to the cottage an hour before their transport was due at the gates.

'I just want you to know, Dax,' said Gina, as soon as they had all sat down around the dining table, 'that I don't hold you to blame for what—what you are.' She spread her hands flat on the linen tablecloth and let out a steady sigh, her face masked with a saintly expression.

Dax looked at her and tried not to narrow his eyes. The scent of her dislike had become thicker than ever and was mixed with fear and repellence now. 'I will always care about you and want the best for you,' she went on, still looking at her hands. 'And I know that your father will feel the same. I'm sure he'll want to come and see you soon—as soon as, as soon as . . . well, we'll cross that bridge soon enough.'

Dax nodded. He couldn't think of anything to say. After a while Alice got up and went outside and he said, 'I'll just go and say goodbye to her.'

Gina stiffened and glanced up now, warily. 'Just—just don't—*do* that . . .'

'I'm *not* going to shift,' he said, through gritted teeth.

Alice was stamping on ants below the apple tree. She broke off from her insect slaughter when he arrived and stared at him. 'What's it like?' she asked.

He smiled. 'Most of the time, it's fantastic. I'd show you . . . but . . . ' He glanced back through the patio doors and spotted Gina standing up, arms folded over her chest, staring out at them. 'Well . . . you know.'

She nodded. 'Will I go Cola, too?'

Dax shook his head. 'No—I think it was something to do with my mum. You've got a different mum, so I don't think it'll happen to you.'

'Oh.'

'You going to keep this a secret?'

'Yes.' She resumed her ant stamping. 'Are you going to tell Dad?'

'I guess so. I—I don't know how really.'

'Just tell him when he phones you,' she said, kicking a few more insects into oblivion as they scrambled up the trunk of the tree. 'I tell him all my stuff when he phones.'

Dax said nothing.

'So when he phones *you* this week, you should just tell him!'

He looked at her and she stopped the stamping and kicking and finally looked back at him.

Dax gave a dry laugh. 'He phones you every week?'

'Well—yeah! He calls you too!'

'No,' said Dax. 'He doesn't.'

She tilted her head to one side as it worked through its nine-year-old logic. 'Oh. Well—I suppose dads just love daughters most.' She shrugged and he heard himself make that dry laugh again.

'Take care then.' He patted her on the shoulder and left.

Owen joined him again as he went back down the lower slopes of the fell.

'It'll be fine, you'll see,' he said. 'Don't think too badly of Gina. She's human, that's all.'

'She wants me locked up.'

'You'll feel better when your dad comes.'

Dax stopped and looked at him and then found

he had to put his hands on his face to stop his mouth shaking. 'Don't you see? Don't you get it?' He hated the hurt sound in his voice—didn't want *ever* to hear it again.

Owen just stared at him.

'He won't come, Owen. If there's one thing I trust about my dad, it's *that*. My dad *doesn't come*.'

11

His dreams were muddled. Pale yellow light seemed to flick on and off and on and off in them and the wolf came and sat beside his bed, its eyes glinting bright and black and bright and black with the shifting light. 'They'll pay money to keep you quiet—they'll pay money,' Dax was telling the wolf—as if a spirit could have any use for money. The wolf just looked at him, shook its shaggy head and sent a telepathic message—as hopelessly strange as they usually were. *Two and three in the land of pom-poms.* Dax actually laughed out loud, Gideon told him later—laughed in his sleep because this one was the daftest message yet. And then that small boy walked past his bed and pointed to the wall above his head—only, of course, that was wrong, because the pointing boy usually pointed to the wall in the medical room. That's how Dax knew he was dreaming. He was dreaming and he knew it, so he woke himself up.

'What's so funny?' asked Gideon, blearily, from his bed. It was early—not yet half past six according to his clock.

Dax sat up and said, '*Two and three in the land of pom-poms.* What do you make of that?'

Gideon yawned. 'You what? Oh—don't tell me. Wolf-boy's been back. Is that his latest message?'

Dax nodded. 'About as useful as they always are. Or maybe it was really just a dream this time. It seemed like a dream.'

'Prob'ly was then.' Gideon pulled his cover back over his head. 'Wish I had a spirit guide to pop in and liven up *my* dreams. All I've had all night is a light going on and off.'

Dax felt the hairs on his neck and arms rise up. 'What kind of light?'

'Oh, I dunno. Sort of yellowy—and then grey and then yellowy again. It creaked, too. Creaky noises. Clicks.'

Dax stared at the back of Gideon's fluffy blond head, wondering whether to tell him he'd had the same thing—he remembered clicks and creaks too, now. It meant something. But Gideon was asleep again and Dax didn't know if it meant anything *much*. Besides, he'd been freaked out all weekend, and all he really wanted was to feel normal again. He decided the shared dream was just another Cola thing. One of too many peculiar things to take much notice of. And 'wolf-boy', as Gideon called him, probably *hadn't* made a proper appearance. The first shapeshifter, who had been murdered before he could join the other Colas, the wolf had helped Dax in the past, arriving in his head and dreams and sometimes as a visible spirit. His messages and warnings were always strange but *this* one was just too ludicrous. It had to be a dream.

Knowing that Gina and Alice were long gone made for a much happier breakfast for Dax. He and Gideon told Mia and Clive about what had happened, in low voices. They didn't want Spook overhearing.

'And she's really taking money from them?' hissed Clive, pushing his spectacles up his nose.

'Yes. Hush money, I think they call it,' said Dax.

'She wants to be careful,' intoned Clive with a sinister glance around them. 'We all know what they're capable of if they're pushed. She could end up encased in the foundations of the new North Hampshire bypass!'

They looked at each other with a mixture of feelings. Clive was being over-dramatic, of course, but in the past year they had all had a taste of just how ruthless the special operatives assigned to the Cola Club project could be, if necessary. There was even a time when Dax and Gideon had been in genuine danger of getting shot by them.

'No,' he said. 'She'll shut up for money. No question of it. And anyway, other Cola families have had financial help, Rosalind said. It's part of a protocol, apparently.'

'What's a protocol? Sounds like something for a bad headache,' said Gideon.

'It's a sort of official rule, I think,' said Dax. 'Or a set of rules about how something is handled. They think that we'll stay happy if our families are happy. That's why they've made that cottage so brilliant to stay in and that's why some of them are getting help with money stuff.' He glanced at Mia, who was looking intently into her bowl of muesli.

'Yes, Dax,' she said, after a pause. 'My dad *is* getting that kind of help too.'

'Sounds like they're all just being bought to me,' muttered Clive and Dax sighed. *The Amazing Boy Tactless strikes again*, he thought, as Mia dropped her head a little further.

Lisa was not at breakfast. She was out running, said Mia. She'd gone out early. But she was back in time for lessons and obviously still in a foul mood. She didn't speak to any of them—not even Mia or Jennifer.

That afternoon in Development there was a knock at the door and Paulina Sartre came in.

'I'm sorry to disturb you both,' she said, as Dax shifted back to a boy. 'Mr Hind, may I borrow you for a moment?' She seemed excited, thought Dax. And anxious too. He could smell both emotions entwined together. Something was happening. Maybe something good.

After a minute, Owen came back in. 'Dax,' he said, 'I think we may have a job for you. You need to come to D3 with me.'

'D3? Isn't that where Lisa is? Is Gideon in with her again?'

'Yes.'

'Are they getting somewhere? Has Lisa dowsed Luke or Catherine?'

'Just come with me.'

They walked swiftly down the corridor and into the little lobby outside D3 where Gideon was surprised to see Mia also waiting. 'What's happening?' she asked Dax but he shrugged as Owen told them to wait and pushed open the door. The Development rooms were soundproofed, and as soon as the door seal broke they could hear Lisa cursing.

'I'm getting a *migraine* here! Just make it *stop*, Sylv! I've *got* it! I *see* it! On—off! On—off! All *right*!'

Mia shivered.

'What?' said Dax.

She shook her head. 'I don't know . . . yet . . . but—'

Now they heard Gideon. He didn't seem to be in a much better temper. 'Ow—ow—*ow*! Look, I am planning to use those fingers again after today!'

Then the door swung closed again and Mia and Dax looked at each other. 'On and off. The light,' said Dax and she caught her breath.

'You too?'

He nodded. 'I was dreaming it last night. Gideon was too. And you?' She nodded back, eyes wide with wonder.

Owen came back and opened the door again, so they could see Lisa and Gideon glowering at each other across a round, polished-wood table. As soon as he saw them Gideon snatched his hand back from Lisa's as if her fingers were molten lava. Even under the rose glow of the silk-covered lamp hanging above the table, he looked pink with embarrassment.

Lisa turned around to stare at them, and rolled her eyes.

'Oh, *great*,' she said. 'It's Furry Face and the Feel Good Fairy.'

'Shut up, Lisa,' said Owen and led them to sit down at the other two seats around the table.

'What's going on?' said Dax and Gideon shrugged and looked weary. The room was thick with the scent of burning incense and candles threw strange shadows in each corner, their twins flickering back from the mirror along the length of one wall.

'We think we have made a little progress,' said Paulina Sartre, her French accent softening her words as she touched his head lightly. His hair rose up to meet her warm palm. This was normal with Paulina Sartre, who was also a clairvoyant and dowser, like Lisa.

'It seems that Gideon and Lisa have shared a vision— and Mia too, says Lisa. We were wondering if you had it also, Dax.'

He nodded. 'Light—going on and off—or . . . sort of light and dark,' he said. 'And a creaking, clicking sort of noise.'

'Why didn't you tell me?' asked Gideon, affronted.

'Didn't seem that important.'

'See?' snapped Lisa. 'Nobody else has a clue!'

'Shut *up*, Lisa,' said Owen again. 'You're getting some help, like it or not. If this doesn't work we'll all admit you're right and you can forget all about it. One last effort, please!'

Lisa looked sour.

'She thinks it's a big waste of time,' explained Gideon. 'She can't get anything definite and it's killing her because she's got such a humungous ego! But now that she's started getting the light thing, I thought it might be a sort of clue. Maybe. She just thinks it's a load of codswallop—but if you and Mia are getting it too, it can't be. So we *all* have to hold hands now! Give her a bit more juice.'

'Can't hurt to try, can it?' said Dax, but Lisa just scowled up at the ceiling.

Mia sighed and pulled something out of her pocket. 'You really should have this on, Lees,' she said and they saw that she had Lisa's bracelet with the moonstone on it.

'I don't *need* any gimmicks, thank you,' grumbled Lisa, but Mia yanked her friend's hand over the table and insisted on tying it on.

Gideon cackled. 'Calms the overly aggressive female!' he crowed. Dax had told him about the moonstone information in the book. 'You definitely need it!'

'Have you both got yours on, too?' checked Mia and they held out their wrists, Gideon's multicoloured stone gleaming gently under the rose light and Dax's dramatic green and black swirls shining. 'Good. They'll help,' said Mia. 'This is part of the reason we got them,' she smiled at Mrs Sartre. 'To help us all connect better.'

She held out her hand to Lisa, who snatched it ungraciously and then took Dax's. Dax and Mia linked hands with Gideon who looked much more comfortable now that he didn't have to have direct contact with Lisa. 'Close your eyes, everyone, and take a deep breath,' said Mia. Dax did so, aware of Owen and Mrs Sartre quietly backing away to the edge of the room and sitting down.

For a long while there was only the sound of their

breathing, becoming slower and more even, like people asleep. He ignored the urge to scratch his ear and tried to use the hypnosis tricks Owen had taught him, to get super-relaxed. It seemed to work. Maybe five minutes or more passed with only the sound of breathing and the soft pink light on his eyelids. Then there was a click. And the light turned yellow. At once goosebumps shot across his arms and back and he heard Mia give a little gasp. The light fell grey, as if a shutter had dropped, and then swung back to yellow. Then grey. On it went—grey, yellow, grey, yellow. And the clicks and the creaks came and went.

Lisa's breathing was getting louder—she seemed to be losing her cool again. 'What? What *is* this? Grit? Birds? It's making no sense! Sylv—tell them to stop that light show!'

'No!' said Dax, surprising himself, his eyes still shut. 'The light show stays! It means something. Wait!'

She *seethed* at him, right into his head and he shoved her back out. *Pay attention!* All at once there was a feeling of . . . cloth . . . cotton against his skin. And pressed across his chest, over his shoulders, as if he were wrapped tightly in a shroud. And the hands that held his began to grip hard. They turned icy cold and their fingernails dug into his skin. A desperate feeling began to well up inside him—fury and anger and frustration and then, suddenly, a bolt of hopelessness seemed to smack into his chest like a boulder from a slingshot and he felt his chair swing onto its back legs and crash right over onto the floor. His head struck the thin carpet over D3's concrete floor and his teeth juddered in his skull.

All around the table his friends were scrambling about on the floor, looking shocked. Owen and Mrs Sartre ran to sit them up and check them over. Lisa lifted her face to Owen and, in spite of herself, a triumphant sparkle was in her eyes.

'I would say,' she smirked, 'that we just made contact.'

'Food!' said Lisa, standing up. 'We need food—pasta and meat. Cheese for Mia,' she conceded.

'What are you *talking* about!' gasped Gideon, rubbing the back of his head and setting his chair straight. 'We've just made contact—and you want a picnic?'

Lisa looked at him as if he was a total idiot. 'It's going to take a *long time*. You won't get through it. We all have to eat. Sylv says so and she's not laughing.'

Owen and Paulina Sartre took them straight to the dining room and sat them down. Owen went to the kitchen to sweet-talk Mrs P and within ten minutes there were bowls of steaming hot fresh spaghetti in front of them, drenched in tomato sauce and ground beef for all but Mia, who had cheese in her sauce instead. Despite their excitement and nerves about what was to come, they wolfed down the food and followed it with lemonade and chunky home-made oat biscuits.

Owen ate too, and Paulina drank lemonade and nibbled on a biscuit. She was excited, Dax knew. She was also deeply anxious. As they finished their food she took

Owen to one side and talked to him quietly. Dax tuned out the babble of his friends around him and targeted his sharp ears to the voices in the corner. He didn't make a habit of this, but he needed to know what was scaring the principal.

'We must be ready to ground them,' she was telling Owen. 'This is . . . this could be dangerous.'

'How?' said Owen. 'They can't really be in physical danger, can they? I mean—yes—they tipped over, and we can put cushions down behind them in case that happens again—but nothing worse can happen, surely? Not while we're there to ground them—bring them back.'

'Mr Hind.' This was slightly chilly. 'With all due respect—you don't know this territory as well as I do. And *I* don't know it nearly well enough. I am trusting to Lisa's spirit guide on this. I am trusting . . . but I am *concerned*. Something *wants* them. Wants their energy and their attention.'

'We don't have to do this,' Owen stated. 'Call it off.'

'I don't think we can, now. Whatever channel has been opened up is still open. And I do not wish to leave Lisa to deal with it alone. I believe she must have her *quatuor* . . . her quartet. These four are required. We must just . . . be ready. Their stones should help keep them grounded.'

'And the scientists? Are they going to be part of this?'

'You know as well as I do, Owen, they have to be part of this. They will not intervene. They never have before.'

'We've never done *this* before.'

* * *

A strange calm had settled upon them all when they returned to D3. The room was fresher but the incense and candles still burned.

'I do not know exactly where you are about to be taken,' said Paulina Sartre. 'But you have to be ready to come back. If you feel frightened or endangered, you *must* come back.'

'How do we do that?' said Gideon, looking pale in the flickering light.

'Use your serpentine, Gideon,' said Mia. 'Like an on or off button.' She looked at Mrs Sartre, who nodded.

'How can I, when we're holding hands?'

He had a point. Dax looked around the table and saw Lisa bending down and taking off her expensive leather running shoes.

'I hate to suggest this, knowing what your socks smell like,' she muttered across the table at Gideon. 'But we can do it just as well with feet.'

Dax laughed and took off his trainers. 'My socks do *not* smell,' said Gideon, peeling them off and holding them aloft. 'Well, only a bit,' he added, after a sniff.

Mia slid off her sandals and they all placed their feet carefully, so they could make contact. 'Ow!' said Mia.

'Sorry,' said Gideon. 'Need to trim me nails!'

With their feet touching they were free to rest their fingers on their stones, their right hands on their left wrists, like businessmen synchronizing their watches. (All the Colas had, without even consulting, moved their watches to their right wrists as soon as they'd got the bracelets.)

'So how does this work?' asked Gideon.

'It's something to ground yourself with—you just tell your conscious mind that this is your on-off button, and you use it when you need to,' said Mia. 'We need to relax again and then, when you're ready, you can press your stone.'

Lisa shrugged. 'Makes just about as much sense as any other way,' she said. 'But don't blame me if it doesn't work.'

'Just do as the Feel Good Fairy tells you,' said Mia, giving Lisa a surprisingly hard stare. 'And if you feel that this—whatever it turns out to be—gets too much, then press again. You should be able to bring yourself back.'

'Back from where?' breathed Gideon and Dax felt a tremor of fear go through him.

'That's what we're about to find out,' said Lisa.

12

After about ten minutes of the breathing and the closed eyes and the gentle flickering light from the candles, Dax was almost certain they were wasting their time. He felt fine—relaxed, open-minded, full of pasta. Nothing else.

He distracted himself with thoughts of the wood. Off fox-trotting around his favourite places in the warm sun, the air drenched with the smells of nature.

Dax. Stop earthing yourself, you idiot! Lisa suddenly snapped, inside his head. *You're holding us all down! Make your mind blank! Get out of the woods!*

He coughed and nodded and then cleared his mind as best he could, concentrating on a kind of pearly light that was nowhere and nothing. Then he remembered, and pressed his fingers against the malachite. There was a creak. Then a click. And then the strange changing light was back. And this time he could see that although it was switching on and off, it was doing so in a kind of turning movement. It made him think of an electric fan—a slow, big fan. Turning and slowly chopping round and round through the air, shutting the light off and on. There was a salty smell in his nose—he could taste it on his tongue—and now the feeling of tightly wound cotton across his skin was back.

At once, the anger and frustration and misery began buffeting him again. All of them gasped and their toes clawed. They would probably all have tipped over once more with the intensity of it, if Lisa hadn't barked out—in all of their heads, he was sure—*Stop it! Get a grip! You can't keep shoving it onto us like that. We can't be of any help if you keep doing that! Stop it!*

Whatever or whoever it was that had been making them feel so bad immediately pulled back and they now felt those feelings much less—as if they were happening in another room.

Then, strangely, a wonderful tingle began to run across Dax's skin, from the top of his scalp, to the tips of his bare toes. *At last. Oh—at last atlastatlastatlast . . .* This was not Lisa. Dax knew this voice. They all did. He heard Gideon making a strange, choking sob.

'I knew it!' he murmured. 'I knew it!'

Atlastatlastatlastatlastatlast . . . went on the familiar voice and might have gone on for minutes on end, keeping them all suspended in that shivery world, if Lisa hadn't cut in.

All right! Get a grip now. We're here—you've found us. Now you need to talk to us.

There was a sigh and the intense tingling subsided a little.

At . . . last . . .

'Luke?' prompted Lisa, out loud, and Dax heard Owen give a small out-breath of shock and excitement. 'Luke—are you dead?'

I don't know, said Luke. *Do you know?*

Lisa sighed. 'I don't think so. But you're not really alive, either, are you?'

No. This is not life.

'Where are you?'

At once, the vision of light and the sound of creaking got stronger, along with the salty smell. Now Dax could hear distant cries. Birds, he was sure.

'Are you near the sea?' said Lisa.

I don't know.

'Are you trapped somewhere?'

Yes.

'Where?'

I don't know.

Lisa huffed with frustration. 'Are you . . . on a boat? Is that the creaking?'

No—not now. I was, but not now.

'Luke,' said Dax, surprising himself with how normal he sounded. 'Who is keeping you there?'

Luke laughed. It was a dry, awful laugh, like the breaking of dead sticks.

You know who.

13

'This is fantastic! Oh—this is the best! Look—you can open your eyes. See me!'

They snapped open their eyes and gasped. Luke was sitting cross-legged on the table. He seemed totally solid, but the air around him curled and eddied like water, making Lisa and Gideon and Mia look *less* real to Dax.

'Don't lose contact,' said Lisa. 'Keep your feet together.'

At first Dax thought Luke was wearing a kind of Roman toga—a sheet draped across his chest and wrapped around his waist and legs. Then he realized that it simply *was* a bed sheet. Luke didn't have his glasses on and looked astonishingly like Gideon, although much thinner.

'I'm in a bed,' said Luke. 'Somewhere. I don't know where it is, but the room is wood and old stone. The windows are high and the light changes all the time.'

Dax looked around at Owen and Paulina Sartre and found he couldn't see them. 'Where are they?' he said, with a stab of concern.

'Where they were before,' said Lisa calmly. 'It's OK—we're on a different plane. We've sort of—*moved sideways*—a bit. They can still see us, but we can't see them.'

'Can they hear us?' asked Gideon.

'Probably not—we're not talking on their level. Probably just sitting with our eyes shut and doing that heavy breathing thing. Stop worrying about them. We haven't got time.'

Luke nodded when Lisa said this. 'No, you're right. She'll be back soon and I won't be able to stay here.'

'You mean Catherine?' said Gideon.

'Yes.'

'What has she done to you? What happened to you both? Everyone thought you'd both drowned,' said Gideon. There was a wobble in his voice.

'Except you, Gid,' smiled Luke.

'Look—as lovely as it is for you to do the family reunion thing,' cut in Lisa, 'we have to get a move on. Time runs out fast here. Luke—shall we see you or be you?'

Dax blinked. He didn't understand what she meant. But Luke did.

'You'd better see me,' he said, gravely. 'You won't want to be me.'

'Fine,' said Lisa. 'I always prefer *not* to be.'

'What are you *talking* about?' said Dax.

'OK, get ready to press our little magic stones again,' said Lisa, with a tight sugary smile at Mia. 'The quickest way to know what's happened to Luke is to watch him. Actually, it's much quicker to *be* him, but you'll only end up throwing up. You're not used to it. Don't go being him. We'll watch and Luke will show us. Take a deep breath before you press—this is going to be . . . intense.'

Everybody sucked in a lungful of air and pressed their stones again. All of a sudden Dax felt as if he were falling. Air rushed upward past his face, making him gasp. By the way Lisa's and Gideon's feet flexed against his at the same time, he guessed they were all experiencing the same feeling.

But he was wrong. Now the air gave way to a cold, gritty, terrible pummelling sensation and Dax felt as if he was being rolled over and over and over, slapped and bashed and clawed at by relentless forces. He gasped again and struggled to breathe and felt terror churning inside him—and yet through it all he could still feel the feet of his friends under his toes. He knew he was still sitting back in D3 with Mia, Lisa, and Gideon, and yet the physical assault was appalling. Now he knew it was water and it seemed to funnel right into his ears and tear at his mouth—he heard himself give out an animal whine of fear and then the noise and the sensations seemed to drop, abruptly, and both Lisa and Luke were clamouring in his head. *Dax! You idiot! I told you to WATCH!* sent Lisa, and Luke, in a much calmer, more sympathetic voice, said, *Dax, you mustn't BE me. Just SEE me. Being me will be horrible for a while. Get out, mate.* And through the weird buffeting of all the noise and violence, Dax actually felt Luke take his shoulders and propel him backwards.

He found himself sitting on a shelf—a kind of see-through shelf. Mia and Gideon and Lisa were sitting on it too—Gideon to his left and Mia and then Lisa off to his right. Lisa was peering around at him suspiciously.

'Are you going to throw up? Because you might as well get it over with and then we can watch properly.'

Dax shook his head but found nothing to say, because he was open-mouthed with wonder at what he was seeing. Ahead of them, below them and above them, curved a three dimensional scene. At the moment all it was, was water—churning, dark blue, green, and black, turning and turning and broken only by an occasional chunk of brick or metal or wood which spun through it and then was swallowed back into it again. The closest thing to this Dax had ever seen was a planetarium, where you could lie down and look at a three hundred and sixty degree silk screen onto which the night stars had been projected, curving up, away, and around you.

But *this*—this was moving! And it curved away beneath them too. The sound of raging water and the dragging of seabed shingle thundered away, but he was no longer pummelled around by those elements. It was as if they were all observing from inside a room-sized bubble—only you couldn't make out where the barrier was between air and water. He could no longer feel what it was like to be inside that cauldron of tortured sea. He sighed shakily.

'This is how it was,' said Luke, from inside their heads. 'I thought it was all over. I held my breath just out of instinct. There was no hope of living, but I was hoping I might bob up and just see that you'd got them all away safely, Dax, before I died. I wanted to know that Gideon was OK. But I didn't come up—not then. Not for ages. She held me down.'

Dax felt Gideon jump as Luke's features, distorted through the tumultuous water, suddenly bloomed into view. His eyes were wide and staring and his hair moved around his head like seaweed. His mouth was tightly shut, but bubbles were escaping from his nose in an upward plume. He could only be seconds away from drowning. Then he jerked in the water and an arm curled abruptly around his throat. Catherine's face now bloomed also, over his shoulder, her longer dark hair curling into his fair hair and her eyes also wide—but in this case, with rage. Dax saw again her expression of fury when he'd last seen her on the grass with Luke, below the suspended sea.

Now something was changing. Among the bubbles escaping from Catherine's mouth, one seemed to anchor to her lips and then grow bigger and bigger and bigger. Before long it had covered her head completely and now it stretched and engulfed Luke too. Inside it, the brother and sister gasped and coughed, and their seaweed hair slumped against their heads. Still the bubble grew larger and larger until they were both bodily inside it—and now Dax, Mia, Gideon, and Lisa seemed to be inside with them, an unseen audience. Luke turned to look at Catherine in amazement, and then his face contorted with anger and he tried to rip her arms away from him.

'Stop it, you lame brain!' she spat. 'You undo me from you and we're both dead. You might have all the power, you cheating liar, but *I'm* the only one who knows how to use it!'

'This isn't possible,' murmured Luke, looking sick.

'It is if you're a Cola,' said Catherine, and she actually smiled, triumphantly. 'Especially if you've got all the power of every other Cola on the planet!' Floating along in a bubble, half a mile under a convulsing sea, she looked as if she was on a ride at the fair.

'You haven't got it all,' said Luke. 'You didn't get Dax.'

'No. Well, that was annoying. Maybe I'll go back for him one day,' said Catherine, running the fingers of one hand through her sodden hair, but keeping hold of her brother with the other. 'But for now we need to get out of here. There's not a lot of air to breathe in this bubble and I'm too tired to make it bigger right now. You'll have to bring us something to sail on.'

'What are you talking about?' coughed Luke, and wiped some gritty dribble away from his chin. 'I can't do that.'

'Luke—don't kid me. You just held back the sea! As far as I know, the last person who did *that* was Moses! Get me a raft!'

'You don't understand,' said Luke. 'I don't know how I did that. I never did know how. I never even thought it was *me* that did it—before . . .'

'So, you *were* lying all the time! Wow! I had no idea. If I'd known I wouldn't have wasted all that time on chocolate guzzling Gideon. *You're* the one! You've got the biggest battery of any of them! How could you not know that?'

Luke shook his head and glanced around the bubble,

which showed curved swirling dark seascapes in every direction. 'I thought . . . I thought it might be, you know, a poltergeist or something. I was scared. I wanted it to stop.'

Catherine looked fascinated, still clinging to his shoulders. 'So how did you stop it?'

'I—I went to see someone. This,' Luke sniffed, embarrassed, ' . . . this kind of hypnotist guy. I'd tipped over a car, and I was really scared.'

'You tipped over a car? Like—over onto the sidewalk?'

'Yeah. Kind of. It was in the road behind us, trying to get by, and this guy was all aggressive and honking his horn and Mum was really scared and I—I turned round and looked at him and . . . and the car flipped over on its top and slid down the undercliff.'

Catherine gaped at him, her eyes glittering with amusement. 'Oh you're full of surprises, big bro! Did they come and get you after that? Y'know—the Cola team?'

'No. Not for weeks. Because I stopped it. Like I said, I went to this hypnotist in Ryde and he set up a sort of *block* thing in my head. Made it stop. Well . . . mostly. Sometimes it came out in dreams . . . '

'Whoa! Like when all your windows smashed in the dorm and everyone blamed Gideon?'

'Yeah. Like that,' mumbled Luke. 'But like I said—only when I'm in dreams.'

'Well, Power Pack Luke, you *weren't* in a dream when you ruined my plans just now, were you? You were awake. So let's get this straight—you're not fooling me. Get me a raft!'

Luke lifted his head and looked at her with an expression colder than frost. 'You don't deserve a raft, *little sister*. You deserve to die. Maybe I don't care if I have to die too. Get your own raft.'

Catherine's pretty face puckered with the tiniest amount of fear before a sneer rested across it. She tightened her hold around Luke's neck. 'Whatever,' she said. And squeezed.

14

'She leeched nearly everything out of me that first time,' said Luke, as the vision of Catherine, nostrils flared and eyes bright, throttling him, faded to soft shades of seawater. 'She didn't really know what she was doing. It's only pure luck that she stopped before I was dead— before we were both dead. I just blacked out, and when I woke up again, we weren't under the sea any more; we were on it. It was daylight and . . . well . . . it was like this.'

The sea shades grew lighter and lighter and there was the morning sky, moving from side to side with the incessant tug-and-tug-back of the deep ocean. Luke and Catherine lay side by side on . . . on . . . yes—it really was—a large wardrobe from one of the dorms at Tregarren. It seemed to be quite whole, with only a dent or two. Even the mirror to one side of it reflected the pale blue sky flawlessly. Catherine held Luke's hand tightly in her left hand and the metal handle of the wardrobe door in her right. Luke's eyes were closed.

'She got it,' said Luke. 'She hung on to me while I was unconscious and moved us up through the sea in our little bubble, almost to the surface, and then found her raft floating by. She used all my energy to suck it across towards us and then got on and dragged me up after her. Nice, isn't it—that she saved my life? And look how she's holding my hand. That's when the habit got started. We were like that for three days. Just lying there, holding hands, sailing out across the Atlantic. A helicopter went by once—miles away—we could hear it and see it on the horizon. If I hadn't been done in, she'd probably have sucked that over to us too and hijacked it, but she was too weak and there wasn't much juice left in her brother battery. Lucky for the pilots.

'Even so, we should have died. There was nothing to eat or drink. We could have gone without food a while, maybe, but not water for three days and nights. You know what she did? She made it rain, over our heads. That was before the helicopter—the last bit of energy we had, just once. She pulled water out of the clouds and opened her mouth and made it pour in. She made me drink too. I was too tired to bother, but she opened up my mouth and made it rain. Then we slept, I think, for quite a lot of the time. Then—'

There was a crack that made them all jump violently, on their invisible shelf above the view of the two triplets on the ocean. 'I don't know if she made her—but Francine came then,' said Luke. 'She smacked right into the raft and then started screaming at us in French. I didn't know what she was saying. I think she was in shock. I mean, you don't expect to see two kids floating on a wardrobe halfway across the Bay of Biscay.

'She threw a rope to Catherine and got her on board first, and then they both got me on. I don't remember much about it, apart from the smell of the yacht and being warm again. My fingers hurt really badly—they'd been so cold and when they warmed up they hurt like they were on fire. Especially the fingers *she'd* been holding. I must have had food and drink, but mostly I just slept while we sailed to the land. Catherine was awake—she was always coming over to check on me, and hold my hand. Sometimes I almost woke up, and I could hear her talking to Francine—in perfect French. I don't know how many hugs it took but she learnt it inside a day.

'I wanted to talk to Francine. I wanted to warn her. You have to know this—I did *try*! I even got up on my elbow that night, and tried to speak. I opened my mouth and tried to speak and then Catherine started stroking my head and pushing me back down and when Francine went up on deck . . . ' Luke's voice, so calm and controlled until this point, now began to crack. 'She opened my mouth up, with both hands, and then dug her fingers in and grabbed my—my tongue. She twisted it in her hand, like it was a bit of cold chicken. She said . . . she said . . . '

They all shrank together—even Lisa had her hands over her mouth, her eyes wide with horror—the dim view of the inside of the yacht that they had been seeing was now replaced with a grim scene. Catherine, grinning and baring her teeth, one hand shoved into her brother's mouth, the other holding down his jaw. She put her face close to his as he struggled and gurgled and flapped his hands weakly at her. 'You,' she said, '*can't* talk. I've already told her you're a mute. And so—' She gave a sharp tug and her eyes rolled up into her head, revealing the whites, before snapping back, open in triumph . . . 'you *are*!'

'Oh no, oh no . . . ' Mia was moaning beside Dax. 'She ripped out his tongue.'

'No,' said Luke. 'She didn't. She wrenched it pretty badly, but it wasn't that. She focused all of her vampire thing on the bits of my brain which are to do with talking, and she emptied them out. Even when my tongue went back to its normal size I couldn't talk any more. I didn't know how to.'

There was a moment of silence. The four Colas along the shelf absorbed this new atrocity in horror and as they did so, Dax realized Mia had been holding his hand, and her fingers became so hot he had to pull away from her. 'No,' she said. She wasn't crying, as he would have expected, and her voice seemed lower, harder, than usual. 'No,' she said, one more time, and then lapsed into silence.

'The tongue thing sort of did me in for a while,' went on Luke, and the view swam away into vague chinks of light and colour, dreamlike and insubstantial. 'I listened though, because they were talking a lot, and I found out that I could understand them when Catherine was holding my hand, which she did all the time we were together below deck. She told Francine that we'd been out at sea with our dad, and there'd been a storm and we'd been washed overboard. She said we'd crashed against a cargo boat and made out that she thought the wardrobe had come from there.

'Francine wanted to do a Mayday then, and get the French coastguard involved and then—then Catherine had to stop her. She said that we'd been beaten up by our dad all the time. That we lived in fear of him and he'd even killed our mum years before, but nobody could ever prove it. She said if Dad found us again we'd go back to being beaten up and she would rather die. She said she missed Mum. Then she said Francine reminded her of Mum and then Francine started to cry. Francine said she used to have a daughter, but the daughter died five years ago from cancer. She would have been the same age as Catherine was now if she'd lived. Francine was a doctor—a surgeon—but she gave it up and went off on her boat after she lost her daughter. And now the sea had given her a new daughter.

'Catherine *made* Francine love her. She knew exactly how to do it. She'd been right inside Francine's head, learning French and poking through her memories and she knew exactly how to do it. Francine believed everything she said. Everything. That we were half French, because our mum had been French and our dad was English, that we'd lost our mum and our dad was a brute—that I was mute and brain damaged, because of all the beatings. That I would never speak again, and probably be a vegetable all my life. Because that's what Catherine wants. And what Catherine wants, Catherine gets.

'She wanted a new start, in a new home with a new mother. So we sailed back with Francine. I guess to

France, but I don't know for sure. She kept me really weak when we reached the land. Unconscious, really. Francine carried me to her car, wrapped up. Nobody seemed to take any notice. Then we drove for a while—maybe an hour, maybe more—and then I think there were stairs. Winding stairs. Then the room. The room with the changing light and the creaks and clicks. And the bed.'

'Are you always in bed?' asked Lisa, and hearing her voice was like waking from a dream for Dax, so lost was he in Luke's bleak world.

'Not always. Sometimes I move to a chair, when Catherine's left me alone long enough to have the energy. And I use a basin to—you know ... They bring food to me; easy food like soups and yoghurts. I don't have enough strength to chew. And then Catherine holds my hand and makes me sleep. Deep down sleep—sometimes too deep even for dreams. I heard women talking on the stairs one day. Francine's sister, I think, came to see her. They said how very kind Catherine was. They said watching her sitting with me, sometimes for an hour or more, was like watching an angel. "*Le petit ange*" is what they call her. They keep us secret, because Francine wants to keep Catherine—she even pays for a private tutor for her. The French aren't as nosy as the English, Catherine says. Nobody asks awkward questions. She really did land on her feet.

'She sits and she takes every last thing she can out of me. Charges herself up with my power and my life force, but not enough to kill me. Never that much. I wanted to die. I wanted to get away from her. If you can't help me I'm going to find a way to die. Sorry, Gid, but I'm just a big battery now. That's all my life is.'

'EVERYONE! Press your stones and get out NOW!' Lisa's shout was like being struck with a plank. Everybody jolted violently and fumbled for their bracelets and in an instant they were back in D3 and Gideon was flinging himself over the table towards Lisa and grabbing her by the shoulders and shaking her.

'What did you do that for? Why did you make us come out? What about Luke? We left Luke behind!' Lisa slapped his face. Gideon gaped in shock and slumped down on the table. There were tears in his eyes.

'What has been happening?' demanded Owen, urgently, from behind them. 'Where did you go? Talk to me, someone!'

'We had to get out. *She* was coming back!' snapped Lisa, wrapping her arms around herself defensively. 'Ten more seconds and she'd have had his hand in her claws and she'd have known straight away that we were with him. And she'd have come after Gideon—or Dax—or all of us! We *had* to get out!'

'But—but what about Luke?' Gideon looked desolate and it made Dax's heart clench to see it.

'He'll find us again. We'll do it again. We'll find him,' said Lisa. 'At least we know what country he's in.'

'What? Where? Tell me!' demanded Owen, banging the table in frustration. Lisa told him what they had learned, briefly and in such a concise way that Dax remembered she had to deal with this kind of stuff all the time and somehow get it across to people in the real world. He would have babbled and mumbled and struggled to explain, but Lisa cut right to it.

'So it's France—that's where he is,' concluded Lisa. 'Not too far from the sea. I might be able to dowse now. I'll try later, when we've smudged in here a bit.'

Smudging was some kind of smoking herb thing they did, remembered Dax, to clear the air of all the supernatural pollution after a big session with the spirit world.

'So he's alive? He's definitely alive?' said Owen and, behind him, Paulina Sartre closed her eyes as if in prayer.

'Well, he's not among the dead—*which* I think I told you anyway,' said Lisa (glossing over the fact that she'd never said Luke was among the living, either). 'He's in a sort of coma, I think. Or a cata—a catatonic state, is it? Because he can move sometimes. And Catherine is keeping him there, never quite conscious. She . . . she sort of . . . ripped out his tongue to stop him talking.' Lisa dropped her head and Dax knew she didn't want Owen to see any tears. Owen patted her gently on the shoulder. It was shocking to see Lisa close to tears. She very rarely cried, unlike Mia.

Dax turned to look at Mia, expecting her to be in floods of tears, but what he saw made him stop dead. Mia remained in her seat, pushed back a little from the table, one finger still resting on the black obsidian stone on her bracelet. Her mouth was set in a flat tight line and her violet-blue eyes had changed. They were exactly the same colour as the obsidian. 'Mia?' Dax stepped towards her and then felt as if he had struck a force field. He couldn't get any closer and as he gasped and looked back at Owen there was a searing, ripping noise and above his head the silk pendant lamp erupted into flames.

15

'Gow—gow—*gow*!' Gideon was hopping up and down, his left thumb jammed into his mouth, nearly hitting his head on the tree house roof. His hammer and nail work hadn't got any better over the last few days and Dax had been very surprised when he'd said he wanted to go back to the tree house, after classes the next morning, and put the handrails up.

'I need to be normal,' he'd said as they walked across to the little woodland. 'I need to stop thinking about it.'

Dax couldn't agree more. He'd slept very little last night and even a run around the moonlit valley as DaxFox hadn't helped much. He kept thinking about what Luke had gone through and couldn't forget that awful image of Catherine wrenching the boy's tongue. It was so—*barbaric*. You just couldn't imagine a thirteen-year-old girl doing such a thing. In the end, Gideon had spoken up at about 5.30 a.m., shortly after Dax flew back in through the window. He said he'd been awake since four o'clock, just after Dax had gone out. They didn't go back to sleep but sat up with their quilts wrapped round them.

They'd talked about the eerie journey they'd made, about what Catherine had done and about the strangeness of being in a place that wasn't among the living *or* the dead. The fire thing at the end had been bizarre too, but Mrs Sartre said she thought the air had been disturbed by all the spirit activity and one of the candles had just thrown a bit of flame into the air and caught the lampshade. It had been dramatic, but pretty small doings compared to what they'd all been through. They'd been ushered outside for fresh air and then sat down on the grass and given hot chocolate to drink. Mrs Sartre released them from classes for the rest of the day and told them to get some rest. Nobody spoke about when they'd all regroup and try again and the following morning they were all back in class like normal school kids, as if nothing had happened.

Gideon was now tap-tap-tapping again, trying very hard to get his nail in straight. It was difficult because the handrails were lightly planed, smoothly sanded bits of thick branch, which Owen had worked, turning them carefully in the woodwork room. The smooth curved surface made Gideon's nail point slide about.

'Let's just put a couple of support nails in under it, to keep it in place,' suggested Dax. 'Then let's go and dig up some roots. We can get really long ones and then bind the handrails in place.'

Gideon agreed it was worth a try and they both swung down over the edge of the tree house platform, found the strong wooden ladder under it, and climbed down to the wood floor. As they turned round, they saw Spook Williams and Darren Tyler trudging across beneath the trees. The pair stopped in front of Gideon and Dax and Spook folded his arms.

'Everyone wants to know,' he said, haughtily. 'You four are off having special Development sessions and we're not being told why. It's not right. You shouldn't be having special sessions—it's not like you're any more special than the rest of us.'

'Oh, Spencer, no one could be as special as you!' sighed Gideon, putting his head on one side with a lovey-dovey expression.

'Cut it out, Reader—unless you want an accurate illusion of your own death,' said Spook. Dax was shocked to scent the anger and resentment on the boy.

'What do you care about it?' he asked. 'You've never wanted to do stuff with us before. Why now?'

'Do stuff with *you,* you mongrel? You've got to be joking!' sneered Spook, and Darren looked at his feet, clearly uncomfortable. He liked Dax and Gideon—but he idolized Spook. 'I don't want to share a *county* with you, let alone a Development room! I just want to know what's so important that you all get hidden away in one room together and then get off double maths! They shouldn't be giving you special treatment, because we've *all* got powers that need developing. And some of us have a future to think about! So go on then—what's happening?'

'It's not your business,' said Gideon, through gritted teeth. A small dust and leaf storm had begun to brew at Spook's feet. The boy glanced down and raised an eyebrow.

'Ooh, I'm scared! Let me guess then—it's her, isn't it? She's not done with you yet, is she? She tried to electrocute you last time and now she's up to something else.'

'*Not* your business,' insisted Gideon and the little storm rose to Spook's knees. 'Shove off, unless you want a nose full of twigs.'

'It *is* my business! Your dead sister nearly flattened *me* the last time she had a go at *you* from beyond her watery grave—don't you remember?'

'Yeah, and *I* stopped her, so you owe me one, don't you?'

Spook smirked. 'You think you're so cool. Want to know how you'd've looked if she'd got you?' The air around him shimmered and Gideon gulped and shut his eyes.

Dax realized that Spook had conjured up another nasty image and was just preparing to punch his smug face when Spook suddenly grabbed his head with both hands and let out a sharp groan. 'Oww—my head! Ow!'

'You not well, Spook?' said a cool voice behind him and Dax peered past the boy in surprise. He hadn't been aware of Mia approaching—the breeze was strong in the other direction. Spook spun round. 'Mia—my—my head,' he whined.

'Go and take an aspirin,' she said, coldly, and Spook gaped at her before striding off, rubbing his temples.

Dax and Gideon stood wordless. Mia watched Spook, and Darren following him, and then turned back to them, her eyebrows arched. 'What are *you* two staring at?'

They shrugged.

'Owen wants you both,' she said. 'In his study.' She turned and went away without another word.

Dax opened his mouth to tell Gideon about Mia's strange eyes the day before and that force field thing, but Gideon spoke first.

'She's getting a bit moody, isn't she?' he said. 'It's bad enough that Lisa's such a witch these days—I can't be doing with Mia getting all stroppy too.'

'Oh, she was just cross with Spook,' said Dax, deciding to talk about the eyes thing later. 'And Jennifer's still OK—for now. They *are* girls, remember—what do you expect?'

'Yeah, too right,' agreed Gideon. 'Girls! Alien species!'

The aliens were both in Owen's study when Dax and Gideon got there. They were curled up on one of his sofas and Mia looked ready to fall asleep, although it was only mid-afternoon. Owen's study was up on the top floor, next to the medical room. It was another attractive high-ceilinged room with a tall Georgian window and a small stone fireplace, currently filled with fir cones. It had two comfortable suede sofas, a large mahogany desk, and a tall glass-fronted bookcase filled with wildlife books, old maps, a barometer, and a couple of bird's nests. A leather trunk stood on the floor between the sofas. On the trunk was a tray with mugs of tea and a plate of biscuits. Lisa had a mug of tea but the biscuits were untouched. Owen sat on the armrest of one of the sofas and Gideon and Dax flopped into it, opposite Lisa and Mia.

'Hang on, Mrs Sartre will be here in a moment,' said Owen, and as he spoke, the door opened again and in came the principal, carrying a small high-tech voice recorder. She fiddled with it for a few seconds and Dax saw the red 'record' light come on as she placed it on the trunk between them all.

'I'm sorry that we have to go through it all again so soon,' she said. 'I know you would probably like to forget it all for a while; it was very traumatic, no?' They nodded. 'But it is sometimes like dreams. If you don't speak of them soon, you can lose them; forget them. And we need to know every detail if we are to find Luke.'

Gideon sat up straight. 'So you're going to look for him? You're going to find him?'

'Of course,' said Owen. 'We've already been on to Interpol and circulated their descriptions. The French special branch is on the case already.' Gideon beamed with delighted relief.

'Come now,' coaxed Mrs Sartre, pointing to the recording device. 'Details, please—all of you—from the start.'

They took pains to explain everything they had seen and felt and heard. It wasn't easy. Words couldn't really wrap around such a huge experience, but when they were nearly finished, Dax felt that they had got most of it across. Lisa was just coming to the bit about sensing Catherine returning when she abruptly sprang up and stamped her feet, swatting around her head as if there were mosquitoes attacking her.

'Oh, will you give it *up*?!' she snapped. They all blinked in surprise and then realized, quickly, that it was another spirit vying for Lisa's attention. Then, much to his surprise, Lisa rounded on Dax. 'Dax! Do you *know* someone called James?'

Dax shook his head, bemused. 'Nope. Why?'

'*See!* I *told* you! Now push off!' said Lisa, actually flapping in the air as if trying to get rid of someone—which she was, of course.

'Who is it, Lisa?' asked Paulina Sartre and Lisa composed herself. She had a lot of respect for the principal.

'Sorry, Mrs Sartre,' she said. 'It's this old boy—keeps going on about someone called James and says he can't get to him—but Dax knows him. He's off his rocker.'

'Can you see him?' asked Mrs Sartre, curiously. Although she foresaw events and could dowse like Lisa, she was not a medium and the whole area fascinated her.

'Yes,' sighed Lisa. 'He's over by the door now. He's a mopey old geezer. In a frock coat-y kind of thing. Early nineteen hundreds, I reckon, when he pegged it.'

'More respect, please, Miss Hardman,' admonished Mrs Sartre.

'Sorry, sorry. I just wish he'd leave me alone. He's been badgering me for days and rattling on about a pocket watch. Anyway, he's gone now. So—where was I?'

She carried on, finishing up their story, with Gideon chiming in here and there. Mia was very quiet, noticed Dax. Then he noticed a movement behind Mia's head.

It was the pointing boy. The boy walked past her, and she shivered, but didn't look up, and then he looked directly at Dax, pointed ahead of him, before simply walking through the wall and out of sight. Dax shivered too now, and glanced at Lisa to see if she'd noticed, but Lisa was leaning towards the recording gadget, finishing her statement and determinedly blocking out any other loitering spirits.

'Er . . . excuse me,' said Dax. 'Be right back.'

He quickly left the study, turned right, and slipped into the medical room. Janey, the doctor, was there, sitting at her small desk and making some notes. 'Hi, Dax,' she said, looking up brightly, her shiny dark hair woven into a plait down one shoulder. 'You OK?'

'Um . . . yeah . . . ' Dax looked past her and saw the pointing boy walk across to the foot of the bed he had spent time in. Once again the boy looked back at Dax, pointed to the wall above the bed, and was gone.

Dax bounded across the room, while Janey stared at him, curiously. He kicked off his shoes and hopped up onto the bed. He patted the wall where the boy had pointed, but it seemed like a perfectly ordinary, rather dull wall, covered with wallpaper. Solid and unyielding. Dax shrugged. Just another mad day in Cola Club, he guessed. He grinned at Janey, who still sat at her desk, watching him with an amused smile, then picked up his shoes, and slipped back next door.

'All better now?' said Lisa, when he came back in. Dax smiled at her and nodded.

Once Owen felt they had given every detail he let them go. 'We will try again, when Lisa is feeling up to it,' he said. 'You all need to relax for a while. Have a laugh, if you can—hang out with Jacob and Alex! I'll let you know if we get any news, Gideon.'

'What did you go rushing out for?' asked Gideon, as they went down to the common room.

'Didn't I tell you? I've got my own ghost!'

'You what? Who? Where? Why haven't *I* got one? It's not fair!'

Dax slapped the back of Gideon's head and laughed. He told him about the pointing boy.

'Probably just pointing out how awful that wallpaper is in there,' said Gideon. 'What's that green swirl thing about, eh? You'd think they'd want you to *stop* feeling sick!'

'I gave it a bit of a prod but there's nothing there. Whatever the kid is seeing is probably from another time. Poor little shrimp seems upset though. I'll try to get Lisa to talk to him.'

'Yeah right!' said Gideon. 'Like *that's* going to happen.'

'Oh, Dax!' called Mrs Dann as they walked through the entrance hall. 'You've got some post! Didn't you see it this morning?'

Dax blinked in surprise. He only went to the post room once a week, to pick up his Cola allowance from his pigeonhole. There wasn't much point any other day—there was never any post for him.

Mrs Dann handed him a small blue envelope with

an Aberdeen postmark on it and went on her way. Dax looked up, wide-eyed, at Gideon and then back down to check the handwriting. The loops and dots were familiar.

'Oh heck,' said Dax, remembering the previous weekend. 'It's from my dad.'

16

Dear Dax

Above all, I want you to know that I still love you. I will always love you, no matter what. I heard about what happened in Cumbria from Gina and although she's a bit of an exaggerator (well, we both know it!) I don't think even she could make up something so strange.

I have to admit it's shaken me up. I always knew you were different—special—but I didn't know how it would come out. Your teacher Mr Hind also got in touch. He seems to think very highly of you. He wants me to come and see you and, of course, I should have come to see you long ago. It's only because things have been very tricky on the rig this last year, what with job lay-offs and so on, that I haven't been able to make the time.

Dax, there's also other stuff you should know—stuff from way back—and I promise I will tell it to you as soon as I see you. I'm going to talk to my boss and see if he will give me some compassionate leave and I will get down to you as soon as I can.

In the meantime, never forget that you are special for a reason.

Look after yourself and don't ever be ashamed of what you are.
Love, Dad
X

Dax found he couldn't speak after reading the letter. Gideon was watching him urgently, wanting to know what was in it, and so he just handed it over and went to sit down on the front steps. He couldn't work out how he felt. The letter was caring, but his dad seemed to think he might be ashamed and that made him wonder if he should be angry. It had never, never occurred to him to be ashamed. Worried, freaked out, confused—yes—all of those things but never ashamed. Maybe that was what Gina had put into his dad's head. She obviously thought he was something shameful, but then, hadn't she always?

'Special'—that was the word. It had too many meanings. Even bad things, like awful disabilities, got called 'special' these days. Maybe his dad thought what happened to him was 'special' in that way. The letter should have made him feel better. All it made him feel was 'special'—in no good way.

'He's coming then!' said Gideon, sitting next to him and handing the letter back. Dax stuffed it into his pocket.

'So he says.'

'Yeah! He says!'

'No date though, Gid. And he's said it before. We'll see.'

'Dax, he might—'

'Look—Gid—can we not talk about it?'

Gideon stopped waving his hands about enthusiastically and let them drop. He nodded. 'Come on,' he said. 'Let's find Lisa. I want to know when we're getting back to Luke. We shouldn't be leaving him out there.'

Lisa wasn't in the common room, and neither was Mia, but classes had now ended for the day and Jacob and Alex were playing Trivial Pursuit, the children's edition, by the fire. Both wore looks of deep, deep concentration, because not only had they to try to answer the questions, but each also had to stop the other brother from nicking answers out of his head. Dax thought it looked quite exhausting but they seemed to be grimly enjoying it.

It seemed as if only the Teller brothers were there, but Barry and Jennifer were also in the room, both glamoured out of sight. Dax spotted the wavy lines on the couch and caught the scent of both of them, but not in time to stop Gideon taking a flying leap and landing on top of them. There was a 'Doof!' and a muffled shriek and both of them snapped into view, struggling and squawking. Jennifer's glasses were askew and she was beating her way out from under Gideon's legs while Barry was shoving his classmate's backside off his head. Dax doubled up with laughter, which came out in gales of relief. He needed a laugh and no mistake. Gideon was now back on his feet looking appalled and complaining loudly that they'd brought it all on themselves.

'You shouldn't sit there in a vanish like that! What d'you want to go and do that for? And not talking or anything! What were you up to—snogging?'

Barry and Jennifer looked disgusted. She had a book which she waved and Barry was picking up his battered, elderly hand-held electronic game. It was always on the blink because of the way Cola powers interfered with computer stuff, but Barry kept on at it, hoping to get to the high score.

'We were just having some quiet time!' said Barry stoutly. 'And sometimes we just fade out a bit without thinking of it! At least we don't break people's stuff or leave feathers lying around for people to breathe in!'

Gideon had once got distracted and dropped a floating hat stand on Barry's favourite mug, smashing it to bits—and Barry suffered from allergies and bird feathers were a particular problem to him. Dax was banned from shifting to the falcon in the bedroom Barry shared with Clive.

At that point Clive appeared in the doorway, holding a book. 'Ah, there you are, Dax. I've been wanting to catch up with you!' Clive looked at Dax over his spectacles, like an old professor, and Dax felt guilty. Clive was a very good friend to him and he hadn't told him much at all about what had been going on. He left Gideon to his argument with the glamourists and followed Clive outside. The air had turned cool and rain threatened in the east—but not for twenty minutes or more, Dax judged. His animal instincts were usually very accurate with weather.

'So—are you going to tell me what's been happening? Or do I have to bug your room?' said Clive—and he was only half joking. He was quite clever enough to bug Dax's room. He'd sneaked that tracker dot on to his schoolmate last year and followed him across four counties, after all.

'I'd hear your bugs! You couldn't,' grinned Dax.

'Ah—you *think*! But there are other frequencies—some that even fox ears might not pick up.'

'Ah—*might* not.' Clive gave him a *look*. 'Sorry, mate,' said Dax. 'I've left you out a bit, haven't I? I didn't mean to. I know we're mates, it's just that . . .'

'You don't have to worry,' said Clive. 'I know that you're *best* friends with Gideon—and that's OK, really. Because I think I'm sort of best friends with Barry now. He's a buffoon, of course, and he's always treading on my stuff, or eating it, but I like him. I just need to know, from time to time, that you're still OK. I feel a sense of—duty—to make sure you're OK.'

Dax lightly cuffed the back of Clive's mousy head. He knew he'd miss him hugely if he ever left the college. 'You don't have to worry about me, Clive,' he said, 'but it's nice of you, anyway.'

'Well—you always looked out for me at our old school,' said Clive, turning slightly pink. 'Anyway, Spook's getting all high and mighty about what they're not telling us about you four—so I thought I really should be in on it, so I can feel nice and superior around him.'

'You definitely should!' said Dax and then he told Clive about everything that had happened in D3. Clive's eyes were round with amazement, and then with horror when he heard about what Catherine had done—*was doing*—to Luke.

'She's a psychopath,' he said, simply, when Dax had finished. 'She should be locked up for life. Are you going to find her?'

'Owen said he's already got Interpol on to it.'

'The international police? Don't make me laugh!'

Dax shook his head. 'What do you mean?'

'There's no way they'd hand this over to another country! You really think all the scientists and government suits who run Cola Club are going to ask another country's police force for help? No chance! They'll want to get them back—both of them—and there's no way they'd let Catherine get picked up by another country. No way!'

'But they're allies! We like the French. Mrs Sartre's French!'

'Yeah! We like them when they cook! And they like us when we buy their wine! But you've got to remember what a Cola *is*. The L stands for Limitless, remember. Limitless power. No country in this world is going to let go of *that* once they've got hold of it. No—they'll send their own. It'll be Owen and a *crack team*!' Clive said 'crack team' with great relish. 'Trouble is, they probably still won't get them. If you go into battle with a Cola, you need another Cola. Maybe they'll take Gideon.'

Dax shivered. He remembered the last time he and Gideon had come into contact with Owen's 'crack team' of special forces soldiers. They'd only just escaped with their lives.

'How do you know this stuff, Clive?'

Clive shrugged. 'I read,' he said. 'I read a lot—which none of the rest of you do much! I get the papers sent in, too, didn't you know? Even some European ones. So I can keep in touch with the world. It's the next best thing to the internet.'

'What are you reading now?' asked Dax, noticing Clive's book. It was large, leather-bound, and old.

'The history of *this* place!' said Clive, sweeping his arm across to the lodge. 'And some of the other stately homes in this area. I haven't really started it yet, but I know it was made of sandstone, shipped across from the west coast of Cumbria. Quite rare around here—very expensive. It used to be a hunting lodge. Good job it isn't now, eh?' Dax nodded and smiled wryly. He'd had more than enough experience of hunting—at the wrong end.

'So who owned it before, then?'

'Oh, several families across the generations. Like I said, I've only just started. I'll make a family tree chart and put it up in the library. It'll be fun.' Dax chortled. He couldn't think of any other boy who would think making a family tree of a bunch of complete strangers was fun. That was Clive, though.

Gideon emerged from the lodge with Lisa. He started waving and shouting but Lisa just stood with her hands on her hips and sent him a telepathic message. *Tell Spock to go and play in his lab. Luke's waiting for us. We're going back in . . .*

17

'At first I thought she could do anything she wanted,' said Luke. 'She'd stolen the power from a hundred Colas and she was capable of anything—as long as she had me to keep boosting her up. Something about my Cola power, which I thought was just telekinesis, like Gideon's, seems to help her to keep hold of all the stolen talent. She has bits of psychic stuff, bits of healing, bits of glamour—she can make herself vanish sometimes, but never for long—and she can definitely throw illusions. She can mimic and dowse, but, with all of these things, only after she's got a battery power boost from me.

'She can't get messages from the dead though. I thought maybe she just blocked them; didn't want them—and then I realized, later, that she had tried, but nothing came through. None of the dead wanted to talk to her. The spirit world blocked her off.

'How do I know all this?' Luke didn't wait to be asked; he could read their questions and sitting cross-legged again in the centre of the table, wrapped in his bedsheet, he smiled and a cold twinkle came into his eyes. 'Because what she didn't know was that when she plugged into me, squeezing my hand and getting her power boost, I was sneaking into her head and finding out what was going on in there. Some of the telepathic stuff seemed to work two ways. She couldn't have got a lot out of *my* head—I was too out of it to think about anything much—but I got plenty out of her.

'A lot of it wasn't nice. Not nice at all. You know her first mum and dad died in a car crash? She made it happen. She got angry with them because they wouldn't let her go to a party. She wanted to pay them back and give them a headache. A lot of ordinary people end up with headaches around Catherine. They get really tired and they get headaches. So she was in the back of the car—an SUV, I think they called it—and she undid her belt and leaned over and touched the backs of their necks. She was in such a mood that she didn't even try to hold back; she just sucked all the energy out of them and her dad—he was a guy called Chase—he just screamed. She'd given him a headache like nothing on earth and then he slumped onto the wheel and the car went off the road. Catherine was thrown out of the window and hardly had a scratch on her. But her first adoptive parents were dead. She was quite upset for a while. A whole week, I think.

'The children's home people started to feel ill after Catherine arrived—and she was hard to like back then, before she learnt charm. If one of the other kids was good at something, Catherine always had to be good at it too, and, of course, as long as she could get close enough, she would be. She'd just suck their talent out of them. But she never stuck at anything. She couldn't, of course. She couldn't keep it, so nothing lasted. They called her Me

Too Cathy and she *hated* it. At school they didn't know what to do with her. One minute she was being lazy and stupid and wouldn't make any effort, the next minute she'd be showing off, doing sums at high school level— but only *after* she'd bumped into the maths teacher and needed to hold his hand to get up, of course.

'So when a second mother took her home to adopt, they were pretty glad to see her go. The next mother, though, was a really serious Catholic and made her go to church every Sunday. Little Cathy hated church; she got bored and she so cannot *stand* being bored. She had to be the best and she had to be more loved than anyone else— even her mother's God. She wasn't so practised, then, at saying the right thing and charming everybody, so she just came out and said it—said that her new mother had to love *her* more than anything in the universe or she was a bad mom. New mom made her go to see a priest. When she came back she was speaking Latin and the priest was unconscious in his vestry. That's when the new mother called in an exorcist. So before long, Me Too Cathy went back to the kids' home—and that's pretty much where she stayed until last year, spreading hugs and headaches all around.'

'No wonder they were so keen to let her come to Tregarren College,' murmured Gideon. He looked pale in the candlelight of D3. The overhead lamp had been replaced, but they'd left it off. It was easier to see Luke without it.

'Oh yes. They even bought her a whole new load of

clothes to take with her, so she looked the part. And, of course, she did exactly the same thing when she got to Cornwall,' went on Luke. 'Only by then she'd learned a lot about people and how to get what she wanted out of them. She'd worked out that she had to have a *lot* of friends, because just one friend got used up so quickly.

'She couldn't believe her luck when she found out about Gideon and me and all the rest of the Colas. She was so souped up with everyone else's talents she could hardly sleep at night. Did you know that, Mia? She used to sit up in bed and just watch you and sometimes she touched your head while you were asleep and got a little extra. That's why you were one of the most done in of all the Colas. And Gideon, of course. She didn't bother with me because she thought I was The Dud. But she was all over Gideon. I didn't like it, but I didn't realize why. I thought I was just jealous. The only other person who seemed to understand was Dax, but then you were jealous too, weren't you, Dax?'

Dax nodded, still ashamed to think of it.

'Luke,' cut in Lisa, 'I'm loving all of this—really, I'm *not* being nasty,' she glared around at the others who were giving her disapproving looks. 'I'm not—but we haven't got much time and I need more help to find you. You have to catch up with *now* a bit faster. We need to know more about what Catherine is doing at the moment!'

'She's hiding,' said Luke, turning to Lisa.

'Hiding? Who from?'

'Gideon.'

Lisa looked baffled. 'How?'

Luke smiled again and that hard, cynical twinkle was back in his eyes. 'We did good, Gid,' he said, looking at Gideon. 'We did really good.

'Catherine found out about this thing called "astral projection". You know about that?'

Mia nodded, eagerly. 'It's when you leave your physical body and travel around like a spirit—but you're not dead. Is that what you're doing now, Luke?'

'Yeah. That's it. Well, Catherine found out about it and started doing it. She must have picked up the talent from one of the Colas. At first she just went around the local area—floating up over houses and so on. I didn't go with her—I couldn't, then. But I got bits of her memory out of her when she was charging up afterwards. She just did it for a laugh at first. She likes a laugh. Then she got to thinking about you, Gideon—and Dax. She especially wanted to get back at Dax. She'd worked out, by then, that the Colas hadn't died. She could tell by the feeling of the powers inside her. They keep wanting to go back to their real owners. The power she gets from me is the only thing that's stopping them. She can also tell *who* she got them from, so she knows about the ten of you that she didn't get to that night. She dreams about coming back for you all— but mostly she wants *you*, Dax. She hates you more than anything else I can think of. She'd like to get Gideon, too, but probably to use him like she uses me. She wants you dead, Dax. *After* she's added shapeshifting to her collection. Of course, she wouldn't mind having all true ten of you.'

Dax nodded and Gideon said, suddenly, 'Eleven, Luke! Not ten. We're going to get you back and we'll be the True Eleven.'

'Yes,' said Lisa, and she sounded unusually kind. 'We will—but for now, keep going.'

Luke nodded. 'Well, when she realized she could travel outside her body, like a ghost, she decided to project back to England and find you both. Only trouble was, she knew she couldn't go that far without recharging from me. She needed power to get her there. Then one night, not far from here, she found an electricity pylon. She found she could pull energy out of it. All the machines went off in the place I'm in—lights went out. She sucked the electricity supply right out and left all the metal on the pylon melted like toffee. It charged her up so much she went halfway across the sea before she had to come back. Then she found another pylon, and did it again and got to the English coast before she had to come back. She was thrilled. She was almost *insane* with delight. She knew she could get there. And she'd learned to control it, too, so that the second pylon she used didn't melt. She worked out how much she could take before she had to get off it. She didn't dare try another pylon here for getting right across the channel—she didn't want another one melting and the local authorities' snooping about and finding us—but she worked out that with an extra long charge from me she could probably get over to England without the local pylon, and then get on to the English power grid and go hunting.

'I didn't realize I could go with her. Not then. She spent about four hours that afternoon holding my hand, and I was so weak I really thought I was dying. I wanted to die. I'd had enough. And that evening, she went to get you. The rest you all know.'

They nodded, astonished, remembering the chase across the west country, trying to outrun first the government patrols who were after them, and then the terrifying electrical entity which was melting pylons wherever they went. Even Owen had thought it might be Gideon causing the destruction, but it was his triplet, leaping malevolently across the sea in spirit form.

'I knew it,' said Gideon, quietly, and looked up at Lisa, who had always been the most sceptical about his insistence that the electrical attacker was Catherine.

'OK, OK,' she said. 'You were right! So—Luke—how did you get to go with her?'

'Actually, *she* did it. It was her doing, although she didn't know it. One night she really did almost kill me.

'She was incredibly excited after that first time. She'd got across to England and moved along the south coast and then inland, jumping from pylon to pylon. She didn't melt them all at first, but as she got closer to you, she had to keep stopping and trying to dowse for you, using the grid of power lines across the country as a kind of map reference. And whenever she stayed too long, the pylon would start to melt. She had to give up that first night, and the next few nights. She had to get back to her body again after an hour or so—she couldn't keep going for ever.

'She was really pumped up with it—crowing and singing and dancing around the room when she came in to me that last night. Said she had worked out where you were and she was going fry you all like pork. She was even leaving a little message for you, Gideon—after her first couple of visits she started burning a "G" into the ground next to the pylons. She was having a brilliant time. She couldn't wait to get out there and she just forgot about what she was doing while she was getting her charge off me. I was lying there, like I do. It's like being under water. You're sort of aware of the world going by above you and you can hear and see bits of it, but you can't do anything about anything. And then I wasn't—I wasn't *under* any more. I was *over.* I was suddenly floating up in the air above the bed and I knew, then, that I was dying. I was glad. It felt so much better.

'But then Catherine came up too. I saw her rise up out of her body and realized she was preparing to go to England again and get Dax—and maybe Gideon too. Then I knew I couldn't die just then—I had to go with her. Try to stop her. And so I did. I attached my spirit to hers, and she never even knew.

'We went across the sea in seconds and then over land. She landed on pylons and I was on her shoulders. She never knew I was there. That was what really surprised me. She never knew. I think it was because the spirit world wouldn't let her know. They shut her off, so she couldn't feel other spirits and she couldn't feel me. Good thing too. I saw her crack that rock in two and I saw her chasing after you in the coach and then I saw her suck up all the power she could in that last pylon and try to skewer Dax.'

'Dax? I thought she was after me,' said Gideon.

'She wanted Dax most, to pick up shapeshifting power, but she guessed he might shift and escape if she tried to grab him. She knew if she got *you* pinned down, Gid, he would try to rescue you and she thought she'd get him that way. She wouldn't have cared if she killed you too.'

'She missed though,' said Gideon. 'She missed us both. Why?'

'I wrapped my arms around her throat—just like she did to me, under the sea, and *squeezed*. I didn't know if it would make any difference, but it did. She got groggy and confused. I couldn't stop her turning over the coach though and nearly crushing Owen and Spook and the others. But *you* stopped her, Gideon. I was never so proud of you as I was then! Except maybe when you looked up at her and told her you were coming for her. I knew then, that I might get up again one day, because she was so scared that you saw her. She was screaming like an animal! I'd never known her scared until then—and *you* did that! You sent her packing!'

'OK—I get it all now. Gideon scared off the big bad sister,' said Lisa, briskly. 'But I still need to know about *today*! Where is Catherine? Where are you? And why has it taken months and months to get to where we are now? Why didn't you just astral project straight over to us the next night?'

'Couldn't,' shrugged Luke. 'I didn't know where you were and I couldn't pick anything up about any of you. I'm just a tele, remember. But then you started dowsing for me, Lisa, with Gideon helping you, and I could feel it. I always thought you *might* be looking for me. I waited and I hoped for ages. But I didn't know how to find you and I didn't know where *I* was either. I still don't.'

'But you must have *seen* something!' insisted Lisa. 'When you were flying around on Mad Sister's shoulders.'

Luke thought for a while. 'It was very flat,' he said, at length. 'The land reaching out to the sea—wide and flat and still.'

Lisa snorted. 'Well, that's a help! What about where you are now? Concentrate—get your eyes open and tell me everything!'

Luke seemed to fade away a little in the middle of the table, and his eyes moved around in a rolling motion. Then he squinted and he peered. 'Like I said before— it's a wooden and stone room. It's round. The floor is wooden and it's upstairs and the light . . . well, you've seen that. And heard the creaks and the clicks. The light kind of goes round. Like a fan.'

Lisa was concentrating hard, rubbing the moonstone on her wrist with her thumb. 'Flat—flat land. Where is it that has very flat land—reaching into the sea . . . ?'

Dax suddenly surprised himself by muttering aloud: 'Two and three in the land of the pom-poms.'

'You what?' said Gideon.

'Remember—what the wolf said in my dream? Two

and three—that's Luke and Catherine—in the land of the pom-poms. What does it mean, though?'

Luke shrugged, looking solid again.

'A round room,' Lisa mused on, choosing to ignore Dax and Gideon. 'Light moving like a fan . . . upstairs . . . stone and wood. Wait! Wait! Luke, does the light and the clicking and stuff always go at the same speed?'

'Um . . . no . . . it changes. Sometimes it's really slow—almost stopped—and then other times it's really fast.'

Lisa slapped the table at grinned at them all. 'When it's windy, I bet!'

Luke looked confused. He bit his lip and then he nodded. 'Yes . . . yes, I think you're right.'

'Gotcha!' cackled Lisa. 'You're not in France! You're in Holland!'

They stared at her. 'See?' she said. 'Very flat land, reaching out into the sea. It's the Polders! Oh—honestly—don't you pay *any* attention to Mrs Dann? We did it just days ago in Geography! The Dutch coast is really flat; some of it below sea level. They call it the Polders. And because it's flat it gets lots of wind off the sea, so it's covered in windmills! You're in a windmill, Luke. The light that's turning and flickering like a fan is the light moving through the windmill sails—and they're what's creaking and clicking. Geddit?'

Everyone nodded, amazed. But when they looked up to see what Luke thought of it, the table top was empty.

18

Lisa insisted she must dowse the map outside. 'There's no point in hiding us under the ground any more,' she argued, hands on hips, at Owen. 'You heard what Luke said—Catherine's not coming after us again. She's scared of us!'

'Well, not to be picky, but I *didn't* hear what Luke said,' replied Owen. 'I just heard what the rest of you *told* me. Mrs Sartre and I had a very dull time of it, watching the backs of your heads and the occasional wobbly candle.' Dax could tell he was quite disappointed that he had not been able to travel '*sideways*' as Lisa put it, into whatever dimension it was that allowed them to talk to Luke.

They had all wondered if it would work to take Owen and Mrs Sartre with them, and they even tried it for a few minutes, getting them to add their bare feet to the circle, but nothing happened. Mia thought it was because they didn't have stones to touch but Lisa said it was because they were the wrong number.

'He's dealing with four, not six,' she said. 'It's a number thing.'

Whatever the reason, they didn't get back to Luke's strange inter-world place until it was just the four of them again. Then Luke had arrived in no time, smiling and wrapped in cotton, as before—but Gideon had been panicked at the end of the session when he had vanished without warning.

'It's OK—he was just running out of time,' said Lisa. 'He knew she was coming back. He didn't have any time left to explain; he just had to go.'

'Are you sure?' Gideon gripped the edge of the table, his face awash with anxiety. 'What if she came back and caught him talking to us? What if she's—you know— *punishing* him?'

'He's *fine*!' sighed Lisa, wiping her hair off her face in a tired gesture. 'Well, as fine as you *can* be when your little sister's tried to wrench your tongue out and is keeping you in a coma for fun.'

'Some people,' said Mia, her head bent but her voice charged with icy anger, 'some people—do *not* deserve to be on this world.' They all stopped and stared at her. Mia said nothing more but she was gripping her bracelet with her right hand and her fingers were flexing along with her pulse.

Lisa went to her and touched her shoulder and then sprang back. 'Whoa! You are really *hot*! Mrs Sartre! I think she might be sick!'

Mia snapped up her head and said, 'I'm *fine*!' in a bitterly cold voice which froze them all to the spot. What made them gasp was her eyes. The violet-blue was totally black.

Outside there had been rain, but the clouds were

clearing away to the east and pale sun was coaxing a fine mist up from the grass. The smell was wonderful after the thick incense fug of D3. They walked together, all four of them, through the wood, taking deep breaths and swinging their arms. Then Dax shifted to the fox and ran lightly beside his friends, glad of the exercise.

'How you doing, Mia?' asked Gideon.

'Fine! I've been fine all along!' said Mia, swinging her arms quite violently. 'I don't know why you're all making so much fuss. It was just a trick of the light—we could hardly see each other anyway!'

Gideon and Lisa and Dax exchanged glances as they walked, but didn't say anything. Mia's strange black irises had changed back to their usual colour with her next blink. It was very eerie.

'You cooling down now?' asked Lisa and slapped the back of her hand against Mia's brow.

'Yes—thank you! Like I said, it was that room. It got very stuffy, that's all.'

Dax remembered when he'd seen Mia's eyes turn black before—during the first encounter with the lost triplet. He might talk to the others about that later, but clearly Mia didn't want to have any more discussion about her health now.

They came to the tree house and decided to climb into it, where they could sit without their backsides getting damp. 'Mind the handrails,' warned Gideon as Dax shifted back to a boy. 'They're not that strong!' They never had got around to binding up the rails with strong root twine.

Under the curved woven-stick roof, which now fanned above them like a parasol, they took the motoring atlas of Europe out of Gideon's backpack. Owen had got it from his bookcase and sent them off with it. 'You need to loosen up a bit first,' he'd told Lisa. 'You're all crunched up with stress. Walk, run; wave your arms about. Then start dowsing.'

Now Lisa was opening the large hardback book and flipping through the pages to locate the map of the Netherlands. She found it and then pushed the others back a bit to make space on the floor. She laid the open atlas on the wooden deck and firmly pressed the pages flat. Then she took a small plastic case out of her jeans pocket and Dax saw, with surprise, that it was a mini sewing kit; the kind of thing you get in a Christmas cracker.

'You gonna do some *mending*?' spluttered Gideon and Lisa narrowed her eyes at him.

'Oh, sorry, I forgot m'lady has servants for that kind of thing,' said Gideon in a mock humble voice, tugging his invisible forelock. Lisa said nothing, but kicked him on the ankle, awkwardly in the tight space. Then she clicked open the mini sewing kit and removed a single needle from it, threaded with fine grey cotton. Everyone fell silent as she passed the thread through her fingers, straightening it out, and then held one end, allowing the needle to fall.

Sitting cross-legged, Lisa leaned her elbows on her knees and propped her chin on her clasped hands, creating a steady steeple with her arms and hands. Between her fingers the cotton—perhaps twenty centimetres in length, swung straight, to and fro, with the needle at the end. Dax could see why she did this. It was a way of turning her body into a frame; one which could keep very still and not influence the swinging needle in its movement.

'Gideon,' said Lisa. 'Put your hand on my shoulder. Please try not to leave a grubby mark!'

Gideon huffed a little, but checked his palm for dirt before placing it gingerly on the top of her pale yellow sleeve.

'Right,' said Lisa and took a long breath. 'Luke.'

At once the needle, which had begun swinging in a relaxed circular movement, jerked sideways and pointed like an arrow at a part of the map. It seemed to strain to reach the paper, holding its weird angle and trembling with the effort. It made Dax think of a dog tugging excitedly on a lead. Mia leaned over and read the name under the fine silver point. 'Gildastaad!' she said. 'It's on the coast! Look! Gildastaad! We've found him!'

'Good,' said Lisa, tugging the needle and thread back into her palm. 'Now we need to get a local map and pinpoint him more accurately. Then Owen can go and get him.'

'*Me* and Owen can go and get him,' said Gideon.

'Yeah, some chance of *that*!' said Lisa, snapping her sewing kit shut.

'I don't care what anybody says,' said Gideon and even

Lisa glanced up because his voice was so full of emotion. 'He's my brother and I was so stupid I didn't know anything about him—and I ignored all Dax's warnings and treated my best mate like a nutter because I was too stupid to see what was going on—and I *let* Catherine keep taking all my power and I was just an idiot—a really thick idiot—and now look what's happened! So I'm going to get him back and if they don't let me I'm going anyway!'

There was a pause and everyone looked at each other.

'OK,' said Lisa. 'OK.'

A silence, heavy and full of dark memories, descended on them for a moment. Then there was a shout through the trees and Owen was coming, carrying a tray. He grinned at them all as he reached them and glanced around at the tree house which looked quite finished. 'Not bad, eh? Aren't you glad you stuck at it, Gideon?' He stepped a couple of rungs up the ladder, passed up the tray to them, and then energetically hoisted himself up.

'Oh—Owen—just—' stuttered Gideon but before he could get any more words out there was a crack and Owen was lying on his back in the leaf litter, a chunk of wood in one hand. 'Sorry—I didn't *quite* finish the handrail!' winced Gideon. 'Are you all right?'

Owen sighed, closed his eyes, and spoke in a voice of strained patience. 'We'll get there, Gideon. I'm not going to give up on you!' He sat up, dusted himself off and then carefully came back up the ladder. Gideon shifted the tray across. On it were five big mugs of cocoa, sending rich chocolatey curls of steam into the air. There was also a tin of Mrs P's best home-made sultana scones which she'd split and lined with cool Cumbrian butter.

'Oh! Just exactly what I didn't know I needed!' sighed Gideon, happily. Owen passed around the goodies with a warm smile. Dax could sense that he was feeling proud of them all. When the mugs and scones were safely delivered, Owen handed Lisa a folded map.

'You got it already?'

'Yup. Amazing how fast we can get things done when we need to. It's a detailed map of Holland. How have you been getting on with the motoring atlas?'

'Brilliantly!' said Gideon, through a mouthful of buttered scone. 'We know where he is! He's in Gildastaad! Right on the coast, like he said. And that's where all the windmills are, yeah, Lisa?'

'Must be,' she said, her face half buried in her mug. 'Open up the other map now and I'll give it another go.'

'It's amazing!' murmured Dax. 'How can you do it? How does it work?'

Lisa shrugged. 'It's about frequencies, apparently. Patterns. It's all maths.'

'How do you mean?'

She put down her mug. 'Well, everything on the planet has a kind of frequency—like radio waves. Or like a mathematical formula. Like—well, think of a computer game you've played (if you can remember back that far!) and you know, don't you, that somebody's made it happen, all bright and clever on the screen, by typing in lots of numbers? Tonnes and tonnes of numbers. That's what computer game programmers do.'

'OK,' said Dax. 'But I still don't get what it has to do with dowsing.'

'Well, stop butting in and I'll *tell* you! Everything you can see or touch in the world was made, right? By something. God, or Allah, or Mother Nature, or just a big bang in the universe—but it was *made*. And it was made to a formula—like a computer game. So, everything has a precise formula or frequency and somehow my brain *knows* what that is. Don't ask me how; I haven't got a clue. But if you say "I want to find *my* sock"—not just anyone's sock, but only your sock—I *know* what the frequency or formula of that sock is, and my brain picks it up like a radio signal and tells me where to look.

'Most dowsers look for water mainly. That's their thing. And water has a very definite frequency in the brain, so it's dead easy to find. Lots of normal people can find water if they're shown how. I can tell you exactly where all the underground streams are in this valley.

'But to find something in particular, I have to be asked by the person who's lost it and who knows what it is, so I can get that information out of their head and go and find it. I need something to link me to what's gone. Or who's gone. That's why I have to make physical contact with Gideon, revolting though it is.'

Lisa sat back, looking quite pleased with herself, and bit into her scone. She rolled her eyes with pleasure. Mrs P's scones were like a poem in the mouth.

'OK,' said Owen, putting his own mug down and spreading out the map. 'Gildastaad, you say? Right— here it is, and you're bang on. This is definitely windmill country. If we can get it down to a village in Gildastaad we can work from there, no problem. I'll go tonight.'

Gideon went to open his mouth but Dax held his arm and shook his head. 'Not yet,' he said, under his breath. 'Not here.'

Lisa finished her scone and got out her needle and thread again. She resumed her cross-legged, steepled-hands position, and let the needle drop. As Gideon rested his hand back on her shoulder, the needle spun around in a lazy circle and they waited for it to pull hard towards some part of Gildastaad.

But it didn't. Lisa frowned and closed her eyes and concentrated. Still the needle spun lazily and made no attempt to point at anything.

'What's wrong?' asked Owen.

'I don't know,' said Lisa, screwing her face up in annoyance. 'It's not picking up anything—which is nuts because we know he's there!'

'Try the other map again.'

They got out the atlas once more and Lisa went through the same business—and yes, this time the needle did point very firmly to Gildastaad. In fact it was so urgent that the needle began to tug against its thread in little jerks and when Lisa paid out a little more cotton it even punctured the paper. She moved back to the local map and the needle resumed its lazy circling. Lisa shook her head. 'It just doesn't want to give us any more than that! I don't know why.'

'Maybe Catherine has set up a protection over her and Luke,' suggested Mia. 'You know, like we all had to do in the woods last year when Owen was after us.' She blinked, embarrassed, at Owen. 'Sorry, Owen. I mean, when *Catherine* was after us.' They had all, back then, needed to imagine themselves protected under pyramid-shaped mirrors—which had worked quite well.

'That would kind of make sense, I suppose,' said Lisa.

'Don't worry. Keep at it,' said Owen, moving to the edge of the platform. 'I'm going anyway. Gildestaad is just a small town and it shouldn't take long to get the gossip on two strange children arriving in the area. Gideon—I'm bringing Luke back, I promise.' Owen got on to the ladder and then jumped most of the way down and Gideon hurried after him and landed next to him a second later.

'Wait! You're not going without me!'

Owen turned to look at the boy and then took him by the shoulders. 'I understand how badly you want to come, Gideon,' he said. 'I would feel exactly the same way. But I *cannot* put you in danger. Remember what happened last time you had an encounter with Catherine? We all nearly fried.'

'So? She won't try that again! She's scared! She's scared of *me*, that's what Luke said. You heard about that. And it was me that stopped her last time. Owen, you *need* me—you have to let me come!'

'Gideon, try to understand. I just *can't.*' Owen turned away and walked back through the woods and Gideon stood, simmering with anger and desperation. His face was set like a mask and his eyes glittered wetly. There was a loud crack, and a small tree a few feet from where Owen was walking split in half. Owen didn't look at it. He walked on without looking back.

19

There was no sign of Gideon at dinner. His chair remained empty. Dax wanted to abandon his food and go and search for him, but Gideon had been quite definite. He wanted to be alone for a while. Dax respected that. He'd given his friend's head a rough pat and walked away, feeling sorry for Gideon—but still excited that Owen was *going to get Luke*!

And Catherine too, of course. He wondered what they would do with her. She might be very difficult to contain at first—but at least she wouldn't be dangerous for long. Away from Luke, her powers would get weaker and weaker, and then she'd be normal again. Well, as normal as someone like Catherine ever could be. Owen's patrol would know not to touch her. Maybe they'd throw a sleeping gas bomb at her or something.

Of course, they still had to find them. Something troubled Dax about that. Owen seemed very confident that in a small Dutch town he would be able to track them down, but Dax wasn't so sure. And what if Catherine decided to start leaping from pylon to pylon again? She could reduce Owen to a pile of ashes. Charged up with Luke, she might even have some psychic power and that could warn her that Owen was coming for her.

Dax shivered as he prodded indifferently at his rhubarb crumble.

Clive appeared at his elbow and sat down in the empty chair next to him. 'Look,' he said. 'It's coming on quite well!' He rolled out a large piece of paper. Dax saw that it was graph paper, criss-crossed finely in blue, no doubt from the science paper store. Inked neatly down the centre was a kind of flow diagram—perfectly drawn boxes with lines connecting them to other boxes and in each box was a name and some dates—births and deaths.

'These are the family trees of the people who've lived here—and there have been quite a few,' said Clive, tracing the lines between boxes with his stubby clever finger. 'I haven't done them all yet. I've got as far back as Clara Mont-Richardson, in the sixteen hundreds though! That's something! And up to the turn of last century with Robert William Jermyn—just doing his family now. They all got diphtheria!' he added cheerfully.

Mia came over and peered at the chart with interest. 'This is excellent,' she said and Clive beamed and turned a little pink, bathed in the Mia Effect. Dax grinned. 'It's brilliant, Clive,' he agreed. 'I'll have a look at it some more later—just have to go and find Gid. He'd like to see it, too.' Clive nodded happily as Mia started talking to him about Clara Mont-Richardson and Dax went to find his friend.

Movement caught his eye as he passed a window and he saw a black four-by-four moving along the gravel driveway. It pulled up fifty metres from the lodge and a man got out, wearing dark clothing. He looked military and there was a bulky black jacket over his black sweatshirt which Dax knew hid a gun holster. The man surveyed the grounds around him through expensive rimless glasses and took a pen out of his trouser pocket. Leaning back against the bonnet of the car, he folded his arms, raised the pen in one hand and began to click the ballpoint in and out, in and out. Dax knew that strange habit. It was Chambers, the top government official who ran the Cola Project.

Chambers had been involved last year when Dax had taken Gideon, Lisa, and Mia on the run. He had headed the patrol hunting them down. He had even recruited Spook Williams to try to fool them into coming out of hiding with an illusion of Gideon's dad. In spite of all this, Dax quite liked Chambers. He was a quiet man with a dry sense of humour. He was also the one who had recommended Tyrone to the Cola Project as Gideon's new teacher, and if Tyrone thought well of him, he must be OK.

As he thought of Tyrone, Dax jolted. There he was now. The lanky young man emerged from the lodge and walked down to Chambers, who patted him warmly on the shoulder when they met. The two began to talk earnestly, and then Tyrone led Chambers inside. Dax stepped away from the window and made for the common room, where he hoped to find Gideon. Jacob and Alex were there, along with Jennifer and Barry, but there was no sign of Gideon.

'Anyone seen Gid?' asked Dax.

'He was upstairs,' said Alex. 'Talking to Janey.'

Dax ran up the steps, two at a time, wondering if Gideon had a headache after their exhausting session with Luke. He found Janey in the medical room, but not Gideon. He also saw the pointing boy again, drifting past mournfully and raising one arm. 'Sorry,' said Dax to him, aloud. 'Haven't got time for more pointy spirit fun.' The boy just vanished.

'Pardon?' said Janey.

'Nothing,' said Dax. 'Um . . . was Gideon here a while ago?'

'Yes. He said he had a headache—that he was going to go straight off to bed,' replied Janey, getting to her feet and coming over to touch Dax's forehead. 'Have you got one too? I gather there's been intense stuff going on in Development today.'

'Yeah . . . um . . . no, I haven't got a headache.'

'Sure? You look a bit peaky.'

Dax felt a shiver run through him. He didn't know how he knew. Maybe it was something he could still smell in the air. There was a definite sense of Gideon's mood left in here. It smelt—*determined*. Janey was rifling the painkillers box now but Dax turned and ran back into the corridor, shouting 'No thanks' over his shoulder, and made for the stairs. He ran down to their bedroom but saw no sign of Gideon, so began to roam the building, looking for him. He eventually returned to the common room where most of the Colas were now lounging after their meal.

'Anyone seen Gideon?' he asked again.

'He was talking to Spook in the garden,' said Darren.

'Oh no,' murmured Dax. The last thing Gideon needed in his present mood was a run-in with Spook. He ran outside and shifted into the falcon immediately, soaring up rather bumpily through the weak evening thermals, and scanned the grounds for Gideon. The large black four-by-four had moved away down to the security gate. Dax could see two dark figures beside it and knew they were Chambers and Tyrone—Tyrone had changed from his usual weathered jeans and shirt into the same black gear that Chambers wore. Dax felt a stab of understanding. Of course! Tyrone was a powerful telekinetic too! They were obviously taking him to help them capture Catherine. It was a very sound idea. He hoped Gideon wouldn't take it too badly.

But where *was* Gideon? Dax arced around in the air and flew closer to the collection of people by the gate. Security guards were talking to Owen in the doorway of the reception centre. The four-by-four's engine was running. They were clearly about to leave for Holland. He wanted to get a closer look—and to check that Gideon wasn't about to arrive and beg to go again. He flew silently down to a small cluster of trees not far from the gate and roosted on a branch, watching.

To his surprise, it was Spook that he saw. The boy was walking languidly across the grass towards the gathering by the gates. As he approached them he turned away into the trees, not far from where Dax was perched. Nobody seemed to notice him. He sat down at the base of a beech tree and crossed his legs, comfortably. He folded his arms, leaned back against the trunk and dropped his head a little. Dax recognized the movement and his heart quickened in its feathered ribcage. What was Spook up to?

A moment later there was a supernatural punch in the air around him, and Dax knew that Spook was throwing an illusion. The men at the car all jolted and looked around in the same direction, towards the perimeter wall. Chambers gave a shout and the security guards raised their rifles and flanked him.

Owen ran around the back of the car and sprinted across the grass. He held up one hand to the rest of them. 'It's all right! I'll talk to him.' He turned back in the direction of whatever Spook was conjuring up, and Dax heard him say. 'Look—I thought we'd had this conversation.'

Dax could see no sign of anyone but the telltale waviness was there in the air. He glanced down at Spook and felt a shiver of anxiety run through him. There was another punch in the air and then Chambers and the guards began to walk fast towards Owen. Owen was shouting to someone who wasn't anywhere in sight. Dax didn't like this. Not at all. He flew down to Spook and landed on the boy's knee, not making any effort to draw back his talons. Spook winced but held his stare. 'I knew you'd be along!' he sneered. 'What do you think you are? The parrot police?'

Dax shifted. He knelt on the grass next to Spook. 'What are you doing? You're throwing an illusion of Gideon, aren't you?'

'Yep,' said Spook.

'Why? What's going on?'

'Shut up or you'll mess things up,' said Spook and Dax glanced around, following his gaze. Chambers and Tyrone were now staring into the middle distance with some concern, the guards still holding their rifles at the ready behind them. Then a short figure emerged from the wooded area on the other side of the drive, a few yards away from Dax and Spook, and behind the party of men in black. There was a click and the mirror-glass rear window of the black four-by-four suddenly slid down. The boy glanced once in Dax's direction, shook his head quickly, and then vaulted into the back of the car. The window slid back up again.

Dax stared, open-mouthed. He was about to race forward when Spook's hand shot out and grabbed his arm. 'Don't *move*, you stupid dingo! You'll ruin everything!'

The men seemed to have relaxed. Owen turned back to the car, shaking his head. 'He'll be OK,' Dax heard him say to Chambers. 'He's upset, that's all. You can understand it. He wants to rescue his brother. He's gone back to the lodge now.'

Prickles of understanding rose all over Dax. He turned back to Spook. 'You did—you conjured up a fake Gideon!' Spook smirked. Owen, Chambers, and Tyrone got into the car and the engine revved. The gates swung slowly open.

'He set this up with you!' gasped Dax. 'He set this up . . . with *you*!'

'For the going rate,' said Spook. 'I don't do it free, you know.'

Dax jumped to his feet and began to race towards the car. His best friend was stowing away. How on earth he thought he'd get away with it, Dax had no idea. He just knew Gideon was in danger and he had to stop him.

Before he could clear the trees he was whacked hard in the chest. A fallen log had shot up to bar his way and now hung eerily in the air, scattering surprised woodlice beneath it. Dax stood, not knowing what to do. As the gate swung steadily shut the log shuddered once more and then dropped back to the ground with a thud.

'I think that was a hint that Gideon didn't want you coming along,' sneered Spook.

Dax was shaking. His mind was in free-fall. Spook got to his feet and then sidled up next to him. 'He said to give you this—once he'd got away. He knew you'd try to stop him. You're like his mother, aren't you?'

Dax snatched the small envelope from Spook and ripped it open. Inside was a bit of lined paper, covered in Gideon's hasty scrawl. He read it.

Dear Dax

I'm sorry about this, mate. I know you'll be annoyed, but I couldn't let you know what I was going to do because you'd get all worried and try to stop me. Or maybe come with me. I wanted you to come with me but it's not fair. She wants to get back at me—but she wants to KILL you. That's what Luke said. I can't have her killing you.

    Please don't come after me. I'll be OK. And sorry that it had to be Spook giving you this. I had to promise him all my Cola allowance for the next two months to get his help. If it went to plan, he threw an illusion of me to distract Owen and everyone, so I could get in the car. Owen knows Spook hates me so I don't think he'll work it out and hopefully he won't find me until it's too late to send me back.

    Please don't tell anyone. I told Janey I was sick, so please make out I've gone to bed early, so nobody will miss me until morning. I'll see you in a couple of days, I hope. With Luke.
Gideon

'Has he put kisses on it?' said Spook, right by his elbow. Dax had to hit him. There was no stopping it. Spook's jaw made a satisfying crack as his knuckles struck it and the boy gave a howl of pain and rage and swiped back, catching Dax in the same place. Dax had the advantage of being so angry he didn't really notice the pain. He staggered backwards but then launched himself at Spook and in seconds they were rolling across the grass, bellowing at each other.

    'You slimy little—*oof*!'

    'Stinking dog! *Eeeuurgh!*'

    'You've put—*eeeuh*—Gideon's life on the—*ow*—line!'

    'Gideon's choice. Makes you—*ooof*—really mad, doesn't it? That he came to *me* because he couldn't trust *you*!'

    There was a sharp metallic click and both boys froze.

Dax looked up and saw a security guard, holding his rifle. It wasn't exactly pointing at them, but it had clearly just been loaded. The guard looked at them impassively. 'Get back to the lodge, you two. Now.'

They scrambled up and walked away fast, Spook limping slightly where Dax had kicked his shin and Dax wiping blood away from his chin.

'If you're such a hero, why don't you fly after him?' murmured Spook, through his teeth, as they left the stony-faced guard behind.

'Because of *this*,' said Dax, waving the crumpled letter and then pushing it into his pocket. Gideon had asked him not to follow, not to tell on him, not to *act* in any way until the next morning. Dax was trembling with fury and fear and indecision. He wanted to go straight to Owen but Owen was gone and Gideon was probably crouching just behind him, under a blanket or something, right now. If he went after them now he'd be ruining Gideon's chances of getting away with them. They *would* find him, of course, but he might be lucky and get found late enough in their journey that they'd decide to keep going and take him along. Were they travelling by ferry? By helicopter or plane? Gideon would never be able to follow them once they were out of the car—would he? He couldn't have a passport, even, could he?

It was nearly dark by now. Dax knew he couldn't go back to the common room. Lisa would pick up his nervous state immediately. He glanced at Spook, still limping along beside him.

'I hope you're pleased with what you just did for a few quid,' he said. 'Of course, if Gideon doesn't come back, you won't get anything.'

'Well, maybe if you didn't keep secrets from the rest of us, I would know *why* he wanted to run away and maybe I would have said no!'

Dax just glowered at him.

'So—are you going to tell me where he's gone?'

Dax smiled thinly at Spook and for some reason a memory popped into his head and he said, 'To the land of the pom-poms!'

Then he shifted and flew up, flipped sideways around the corner of the lodge and glided into his open bedroom window. Gideon's empty bed seemed to stare at him accusingly—although how it was possible for a bed to look accusing he couldn't guess. It accused him of letting his best friend go off into danger, but the minute Dax shifted and stood on the floor, thinking of going to Mrs Sartre, it accused him of betrayal. He slumped onto his own bed and put his head in his hands. It was going to be a tough night.

20

He realized he'd dozed off when he woke up in the early hours. He was curled up, fully dressed, on the bottom half of his bed. He had lain there awake, anxiously trying to guess what was happening with Gideon, for an hour or more, before exhaustion overtook him.

Now he opened his eyes and saw movement in the gloom of the unlit room. He sat up and stared. The wolf was back. It was curled up on Gideon's bed and as Dax sat up, it sat up also.

'What?' said Dax, aloud. 'What?'

The wolf lifted its dark snout and its eyes shone like twin moons. *Two and three in the land of pom-poms*, it sent.

Dax clicked his teeth in annoyance. 'Can't you do any better than *that*?' he said. 'Why do you have to be so weird all the time? Can't you just talk to me normally? Lisa's spirit guide can manage it! Why can't you?'

The wolf just regarded him from Gideon's bed. *Two and three in the land of pom-poms.*

'Yeah—yeah I got that bit,' muttered Dax. He shrugged and sighed. 'It's not that I don't—you know—appreciate it. It's just that it's not much help. I mean, I know that two and three has got to be Luke and Catherine. He was born second and she was born third. But land of pom-

poms? What's that about? Do they have pom-poms in Holland?'

The wolf shook its head very firmly. Then it disappeared. Dax sat frozen—all the hairs on his arms and neck rising up. They were wrong. Luke *wasn't* in Holland. Lisa had sent Owen to the wrong place. He was as certain of this as his own name.

He checked his watch. It was 3.42 a.m. Lisa wasn't going to like this.

'Too bad,' he said, aloud, to himself, before shifting and flying out of the window.

Peregrines are not night fliers, but he needed only to go along the ledge a few feet to find the girls' window. He landed on the stone sill and listened through the thick velvet curtain drawn against the window, which was, fortunately, open. He didn't want to wake them up and have them all screaming in a girly way. He just wanted to wake up Lisa. He wasn't even sure what bed she was in. He shifted to the fox, perched precariously on the high sill, and let his nose guide him. She was on the far left. Good. He pushed through the curtain with his snout and dropped quietly to the floor. Fortunately there was a thick rug between the beds, below the window, so his claws did not click as he landed. The room was dark but his fox eyes easily made out Lisa, sleeping peacefully on her side. He walked across to her, aware of the steady breathing of Mia and Jennifer behind him.

He tried to wake her by calling to her telepathically, but she just snorted a little and seemed to press her eyes tighter shut. Maybe she thought he was just one more spirit in her queue. He prodded her with his snout and now her eyes shot open. She opened her mouth to say something—probably rude and loud—to him, but he gave a low warning growl and she shut her mouth again and eased up on one elbow, staring at him in confusion. *What are you doing in the girls' bedroom, you weirdo?* she sent.

You got it wrong, Lisa, he sent back, angrily. *You've sent them all to the wrong place.*

'I have *not*!' declared Lisa, at full volume. Mia immediately sprang up in her bed and Jennifer mumbled in her sleep.

You have! insisted Dax, glancing around at the others. *They're not in Holland! The wolf came and told me!*

'Oh, bully for him!' She sat up in her crumpled silk pyjamas and glared at Dax. 'What makes you think *he* knows? And if he's so clever, has he told you where Luke *is*?'

Dax shifted and sat on the end of her bed. He didn't bother to keep quiet any more as both Mia and Jennifer were now awake and staring at him. 'The land of the pom-poms,' he said, feeling both righteous and embarrassed.

Lisa gave a hard laugh. 'Yeah—I thought so!'

'I know it doesn't make sense—*that* bit—but when I asked him if Luke was in Holland he shook his head. Very firmly. It's not Holland!'

'My dowsing has never been wrong yet,' said Lisa.

'Well, maybe there has to be a first time!' Dax and Lisa glowered at each other, and Mia switched on her lamp, got out of bed, put on her dressing gown, and then went to the long wardrobe at one end of the large room. From it she brought the map book of Europe they had used earlier. She flicked through to the page mapping the Netherlands and lay it open on Lisa's lap.

'I am *not* dowsing in the middle of the night!' said Lisa.

'This is important,' said Dax. 'Gideon has gone with them.'

'What?'

'He got into the back of the car. He paid Spook to throw an illusion of him—being somewhere else. And then, when they were all looking at fake Gideon, real Gideon got in the car.'

Lisa, Mia, and Jennifer looked at him, open-mouthed.

'How do you know all this?' demanded Lisa. 'And why didn't you stop him?'

Dax pulled the letter from his pocket and handed it to her. She read it quickly and shook her head, before handing it to Mia, who shared it with Jennifer. Dax stared at his shoes, waiting for them to start laying into him.

'Puts you in a kind of awkward position, doesn't it?' said Lisa, much to his surprise.

'Well, at least if they're going to the wrong place there's less chance of Gideon getting killed,' said Mia. This bluntness from her was strange. She wasn't making any attempt to send out soothing vibrations to them all.

'It is *not* the wrong place!' insisted Lisa. 'I've told you—I don't dowse wrong. It's never happened.'

'Maybe you should just do it one more time,' said Jennifer, who Dax guessed must know about the situation with Gideon and Luke. She shared a bedroom with Lisa and Mia, after all.

Lisa switched on her own lamp and picked up the map with an angry jerk. 'I'm not doing the needle—it's in the bathroom. I'll just do fingers.' She shut her eyes and allowed her fingers to wander in a lazy random pattern across the page and after a few seconds they settled again, over Gildastaad. Dax sighed with frustration and then reached over and whipped the map book away from Lisa. He stared and stared at it—looking for *some clue*. Anything about pom-poms? The clue seemed more American than Dutch. He sighed again and then caught his breath. The needle Lisa had used earlier had been desperate to get at the page. So urgently it had actually gone *through* the page. Dax felt a stillness fall over him, as if the planet had slowed down in its turning. He looked at Lisa and Mia and then Jennifer, and then flicked over the page of the map book.

On the other side was a map of the northern half of France. Dax pulled the page up so the lamp shone behind it. A pinprick of golden light glowed. Right above it was a name. *Troisenfants.* The earth stood still. Dax stared up at Lisa. 'You *were* wrong. And you were right.' He showed her the map and she nodded, slowly, understanding.

'It knew where we had to go,' she murmured. 'We made our minds up about Holland, but we were on the wrong page. It meant us to go to France, so it poked right through the paper to France—on the other side! *That's* why it wouldn't work on Owen's other map of Holland. No! I've been an idiot! You should *never* make your mind up about *anything* before you dowse! We should have had a whole map of Europe—not just the Netherlands. Oh—I'm so sorry, Dax.'

'But ... the windmills ... the polders,' said Mia. 'That's Holland, isn't it?'

'No,' said Jennifer. 'There are windmills all over the place. We've got loads of them near where I live in Norfolk. And polders are just flat lands. You get those in Norfolk too.'

'And we know the woman who saved them—Francine—is French,' said Dax.

Lisa took back the map and studied it intently around the tiny needle hole. 'Look,' she said. 'Between le Mont-Saint-Michel and Cancale—there's this long stretch of marsh. That's got to mean a lot of flat land, before the sea starts. Is that polders?'

'Yeah,' said Jennifer. 'That would work—and I bet there are windmills. Right by the sea with all that flat land. That's exactly where people put windmills. And hey—in case you haven't noticed—*Troisenfants* is "trois enfants". That's French for "three children". Might just be coincidence, I suppose ... ' They looked at each other in silent awe.

The planet was on the move again. Dax sat up straight. 'It's right. I know it is. I'm going there. Now.'

'Why?' said Lisa. 'Just go to Mrs Sartre and tell her

what we know and she'll get a call through to Owen in minutes. Why should you go?'

'Because I have to. If I wasn't meant to go, why would the wolf be coming to me? It's no good ignoring it. I can't just do nothing any more, while Gideon's out there. I need to get there, find out where Luke is, and then fly to Owen and Gideon and tell them where they have to go. At least I can do it easily without anyone noticing, and they'll be extra safe if they know exactly where Luke and Catherine are before they even get to the place.'

'Dax,' said Mia, gently, 'I know you're worried about them, but why put yourself at risk? Luke has been stuck where he is for months and months. He'll be OK for a bit longer.'

'Oh, hell!' said Lisa, suddenly grabbing handfuls of her hair and screwing up her face. 'Oh, hell! I don't think so.'

'What are you getting?' asked Dax.

'Oh—it's not good. It's . . . a boy. I can't see him too clearly for all the blood. There's an awful lot of blood.'

They all stiffened and stared at her.

'What does Sylv say?' prodded Jennifer.

'She says it's a boy who means a lot to Gideon. She says there's not much more time. Something about . . . oh, for heaven's sake, woman! Stop speaking in riddles! Yes—yes?' She opened her eyes and looked around at them. 'She says he's trying to speak, but he can't. That's got to be Luke.'

'When? Is this *now*?!' demanded Dax.

'No, it can't be—looks like late afternoon sun. I think it's very soon though. Tomorrow. Oh, hell—I think Catherine must have found out.' Lisa sighed and shut her eyes again. 'You're right, Dax. You have to go. But Sylv says to watch your back or you'll be up and over. *Don't* ask me what that means, because I haven't a clue!'

Dax was very relieved that Sylv was backing him up. 'OK—I want *you* to go to Mrs Sartre so she can call Owen, but only after you've given me five minutes to get clear of this place. I can't risk anyone trying to stop me. The others might not be able to get there in time.'

'How long is it going to take you to get to France?' said Mia. 'It's a really long way! Even for a falcon.'

Dax shrugged. 'Peregrines migrate—and I think I'm a bit faster than normal ones. I looked up how long they usually take to get places after I flew back from Cornwall that time, and I think I'm about twice as fast—bit of extra Cola boost. I ought to be able to get across the Channel in about ten or twelve hours. I can always land on a ferry if I get tired. Shift and have a cooked breakfast.' He grinned, with more cheer than he felt.

He went back along the corridor to his room with the map book, leaving the girls murmuring excitedly to each other, and found his backpack. He put the map book into it, along with some money (although it might not be much use to him in France), a compass, a warm fleece, and some of Gideon's chocolate from his bedside drawer. In fact, he wasn't sure he even needed any of this, apart from the map. As a falcon or a fox he could easily find his own food and keep warm. It was comforting, though, to take a few things. He slung the backpack on and returned to the girls' room. They were all huddled on Mia's bed, talking quietly.

'Have you got your bracelet on?' said Mia. He nodded.

'Oh, not *now*!' said Lisa and Dax at first thought she was talking to him, but then he realized she was in conversation with another spirit. 'I *told* you,' she said. 'He doesn't know him—and he's *busy*!'

'Who's that?' he asked.

'Oh, that old bloke who keeps asking for James. Still seems to think you have some connection with him. Makes no sense. Don't worry about it. He's gone now.'

Dax wished she would be kinder to her spirits. 'Tell me more about it when I get back,' he said. 'Wish me luck.'

They did, and Mia gave him a quick hug and surprised him by whispering, 'Don't let that girl fool you. And don't spare her.' He gave her a startled look but she just smiled as if she'd said nothing strange at all.

Dawn was reaching across the sky—easily light enough to fly by. It would be a little bumpy in the cold of early morning, but it couldn't be helped. Dax said, 'Another five minutes before you go to Mrs Sartre, OK?' and then shifted and flew away.

21

The furthest he'd flown before was from Cornwall to North Hampshire—and that had taken him just under three hours. He had no idea how long it would take him to reach France, but felt confident he could do it by the middle of the afternoon. Only an hour into his flight, though, as he reached the lower end of the Pennines which ran like a ridge down the centre of the country, he was cursing himself. He hadn't eaten anything for hours! Idiot! Whenever he shifted he got hungry—ravenous sometimes, and that was just while coasting or running around the valley. Now he was riven with desperate hunger and he would have to stop and hunt. He looked for woodland below him, thinking he would have to shift to the fox for a while—but then he realized that the quickest way would be to hunt as a peregrine. He had never yet done this. He had killed rabbits and a wood pigeon before, as a fox—out of necessity—but never yet eaten as a falcon. Dax looked down through wisps of fine cloud and dropped sixty metres lower to examine what was on offer for breakfast.

Below him the country spread out like a tapestry, rolling hills easing into fields; a small village to the east, a larger town, glowing with lights in the early morning, to the west. Forest stretched along a river valley to the south, and this is where he was heading. He couldn't hunt in the trees, however, not as a falcon. Peregrines hunted high and wide spaces; cliffs and coasts and sometimes the pigeon-packed parks along rivers running through cities, especially if they could find a safe place to nest, high on the box-girder of a bridge or the roof of a tower block. They left the woody spaces to the lana falcons and sparrow-hawks. Dax knew this from the books he had read—he also knew it instinctively as he flew. He must take prey now, or wait until he was beyond the forest that lay in his direct path south. It was now. Right now.

His eyes were beyond keen. He could see every flicker of life in the land and air below him. He could take a rabbit or a rat if he chose, but peregrines would always choose to hunt in the air. A crow flapped by thirty metres below him, unconcerned. Too much trouble. Too heavy. A bang from a misfiring car engine below sent up a cloud of spooked pigeons, just as high as a house, on the edge of the trees. Dax picked one, stooped in the air, flipping over like a dart, and then plummeted towards his target, riding gravity down and down and then—crack—the bird was his.

It made a shocked whoop as he took it in his talons, and shuddered. With instinct taking control, Dax ratcheted his claws tighter into its plump body and drove the vicious tip of his beak into the bird's rainbow-feathered neck. Its spinal cord snapped and it was dead in a second. The pair fell to the ground and Dax only just pulled up his wings in time to save himself from the same fate as his breakfast. On the cool wet grass, as the other pigeons wheeled away in panic and a scared jay chack-chacked loudly in its nest, Dax's wings spread around his catch in a protective mantle and a second later, he feasted.

Later, as he left the forest behind him and flew steadily down into Southern England, Dax wondered if he was a killer. What did it make him, this taking of life, if not a killer? But how could you not kill, when your life depended on it? And that's how it was for fox or falcon. You couldn't apply the same rules. If your life depended on it, sometimes, you had to kill.

He reached Portsmouth by mid morning and roosted on top of the elegant Spinnaker Tower, a white steel sail on a needle that reached a hundred and fifty metres into the sky. Below him the ferries to France edged in and out of the busy port. Could he really fly all the way over the channel? He needed to remind himself where he was going. He saw, below him, the topmost observation deck of the tower where one or two visitors were marvelling at the view. There was netting pulled across it to stop birds, but he noticed a large tear in it, and knew he could easily drop through it. He waited for the people to go and a minute later they did. Instantly, he dropped down and through the netting to the deck and shifted to a boy as he hit the floor. He took off his backpack and rummaged through it for Gideon's chocolate and the map book. Stuffing the chocolate hungrily, he looked at the two-page spread of northern Europe and traced his route from Portsmouth to Troisenfants, which lay near the coast on the Normandy/Brittany border. The quickest way was to follow the ferry route to Cherbourg in the north-west of Normandy and then fly south across the land. He folded the map, put it in his backpack and put the bag back on.

'Amazing view, isn't it?' said a woman and Dax glanced up to see her, standing with a man, peering down over the high railing, their backs to him. 'Imagine jumping off this!' Dax glanced around, shifted, shot up through the gap in the netting and plummeted away in front of her. He heard her cry—'Look! Isn't that a falcon?'—and then she and her man were far behind him.

He skimmed across the Solent and glanced west to the Isle of Wight, thinking of Luke's adoptive mum. If things went well, her beloved boy would be coming back from the dead. He wondered if she would ever let him go again, once he did.

Flying over the sea was exhilarating, but scary. He didn't feel as if he would need to, but if he *did* have to rest, where would he stop? Only thirty minutes out from land he spotted his answer. Below him a cross-channel ferry churned its way across the sea, leaving a wide, steady wake behind it and a plume of pale smoke trailing from its funnel. Dax looked wide to east, west, and south and saw two other vessels ploughing through the water. It was, he had heard, one of the busiest shipping lanes in the world. After another two hours, hunger was nudging at him again. He didn't fancy tackling a seagull—they were huge and bad-tempered and would probably mob him if he tried. *Nope,* thought Dax. *I'm in the mood for sausage, beans, and bacon.* He circled once before dropping to the fourth ferry he'd spotted in that hour—this one travelling to France, rather than to England. It wouldn't have made much difference—he'd have made up the time backtracking in minutes after stopping for breakfast on a Portsmouth-bound ferry. But it felt good to stay in the right direction. He landed on the bridge, his talons catching at the metal ridge of the captain's viewing deck. He swept 360 degrees with his astonishing eyes before he was certain that nobody was watching. It was a bright but cold morning, and most of the passengers were below. He flew down another level, to the rails of the upper deck, glanced around again and then hopped to the green-painted metal floor and shifted to a hungry passenger.

Inside the ferry there was a short queue in the restaurant for breakfast and Dax joined it, fishing the money out of the backpack. He lined up with a plastic tray and collected a hot plate of bacon, sausages, beans, egg, and fried bread, as well as a big mug of brown tea. He paid the French girl on the till in English money, relieved that they took both sterling and euros. In a moment of quick thinking, he asked the girl to give him his change in euros, and then found a table by the window and sat down to eat. Around him families squabbled over drinks and truckers ate heartily and read the sports pages of newspapers. Uniformed stewards stacked cutlery and collected abandoned trays. The tannoy announced a film starting in the on-board cinema. It was so normal it was weird.

'Looks like that's going down well,' said one of the truckers (at least he looked like one) grinning over his paper from the next table. Dax nodded and beamed back, his mouth full of fried bread and his hand wrapped around the hot mug. 'You travelling on your own, son?' said the trucker and his mate looked across now.

Dax felt slightly alarmed. He shook his head. 'No, Mum and Dad and my sister are all in the cabin. They get seasick. Not me though.' He grinned and took another forkful of sausage and the truckers nodded approvingly.

'Good sea legs,' said the second one. 'You should be a sailor.'

'Oh, I'm thinking of the air force,' said Dax, cheekily. 'I like to fly.'

They laughed, not taking him at all seriously, and Dax concentrated on his food. He couldn't spend too much time enjoying normal people. He wondered what was happening with Gideon. Had Owen discovered him yet? He felt sure that he would have. Without Spook's glamour to help him, Gideon couldn't distract attention from his presence for very long, and Owen had a hunter's instincts. He must have found Gideon by now. He just hoped that he hadn't forced Gideon back to the college. With any luck he would have decided to take him along and keep him well protected.

More importantly, by now Owen should know about Lisa's mistake. The girls would have waited for their five minutes, and then one of them would have gone straight to Mrs Sartre's room and woken her up. Mrs Sartre would have contacted Owen immediately and they would have changed their route to head for France instead. Suddenly Dax felt a stab of concern. What if they were helicoptering down right now and he missed them? What if they were already there? He hadn't thought of that before. He had relaxed a great deal about Gideon, because they'd been going to the wrong place and were in no danger. Now, though, they might be there already and anything could happen.

Dax finished his breakfast, hurried back up on to the top deck, glanced around quickly, and then shifted. On the bridge the first mate gave a cry of surprise. 'Well, blow me down! I've never seen a bird of prey this far out before!'

Why was he so worried? Dax pondered this as he rose higher and faster through the air, leaving the ferry far below and behind. Owen was the best. He would protect Gideon. Owen would find Luke in time, with his help, and get the boy away, and then go back for Catherine and—what? *Contain* her. Could Catherine *be* contained? They would know not to touch her, at least, he told himself again.

Lisa's premonition of Luke lying in blood needn't come true. Other premonitions she'd given him in the past hadn't—not exactly. They were warnings of what might happen if they *didn't* act. Nothing was set in stone.

He flew on, rising high where he could move faster, and flipped in the air with excitement two hours later when he saw the coast of France. It looked very much like England—green and cut through with haphazard road networks. He had to go directly south now, he knew. The journey would take him across land and down the Normandy coast until he reached the polders in Northern Brittany. Le Mont-Saint-Michel—an unmistakable island with its impressive church spire, which he'd often seen on postcards—would be his landmark. Troisenfants was only minutes away from it by air according to his map. Then all he had to do was find a windmill.

He reached his landmark after forty minutes flight. The island rose like a tiny mountain, with medieval buildings clustered around its steep sides, their dark slate roofs gleaming in the mid afternoon sun. Tourists were swarming along its narrow streets like ants. Cars moved steadily across the long causeway towards it. Crowning the small peak was an abbey, with tall straight walls, elegant turrets, and a high spire. Dax dropped to the spire and landed on a small gold figure that was poised on it. The figure must be some kind of angel. It had wings and a sort of spiky halo. It wasn't a very comfortable landing, so he dropped to one of the more forgiving ledges, some way below the spire, and took in the view.

It was the flattest, widest coastline he had seen. To the west the sea stretched calm and still, like a dull blue mirror. Shadows of clouds moved languidly across it and he could see the shape of the seabed beneath the shallow saltwater for miles and miles before a deeper blue seized it on the horizon. Towards the shore the water did not even seem to trouble the land—it just disappeared into marsh. Tidal rivers cut deep scars into the mud and tussocks of grey-green weed grew out along them. Further into the land the weed grew thicker, shorter, and greener and sheep grazed along it. Sea and land seemed to merge eerily in a denial of what a normal seaside *was*. This, then, was 'the polders'—the flat coastal plains that Jennifer had described.

Dotted along the coast were small villages and the occasional campsite, beside the quiet strip of road that wound towards another headland further south. Cancale, Dax remembered, from the map. Now where was Troisenfants? Set back maybe a mile or two from the polders, he thought, going by the map. How was he to find it? Dax flew away from the abbey roof and headed inland. A windmill was what he was looking for and that shouldn't be hard to find from the air. It wasn't. He found a windmill almost immediately, sitting prettily on a small hill above the causeway road, almost as soon as he reached the mainland.

It was round and made of stone and his heart beat rapidly inside him when he remembered Luke's words. He was in a round room—of stone and wood! Dax flew to a low wooden fence that surrounded the windmill, but almost immediately he realized it was wrong. There was a plaque for visitors and a car park nearby. It was a 'working windmill museum'! There would be no foreign brother and sister hiding here. To be sure he flew up to the window between the tethered sails, and looked inside. It was cool and dark, but he could see the beautifully preserved workings of the mill and more plaques and pictures with the history of the mill worded in French. Three people were wandering along inside, reading the plaques and reaching out to touch the dormant mill workings.

Dax shook his head and flew on. And that's when he first noticed it. As he rose above the land he surveyed the shape of it, the fields, the polders, the winding roads, and the trees. The trees. What *was* it about the trees?

He landed on a farm building and shifted back to a boy, sitting eight metres up on an old tiled roof, staring out in wonder. High ridges of trees, tall, thin ones, like poplars, ran across the countryside in all directions, edging the roads and bordering fields. In the trees were hundreds and hundreds—perhaps thousands—of dark round pom-poms. Dax felt a shiver run from his neck to his knees. He was in the land of the pom-poms and he knew what the pom-poms were. They were infestations. Parasites, like Catherine. Pretty round pom-poms, in almost every tree he could see, in every direction. They were mistletoe.

22

A bell rang cheerily as he pushed open the door of the small grocery shop beside the road. He looked around, his mind turning feverishly, trying to work out what he would say. A young woman in a blue overall looked up from behind the counter where she was resting her arms along the till. '*Bonjour, monsieur,*' she said, with a smile that meant she found it rather sweet to be calling him '*monsieur*'.

Dax flushed. He was thirteen now, but he was small and had a young-looking face and could probably have passed for eleven. He took a deep breath and replied, '*Bonjour, mademoiselle*—' She raised an eyebrow at him and he remembered instantly what Mrs Sartre had said about addressing French women. You *never* called a young woman mademoiselle! It wasn't like 'miss' in England—it was more like calling her 'little girl'. 'Um . . . pardon—*madame*!' he spluttered and her smile returned. She must know he wasn't French.

Dax neared the counter nervously and took a deep breath. 'Um . . . *je vou—je voudrais . . .* um . . . *trouve—* no—no—*je cherche un ville. Le nom est Troisenfants?*' He hoped he had just said he was looking for a village called Troisenfants but he had no idea if his pronunciation was right. He had said 'Truz-en-fanz' and hoped for the best. She screwed up her dark eyes for a moment and then replied, '*Ah—Troisenfants.*' She pronounced it *Twazenfon.* '*Mais oui! Vous suivez cette route-là, vous prenez la première à gauche et alors Troisenfants est sur la colline.*'

Dax gaped and tried to work it out. She sighed and smiled again and then said: 'You go on here—along one road—you turning to the left and Troisenfants is being on the hill.'

Dax beamed with relief. 'Thank you! I mean— *merci* . . . ah . . . *bonjour* . . . er . . . no—I mean *au revoir*!'

'*Au revoir!*' she sang back at him and he hurried out, keeping her instructions in his head and wishing he'd worked harder in French. He walked swiftly along the little parade of shops, past the small pharmacy, the bakery, and the greengrocer's. Dax smelt the bread and felt an ache inside. He was hungry again. He felt the euros in his pocket and turned back to the bakery (here it was called a *boulangerie*) and suddenly there was that feeling again, of the world slowing down. He stopped dead in his tracks, his senses straining. A young lively voice was drifting from the bakery. A girl's laugh, bright and musical. Dax turned and stared in dumb wonder. It couldn't be! But he knew it was.

Inside the shop, standing next to a dark-haired, middle-aged woman and holding a wicker basket with baguettes of French bread in it, was Catherine. Dax gasped and stepped back. He had nearly ruined everything by walking straight into her!

He sidled quickly back around to the next shop doorway and stood, his heart racing, wondering what to do. There were too many people around for him to shift and fly away. He stayed still, listening hard, and heard Catherine chattering on animatedly to the shopkeeper in the bakery. Her French sounded faultless. She had been, of course, arm in arm with the woman—and was undoubtedly sapping her fluent language straight out of her. A few seconds passed and then he heard them both say *'Au revoir! Bonne journée!'* and the bell on the door jingled and they were both out on the pavement and walking away. Happily, they did not pass the doorway where he stood, rigid, against one wall, but turned in the other direction. The pharmacist was giving him a hard stare from inside the shop so Dax nodded politely and stepped back onto the pavement. Catherine walked away, still arm in arm with the Frenchwoman, both in step and carrying baskets. Her hair was much longer and woven into a loose dark plait which swung down between her shoulderblades. She looked tanned and healthy and taller, too. In a yellow dress and leather sandals, she looked, as well as sounded, vibrant. Dax felt a welling up of anger towards her. He knew where she got a lot of that vibrancy.

He expected her to sense him, to look round and gasp—and then maybe to fly into an attack, but she didn't look back. Dax remembered what Luke had said about the spirit world not allowing her in. It looked as if her sixth sense wasn't helping out either. Dax walked quietly behind the woman and the girl, noticing that the woman's shoulders were rounded and her walk not as energetic as her young companion's. He wasn't surprised to see it. He wondered if Francine had any idea about what Catherine was doing to her. Was she so happy to get a 'daughter' back in her life that she didn't care about her failing health? Because it must *be* failing. You couldn't spend that much time alone with Catherine and not be worn out.

Maybe though, Catherine had learned enough to keep her distance—but it didn't look like it, as she skipped along, hand clamped on her latest mother's arm.

Dax found a rather dank side alley which led away behind the shops, past some large bins. He turned down it and found a sheltered patch of weeds in which to shift. In seconds he was in the air and following them home.

The windmill was quite similar to the tourist attraction near le Mont-Saint-Michel—a round, chubby looking stone tower, perhaps ten metres high, with small, deep-silled windows. A stone extension had been built out of one side of it, which marked it out as a home, rather than a working mill, and yet the sails were in good condition, although the light wooden slats along them were bleached silver by the sun and the wind. They were untethered and turning gently in the light breeze with a rhythmic creak. It sounded very familiar to Dax as he came down to rest in a tree at the end of the garden of Maison Moulin Gris (Grey Windmill House he managed to translate). The tree he was in was tall and slender and festooned with mistletoe pom-poms. Dax perched well clear of them. He found them creepy. They rustled in the wind like whispering ghosts.

Maison Moulin Gris was set on a small hill which rose above the village of Troisenfants. The village was just big enough to have its own inn, a tiny shop selling bread, newspapers, and wine, and a couple of chambres d'hôtes (bed & breakfast houses, Dax remembered, from his lessons). There were no more than fifty houses in the village and the windmill was the most interesting thing about the place. Clearly Francine had done well as a surgeon before she lost her daughter and her will to carry on in medicine, because the garden was beautifully kept, the windmill house well maintained and pretty, with window boxes full of flowers—and an expensive French car was parked in its gravelled drive. Catherine had been lucky.

Dax gazed across at the small window in the centre of the mill tower, just below the central pin of the windmill sails. He could see nothing through it other than a dim grey light but he was certain that this was the room in which Luke lay. He was about to fly across to the window when he heard voices and saw Catherine and Francine coming in through the gate, between neatly cut yew hedges that enclosed the garden. He had overtaken them as soon as he spotted the windmill. Catherine was still talking and laughing and lively, exactly as he remembered her at Tregarren. Francine was nodding, smiling, but looking tired.

As they turned into the garden, Francine said something back to Catherine and then gave her a quick hug, smiling down at her. This was the main difference, thought Dax. Francine loved Catherine. They paused at the front door as Francine took out her key and in their conversation Dax heard 'Luke' mentioned. Then they disappeared into the house, leaving the door open, and their voices became more muffled. *Now what?* thought Dax. *Go to Owen,* said a sensible voice in his head. *You know where they are now—so go to Owen and bring him here.* Dax nodded at his own instructions. *I will—but first I have to see that Luke is OK.* He winged across the garden, easily timed himself to dodge the gently turning sails, and landed on the thick sill of the high window. The glass sash built into it was pushed up, allowing the May air inside, and Dax crouched quietly on the sill and looked down into the room. It was round, as Luke had told them, with a wooden floor and stone walls. Old wooden beams criss-crossed at ceiling height and dark oak rafters angled up into a vaulted roof beyond them.

Dax flew silently across to the lower rafters to get a better view and shivered at the ever changing light, the creaks and the clicks which he had seen in dreams and visions and now here—in reality. There was little in the room to look at. An elderly wooden table stood beneath the small window, with a lace cloth laid upon it and a large china basin and a jug resting on the cloth. A wicker easy chair stood just inside the door into the room and a wooden upright chair was positioned right next to the bed, with a stack of books beneath it. The bed was iron and on it lay a thin boy whose flesh was almost as pale as the white sheet which was tucked tightly around his skinny form. His eyes were closed, blue veins spidering across the lids. His hands rested on his chest and his breathing was even and shallow. Dax felt as if a strong gust of wind could blow him apart. His heart clenched inside him when he thought of Luke as he had been. Quiet and steady, but bright and funny at times, often reading or simply watching them all with great interest. 'The Dud', the plodder, the quiet one—the boy who'd saved more than a hundred lives. And now here he lay, unable to wake; and if he did wake, unable to speak.

Go and get Owen! spoke up the sensible voice again, but before he could move there were footsteps on the stairs and he froze, hidden behind the cross of the beam, and in came Francine, followed by Catherine. Francine went to Luke and touched his forehead. She looked worried. '*Il est très malade.*' She looked at Catherine and spoke urgently, pleadingly. '*Je dois appeler un autre médecin. Je ne peux pas le traiter moi-même. Il a besoin de l'aide d'un spécialiste!*'

Dax didn't understand all she said, but he made out '*un autre médecin*'—that meant 'another doctor'. She had also said 'specialist'. She wanted to bring somebody to help Luke. But Catherine was shaking her head. She clutched at Luke's hand and tears spilled from her green eyes and trickled down her face.

'*Mais tu peux le guérir toi-même. Je sais que tu peux! Si un autre médecin vient il posera des questions à notre sujet et mon père nous trouvera. Il nous prendra loin de toi.'*

Whatever Catherine was saying to her, it was clear that she did not want anyone else tending to Luke. Francine seemed to accept what she said, although she still looked worried. She nodded slowly and left the room. There was a long pause during which Catherine simply sat and stared at Luke. Her tears dried unheeded on her cheeks and then she leaned down to her brother's pale face and opened her mouth to speak. From it came English, with an American accent.

'I bet you thought you were real smart, didn't you? You thought I wouldn't figure it out, but I'm *not stupid*! You did like I did, huh? You went skipping off on the power lines or something and tried to get help! You got into Lisa or someone's head and told her to run and tell Gideon, didn't you? You didn't think I knew, but I knew—oh yeah—I saw it in your head!

'Well, good for you, big brother! Thanks! I'll be real glad to see Gideon again because, you know what? You are nearly out of juice! There's hardly anything of you left worth having. I'm gonna finish you off tonight, while she's asleep—then she'll take me somewhere safe. And then I'll get Gideon instead. I'm not afraid of him any more—he's just like you. Weak! Weak in the end. But I'll be careful and make him last a bit longer than you. And when he's all gone I'll get Dax. That'll be *real* cool. I can't wait for *him*! I could make him stay a bird and keep him in a cage and carry him around with me.'

Dax found he was gripping the wood viciously with his talons. *Go for Owen! Now!* But he was rigid with fear for Luke. What did she mean by 'tonight'? When did tonight start? Lisa's premonition had been at sunset. How long did he have to get Owen here before Catherine chose to finish off Luke? Already it was late afternoon and he had no idea where Owen and Tyrone and Gideon were. He hadn't thought this through! What should he do? He fought the wild urge to fly at the mistletoe sister now, and tear at her face. He remembered how she had used her stolen telekinetic power to hurl him into a cliff the last time he'd tried that. He couldn't risk getting killed or stunned when he might be the only one able to help Luke.

'Katrin! Katrin!' called Francine from downstairs and Catherine called back to her, putting a sorrowful sigh into her voice, before leaning once more down to her brother.

'See you later, Luke!' she murmured, a nasty smile on her pretty face. Then she went down.

Dax stayed still, listening hard. He heard more conversation, muffled, downstairs and perhaps five minutes passed before he heard Catherine call, '*Au revoir! Je serai de retour bientôt.*' He flew to the window and saw her walking back up the garden path, holding some books. Now was his chance. He flew to the floor and shifted and ran across to Luke. He grabbed the boy's hand. It felt cool and lifeless, but there was a slow pulse in his wrist. 'Luke! Luke!' he whispered urgently into the boy's ear. Luke did not stir. 'It's me—Dax! I'm here! I've come to get you!' Luke sighed and his eyes rolled under their thin lids. Dax took Luke's face in his hands. 'Luke! Try to wake up!' A sliver of white showed along one eye and Luke sighed again.

Dax sat back, trying to think. He looked around for water to throw on Luke's face, but there was nothing in the bowl or jug on the table. Dax clenched his teeth with frustration and then noticed Luke's eyes. Now they were open and they were staring, but not at Dax. Dax spun round.

Standing in the bedroom doorway, holding a kitchen knife, was Francine.

23

The woman was staring at him and the knife—still wet from slicing tomato (Dax could smell it)—shook in her clenched fist. Her face was attractive but had many worry lines etched into it. Her eyes were grey and large and fixed upon him.

'*Qui êtes vous?*' she said. Dax could smell fear on her rather than violence. He could also smell anxiety and sorrow and confusion. He felt calmer. This was not a killer.

'*Je suis* Dax Jones,' he said, in a voice that sounded stronger than he felt. '*Je suis Anglais. Parlez-vous Anglais?*' He was amazed at how the French flowed out of his mouth. How had he remembered all that?

'English,' said the woman. 'Yes—I speak English. Now tell me—what are you doing here?' Dax stood up and she gripped the knife tighter and gulped.

'I've come for Luke,' he said. 'He needs rescuing, don't you think?'

She stared at him and then glanced at Luke who was still regarding them both silently from the bed.

'And who are you to rescue him?' she said, lifting her chin. 'He is being taken care of here.'

'Oh, yeah—he's being taken care of,' said Dax. 'Just like Catherine takes care of everyone.'

'What do you mean?' she demanded, but her eyes flickered back to Luke and the scent of fresh anxiety gusted from her.

'I think you know what I mean,' said Dax. He wished Owen was here. Owen would be able to deal with this so well. He would make her understand what was happening. *Where are you, Owen?* he sent inside his head, but nothing came back. Why should it? Owen wasn't telepathic, even though he had, on occasion, been able to pick up messages from Lisa. Dax didn't have Lisa's power to connect with him. Dax decided he must try to be as much like Owen as possible. He took a deep breath and sat back down on the bed, folding his hands together. 'You don't really want to use that on me, do you?' he said.

She looked at the knife as if she had forgotten it. She allowed her hand to drop to her side, but she kept the knife tightly in her grip.

'Who are you?' she said, again. 'How do you come to be here?'

'I come from a special place, a kind of college, in England. Catherine was there last year. So was Luke—and another brother, Gideon.'

'There is another?' she asked.

'Yes—they are triplets. They're very special triplets. I think you know what I mean. They're—different.'

She narrowed her eyes at him. 'How?'

'They have some unusual powers. They can do things that normal people can't do. Have you noticed that, in Catherine? Do you see how she's different?'

She closed her eyes for a moment and then fixed them back on him. 'And you—are you different too?'

'Oh yes,' said Dax. 'Do you need me to show you?'

She nodded.

'You'd better sit down,' said Dax. 'No, really—you should.'

With a suspicious glare, she reached across and dragged the chair from beside Luke's bed to the doorway. She was taking no chances on Dax getting past her. She sat down on the chair and held the knife firmly. 'Show me then,' she said.

Dax shifted, first to a fox, standing on the foot of the bed, gazing straight at her and flicking his magnificent tail, and then to a falcon, balanced on the iron bedstead.

She moaned '*Mon dieu!*' and put one hand to her throat, but she didn't scream or faint. Dax guessed she had already witnessed some very strange things since Catherine and Luke arrived in her life. He shifted back to a boy and remained seated on the bed.

'That is my power,' he said, keeping his words simple. 'Luke and Gideon have a different power. They can move things around without touching them—with their minds. Do you understand?'

She nodded again and her expression was less than surprised.

'You've seen Catherine do that, haven't you?'

She didn't answer for a moment and then she sighed. 'And that is Katrin's power? That moving with the mind?'

'No,' said Dax. 'It isn't. Catherine's power is nothing like Luke's or Gideon's. Catherine is a parasite.'

'Parasite?' She pronounced it 'paraseet' and Dax realized it was pretty much the same in French. 'Like a—a *worm*. A bloodsucker? No! This cannot be! She is a good girl!'

'Is she?' said Dax and watched the woman's face as it went from distress to defiance and then back to distress. 'How do you feel—since you met Catherine?'

'She looks after her brother,' insisted Francine. 'She loves him and she holds his hand and—'

'Physical contact is how she does it,' said Dax, bluntly. 'She touches you and she takes whatever she wants. From Luke she takes power, like he's a battery. She has stolen many other powers from the children at our college and Luke's energy helps her to keep them and use them. She can move things with her mind, she can make illusions, she can probably even disappear a bit, when she tries. She might be able to heal wounds—probably her own wounds. She can read minds too. But she can't do any of these things without Luke. She gets all the energy from Luke. That's why he can't wake up.'

The woman looked from Luke to Dax, and back to Luke again, her mouth open with shock. She suddenly got up, dropping the knife, and walked across to the boy in the bed. She touched his face and knelt down next to him. 'Is it true? Luke? Is it true?'

Luke nodded at her and his eyes flickered with the exhaustion of it.

'*Oh mon dieu*,' she murmured again.

'He would have told you,' said Dax. 'He tried to warn you on the yacht, but Catherine stopped him. She made him a mute.'

'I cannot believe it! I cannot. There must be some mistake.' She stood up and wiped her hands through her hair, staring into the air between them.

'And yet,' Dax stood up, 'you're not calling the police. Are you? You know what I'm saying is true. How long have you known that something wasn't right? How long did it take before you started feeling tired and getting headaches?'

Francine snapped her attention back to him. 'Headaches? What about the headaches?'

'You are getting them, aren't you? That's because Catherine is your parasite too. She needs you. She had to learn French right away—so she could talk you into taking her home with you. She got into your head as soon as you got her on board your boat. She found out all about your dead daughter and how sad you were and she realized that all she had to do was be a replacement daughter. She pokes around in your head, so she always has the advantage of you. How often has she said *exactly* what you're thinking? How often?'

Francine was drawing slow breaths, trying to keep control, but realization was flooding her face.

'I can't give her back,' she said. 'I can't. I love her—she is like my own.'

'That's how she works,' said Dax. 'And when you're

all used up, she'll find someone new to look after her. She'll dump you like rubbish, if she hasn't killed you first. Nobody, not even Luke, has enough in them to last for ever. That's why she's going to finish him tonight. That is her plan. If I leave him here with you he'll be dead before morning.'

'Maybe—maybe she doesn't know what she does . . . ' said Francine, and tears welled in her eyes. 'Perhaps she cannot help it?'

'You believe that?'

She sank back down onto the chair by the door and put her hands over her mouth.

'Francine, you have to help me! I've got to save Luke. Let me use your phone and call someone who can get him away.'

'No! No! If someone comes they will take Katrin! I cannot have this!'

'Even if Katrin is *killing* him—and *you*?'

'I will make her stop. I know I can. She cares about me too. She will stop if I ask her to. She will do it for me.'

'Oh, Momma!' said a low voice from the door. 'I *wish* I could! I really, really do!'

Francine spun round and Catherine stepped into the doorway. Dax cursed himself. The intense drama in the little bedroom had blunted his other senses and he hadn't picked up Catherine's return with ears or nose.

Catherine leaned into the doorway and smiled. 'Hey, Dax! Good to see you! You're just in time to take over from Luke.'

221

Francine stared at Catherine. 'What does this mean? What this boy is saying! It cannot be true!'

Catherine squeezed her on the shoulder. 'Don't upset yourself. It can't be helped. I am what I am.'

'But you wouldn't—you couldn't . . . '

'Hurt Luke? Well, you know, it's not that I *want* to. I just *have* to, or I'll run out of all my powers. I can't have that. I'm going to be the most powerful Cola on the planet. You gotta be a bit hard to get to the top, don't you think? But don't you worry, I won't hurt *you*! You're the best mom I ever had. I won't hurt you. Well, not unless you *make* me.'

Francine made a choking noise, as if she might be sick, and Catherine put both hands on her shoulders. 'My—my head!' breathed Francine, and the colour ran out of her face.

'Yeah, it's bad, isn't it? *Pauvre petite maman. Ça te fait mal, non*? I'll make it better soon—as soon as we're OK again.'

'Get off her,' said Dax. 'You're hurting her!'

Catherine's merry green eyes regarded him and now she rested her hands on the pale Frenchwoman's head. 'Mmmm. I am. She's thinking about letting you take Luke away, and she needs to understand that it won't do. Luke is mine. I'm nearly finished with him. You're too late, Dax.'

Francine moaned and began to slump sideways. 'Get off her!' shouted Dax.

'Or what, Dax Jones? What are you going to do? Peck me to death? Go on—I want to see you try!'

Dax shifted instantly and flew at her. He could do

better than peck. He could rip her eyes out with his talons. But before he'd got a foot into the air he was belted backwards with a huge telekinetic swipe. Of course—she had been leeching power out of Luke only fifteen minutes ago. She was fully charged. Dax hurtled backwards and shot helplessly through the small window, where the hard edge of a sail suddenly sliced quickly down and dashed him to the ground.

He lay on the gravel, still a falcon, his head and wings stinging with pain and shock and his heart thundering in his chest. There was another powerful belt and suddenly he was airborne again—but not flying. A rush of warm air threw him up high in front of the windmill and then flung him flat on to one of the turning sails. The sail shuddered to a halt despite the breeze and the falcon, wings spread, was immobilized against it. Dax's bird's eye view closed on Catherine standing in the garden, her arms folded.

'Come and see this, Francine!' she crowed, jubilantly, like an infant showing off a new trick. 'Watch me! Watch *me*!'

In an instant there was a metallic crack and a terrible stabbing pain in Dax's left wing. A second later there was another—this time striking his right wing. Dax's vision swam pink and black and he felt wave upon wave of dizziness wash over him. The pain was so great he could not stand to look at what had caused it.

'Neat, isn't it?' giggled Catherine.

Francine stood behind her and her face was a mask of horror. Dax finally turned his head to the right. Embedded in his wing was a thick rusty nail. It skewered straight through to the wooden sail behind it and pinned him in place. On the other side was a shard of glass, doing the same job. Twin rosettes of blood were seeping out into his feathers. Horror and misery engulfed him. He had failed.

'Go on, Dax! Try to shift *now*!' said Catherine, with a hoot of laughter, and then the sail began to move, turning on through its arc until Dax hung upside down, the nail and the glass tearing against gravity through his brutally pinned wings. 'Go on—shift! Let's see how you manage up there as a fox! Or a boy! You'll never stay up there! You'll be down on the ground again in no time!'

She was right, of course. Shifting now would probably mean a broken back or a broken leg. It was over. She had won. And now she was going to enjoy herself. The sails continued to turn, a ghastly vertical roundabout which he could not leave. He turned faster—faster—swept up and over and down and round as the world streaked into a gaudy blur of colour. '*Up and over*' he remembered Lisa telling him; the message from Sylv. '*Watch your back or you'll be up and over.*' Once again, too little information, too late. The air whipped past his feathered brow and the smell of his own blood and fear built up inside his head. He could hear her laughing and laughing, and in the background, Francine was crying and pleading with her to stop. Finally, the Frenchwoman got Catherine's attention.

The sails slowed to a halt, with Dax pinned upside down on the lowest, as Catherine spun around to deal with her French mother.

'Don't *you* tell me what to do! *Nobody* can tell me what to do!' she spat, her back to Dax. He could see Francine, upside down in her upside down garden, mumbling at Catherine in French and shaking her head. 'Speak English!' commanded Catherine. 'It's rude to speak French when my birdy friend can't understand it!'

'You don't know what you do!' cried Francine. 'This is wrong! This is all wrong! You are a *good* girl! Stop this and we will go away! We will take Luke and go far away! We will go to Nice! I have friends in Nice.'

Catherine put her hands on her hips and her head on one side, considering. 'I guess you could be right,' she said, and she sounded so utterly reasonable it was terrifying. 'If Dax has got here the rest of them won't be far behind. We can't stay here. Luke probably won't live long anyway—we can always find somewhere to bury him along the way.'

'Then help me get Luke to the car. We have to hurry!'

'OK,' said Catherine, as if she'd just agreed to fetch something from the fridge. She and Francine went back into the house. Dax could feel the blood dripping from his wings but he couldn't see or hear much at all. His head felt as if it was filled with fire and his body raged with pain. He began to lose consciousness but was roused by the sound of Catherine and Francine struggling out of the house with Luke. They had put pyjamas on him and he hung between them like a rag doll. They hauled him across to the car and bundled him on to the back seat, where he sagged, face down, and lay still.

'*Vite, vite, chérie!*' begged Francine, her bag on her shoulder and her car keys jingling. 'We must go! They will come!'

Catherine paused at the car and looked back at Dax, a broken bird suspended upside down on the windmill sail. A small pool of blood was spreading on the gravel beneath him.

'Wait! I want Dax! I *want* him in a cage!'

'*D'accord*—OK, little one,' said Francine, breathlessly. 'I have a cage. We will put him in there and take him along. You go to the garage for the cage and I will take him down.'

'No—*you* go for the cage. I want to get him. I really want to get him!'

Through the whirl of unending pain that tore around his falcon body, Dax realized what she wanted. She was finally going to get the chance to pick up shapeshifting power. He tugged desperately against the nail and the glass, despite the awful splinters of agony this sent through him. She must *not* get to shapeshift too.

Catherine walked towards him, her face filled with triumph and excitement. The end of the sail hung just two metres from the ground and she had only to reach up to collect him to get the power of shapeshifting. She lifted her arms like a ballet dancer, her fingers outstretched.

There was a ringing metallic thud. Catherine froze. Then her arms dropped and she slumped to the ground.

Behind her stood Francine, her face streaming with tears, holding a garden spade.

2 4

Francine moved rapidly. First she checked Catherine's pulse and nodded briskly to herself. *'Bien!'* Then she hauled the girl up into her arms and dragged her over to the car. She put her into the front seat and buckled her in, before tenderly pushing her hair back from her face. *'Je suis vraiment désolée!'* Dax heard her murmur.

Then she returned to Dax and her face puckered with distress as she stared up at him, hanging limply on the sail. 'I am so sorry,' she said. She supported his body with one hand while she wrenched at the nail with the other. Dax heard a shrill scream and realized he had made the noise himself. He hadn't thought such pain was possible. The glass came out with an equally agonizing tear and then she carried him to the grass and laid him under the tree. Dax willed himself to shift and the weight of his human form returning brought another nauseating wave of pain crashing across him. Francine gave a cry of shock, and then knelt beside him and looked at the wounds in his arms. Above his left elbow and just below his right elbow were deep ragged punctures and splinters of bone. Blood flowed freely from them.

'I am so sorry,' she said, again, and made a series of short beeps. 'Take this—dial your home. Get help. I must go.'

She ran back across the garden and he heard the car engine start and the shriek and skid of the tyres over the gravel and then they were gone. Dax felt something in his left hand. He could not move his right hand or arm at all but the left one seemed to be still working. With immense effort, feeling sweat running off him like rain, he lifted his left hand up and saw what was in it. A mobile phone. He stared at it, trying to remember what it did. *Think! Stop fading out!* shouted a voice in his head, which sounded like Lisa. He stared at the little square screen on the phone and saw that there were already numbers on it—the code for the UK, he was sure. Francine had helped him that much. Now he just had to remember the number for Fenton Lodge. It could have been all over then. Dax was not normally good at remembering phone numbers. But by happy chance, the phone number at the lodge was easy to remember because part of it was his dad's birthday—the twenty-third of September. The code for Cumbria he knew and then it was eleven—like the True Eleven that Gideon spoke of—and then 2309.

It seemed to take forever to press the numbers. His fingers slid around and left blood on the buttons. He began to think he would never be able to do it but then he pressed the OK button and heard a series of clicks and then—amazingly—the double beep of an international exchange ringing. He cried with pain as he bent his arm fully to bring the phone to his ear and his vision swam and turned grey at the edges. *Don't faint now! Not now!*

The phone rang three times and then someone picked up and a flat voice said: 'Eades.'

'Mr Eades,' said Dax and his voice came out thin and faraway.

'Who is this?' snapped Mr Eades.

'It's me—Dax . . . '

'Who is it?'

'Dax . . . '

'Is that Dax Jones? Where the devil are you? You are in a lot of trouble, young man.'

'Mr Eades . . . please . . . I . . . ' The grey closed in and the phone tumbled out of his hand with a click and a beep. Now the grey claimed him. The world went away.

25

'I like this place,' said Luke. 'It's cool.'

Dax nodded and swung his legs happily from the deck of the tree house. 'We built it—all of us,' he said. 'Even Gideon banged a few nails in, but he made a bit of a mess of them—look!' He showed Luke the mangled spider of nails on the oak tree branch and they both laughed. It was such a good feeling and his arms were so much better here.

'I guess we must be dead then,' said Dax. 'I never thought I'd come back here. Oh, look—it's Pointing Boy!' The pointing boy sat a little way along the deck of the tree house and he smiled at them both, a soft breeze rummaging through his hair. There was something in his hand, something glittery. 'He doesn't come,' said the boy to Dax and Dax sighed and said, 'No. Sometimes they don't.'

'You're not dead, Dax,' said Luke, stretching and yawning with a relaxed smile. 'I'm not either—yet. I might be dead soon though.'

'How can I be here with you if I'm not dead?' asked Dax. A flash of unpleasant recent memory went off in his head and he did his best to ignore it.

'You're in the place where we met before,' explained

Luke. 'It's the same place, but you chose to make it be here, in the tree. We are *nearly* dead, though!' he added, comfortingly.

'So we're just sort of—on a day out?' asked Dax. 'A day out in dead-land.'

'Something like that. You can pop right out of your body sometimes, and come here, if you know how, or if it hurts so much you can't stand to stay there any more. Or if someone like Lisa takes you here. But you're still alive. You're probably going to have to go back in a minute. Stay here much longer and you won't be able to.'

'Doesn't seem so bad here,' said Dax.

'Yeah, I know. But you'll miss Mrs P's cooking. And Gideon will be wrecked. That's him now.'

The phone began to ring and Luke and the pointing boy and the tree house winked away and the pain shot back into him. Dax wailed with it, and grabbed the phone. 'What do you *want*?' he gasped into it and Gideon's tinny voice yelled back, 'Dax! Dax! Where are you?'

'By the windmill,' said Dax. The pain was still awful and he felt weaker than ever, but his head seemed much clearer now. 'In Troisenfants. Where are you? You're taking ages.'

'I know, I know—we had to go back for Mia. But we're nearly there—we're following your mobile signal. We can see the hill and the windmill. Are you OK? Is Luke still there?'

'He's gone. So has Catherine.'

'Oh no!'

'Why did you go back for Mia?' Dax felt soaked. He hoped it was sweat or rain, but he knew that it wasn't.

'Owen found me—*yeah, to the left, Ty!*—Owen found me at the airport and was going to string me up, but I got him to agree to take me. Then, when we were in Holland, Mrs Sartre called and said we had to come to France and meet you. And then she called again an hour later saying Lisa was hysterical and going on about a boy covered in blood and there was not enough time and we had to take Mia to save him. Dax! Did Catherine hurt him? Was Luke bleeding?'

'No, but he's gone now. I can't tell what's happening to him,' said Dax quietly, and it took all the strength in him to get the words out. He didn't know how much longer he could hold the phone to his ear.

'Oh no, oh no, this is so not good,' groaned Gideon. 'We're coming up the hill now. Dax! Mia had to come to save his life! He's out here somewhere, lying in blood! I think we might be too late.'

Dax's strength gave out and the phone slid from his grasp. The scarlet pool he lay in grew larger.

The sound of the car engine roused him again. He felt oddly embarrassed. He didn't want to be found like this. There was a crunch of gravel and then he heard Owen give a low cry of despair. He heard him say, hoarsely, 'Gideon—stay there! Stay in the car!' and guessed he must look dead.

He felt Owen kneel down at his side and touch his face. 'God alive, Dax. What did she do to you?'

Dax couldn't speak. He simply didn't have enough energy, but he opened his eyes and saw Owen gasp and then close his own in relief.

'Mia! I need you here now!' shouted Owen and Mia arrived seconds later. She, too, looked horrified. She dropped to the grass behind his head and immediately placed both hands on his wounded arms.

'He's lost so much blood!' she said. 'I can knit the bone and the skin—but I don't know if that's enough! I can't put blood back in him. It was *Dax* that Lisa saw, not Luke. Dax in a pool of blood. Oh, Dax!'

'Do whatever you can,' said Owen, smoothing Dax's hair back from his forehead.

A pulse of warmth ran into his wounds from Mia's hands and immediately the raging pain in them eased. He felt incredibly calm, like he had on the tree house with Luke. Luke! Now he remembered! Luke was in the car with Catherine! As the energy and healing from Mia flooded into him he took a ragged breath and spoke, looking urgently into Owen's anxious blue eyes.

'Luke . . . in a car with Catherine and Fra—the Frenchwoman. Catherine was . . . unconscious . . . but she'll wake up and kill him and bury him . . . somewhere on the way to Nice. Francine might stop her . . . if she can. Saved me.'

'What does the car look like?' asked Owen, and up beyond his shoulder, Gideon's face appeared. It crumpled when he saw Dax.

'Dax! Oh, mate!' gulped his friend. 'It was *you*!'

233

'I'll be OK . . . You brought Mia for me,' said Dax. And then he sat up. Mia tried to keep him down but suddenly the energy seemed to be pouring into him. 'You OK?' he checked with Mia, wondering if her healing would have a bad effect on her.

She nodded. 'Yes—I'm much, much stronger than I used to be. I'll be fine.'

The bleeding had stopped and the wounds were already scabbed over. It was astonishing. It felt as if Mia *had* put back the blood in his veins, but that couldn't be—it was still seeping into the grass all around him.

'The car is red—a Renault. A hatchback,' said Dax. 'I'll find it and come back to you.'

'You can't shift *now*!' said Owen, as Dax got to his feet. 'You've just come back from death's door! You'll never make it.'

'Gideon,' said Dax, holding out his trembling—but *working*—right hand. 'I need chocolate.'

Gideon fumbled in his pocket and pulled out a chunky bar of Cadbury's. 'Excellent,' said Dax, trying to keep his voice strong. He wolfed the chocolate down at speed while they stood staring at him.

'Right—I'm good to go,' said Dax, although he knew it was at least half not true. They looked at him, fearful and unconvinced.

'Well—do you have a helicopter?' he demanded.

'No,' sighed Owen. 'We . . . er . . . ran into some trouble with the French and had to do a runner from the airport in a stolen car. Tyrone and Gideon had to—

well—squash up a fence or two. And I think Chambers is in custody!'

'Right, then all you've got is me. Get in the car and follow me. I'll spot them and come back to you.'

They looked at one another. Mia shrugged. 'Sometimes people get some extra strong energy boost in them when they're newly healed. That should keep him going for a while.'

Reluctantly Owen agreed. 'OK—do it. But, Dax, remember, you are as important to us as Luke.' He lowered his voice and steered Dax away from Gideon's hearing. 'Maybe—maybe more so. I'm not interested in trading you for anyone else, you understand?'

Dax nodded once and then shifted before Owen could change his mind. He flew above the tree with its nasty pom-poms and saw them all hurrying back to the stolen green people-carrier below. Owen stared up at him before he got in and called: 'Straight back! As soon as you see them! Straight back to me! We'll head for the main road towards the south.'

Dax rose high, scanning the land below him for a red car. He saw nothing on the coast road, but as the land spread out beneath him he saw a main road going south-east, inland. He turned in the air and flew for it. Below him cars of all colours sped along, but he remembered a sticker in the back window which featured a black bat. This is what would help him. He reached the road and began to follow it, coasting steadily ahead of the traffic and dropping lower to inspect every red car. And then he saw it. The red car carrying Luke and Catherine—the sticker was there and his peregrine eyes could not mistake it. The car moved along the right-hand lane and then turned off onto a smaller road, winding along through trees. Dax could see that the road led to a lake beauty spot two or three miles away and ended at a car park. He flew lower, pulling ahead and looking through the windscreen. His eyes missed no detail.

Catherine was now awake in the front passenger seat and her hand was clenched tightly on Francine's shoulder. Dax had no doubt about what she intended to do at the remote lake. Luke still lay as if dead on the back seat.

Dax knew everything he needed to know. He turned and shot back the way he had come, finding the people-carrier just as it reached the main road inland. He swooped down beside it as Tyrone drove on. Gideon wound down his window and the falcon shot inside. Between Gideon and Mia, Dax shifted and gasped out: 'She's made Francine drive them to a park by a lake—you need to come off at the next exit! We have to be quick! I have to go ahead again.'

'No!' shouted Owen and Gideon together.

'You stay with us now,' said Owen and the window next to Gideon rolled up. There was a clunk as Tyrone locked all the windows and doors from the driver's controls. He shot off at the next exit and Dax sank between his friends, his heart thumping in his chest, desperate to fly, but understanding that he must stay.

'You need to drink,' said Mia, and handed him a bottle of mineral water. He took it wordlessly, realizing how parched he was. 'I think you must have lost at least four pints of blood,' she said. 'You're a miracle right now. You should be unconscious! Even *with* the healing!'

Dax emptied the bottle down his throat and gave her a tight smile. 'You're better at it than you thought,' he said, although he knew he could crumple at any time.

Gideon compressed his lips. He didn't speak. He had a cricket ball in his hand, obviously a find from their stolen car, and he flexed his fingers around it repeatedly as he stared through to the windscreen in front.

'They got me on a helicopter, straight from Fenton Lodge,' went on Mia. 'It was amazing! Then when we got to France they got all official with us and wouldn't let us go straight through—Gideon didn't have a passport—and we knew we didn't have enough time for it all. Chambers went off to "pull strings", but then they insisted we had to take these French agents with us and Owen wouldn't have it. Tyrone made the roof of the airport fly off—he really did! Everyone thought it was a freak tornado!' Dax saw Tyrone grin self-consciously in the rear-view mirror. 'And then we ran for the car park while everyone was screaming, and stole a car! Can you believe it? Gideon broke the locks with one look and Tyrone got it started with just a hard stare at the dashboard! Incredible! Then they just mashed holes in the fences between the two of them so we could drive straight out. It was amazing!'

Mia seemed really bright considering the grave

situation, thought Dax. Or maybe she was just trying to distract him from his horrible experiences that day.

They sped at high speed along the winding road, past tourist signs for Lac du Barragne, with symbols for picnic areas and camping. Minutes later they slowed down and turned into a car park amid the trees. They all got out of the car and followed Gideon past the red Renault, which was standing at the far end of the car park, empty.

'This way! Can you smell them, Dax? Am I right?'

Dax nodded—the scent was clear. Gideon began to run into the trees, away from the lake and the picnic areas and into a dense dark plantation of firs. Owen and Tyrone chased after him and Dax saw them both haul military rifles from under their black jackets. Mia chased on, too, but Dax simply shot up through the trees, a falcon before he'd even thought about it. His weakness fell away with the earth. They were so close—so close.

A quietness fell into him. His flight was serene and the dark woodland below looked like emerald green fur. Chinks of silver glittered through it; streams running to the lakes. He zoned his eyes in, seeking movement of a different kind. He could see his friends running after Gideon, zigzagging through the trees, and knew that Gideon was going the right way. Because a quarter of a mile from him he could see Catherine and Francine. They were digging. Dax stooped, flipped, and plummeted to earth.

He dropped through a chimney in the thick conifer foliage. If he had struck a single springy twig she would surely have heard him and looked up, but he avoided them and landed softly on a branch three metres above them Luke lay on the dark needly forest floor, his eyes closed. Was he already dead? No—Dax could see him breathing. Catherine and Francine were hauling lumps of peaty soft earth away together. They were digging a grave.

'You don't have to be sad,' Catherine was saying. 'He's going to a better place!'

'But . . . but, Katrin—*chérie*,' sniffed Francine. 'He is not yet dead. He might live! We can save him.'

'Oh, I think it's a bit late for that, don't you? And hey—don't think you're fooling me with that "*chérie*" business. You hit me with a spade!'

'Only because you were—hysterical. Not well . . . You didn't know what you were doing. I know you didn't really want to hurt that boy.'

'Well, you got *that* wrong!' cackled Catherine. 'I most definitely *did* want to hurt him. And now I want to hurt *you*! But you'll be OK. You love me, don't you? You want to help me. So, just as soon as we've buried Luke, I'll make your headache go away. Deal?'

'Yes,' said Francine, and it came out as a sob. 'You— you won't bury him alive? Please say you won't do that.'

'Oh, stop your squalling! He's mostly dead anyway. I should have killed him ages ago, really, when he still had a lot of power in him. Then I could have kept it all for good! But I never knew in time, and I couldn't ever let him power up again properly, because he would probably have killed me. If he had any sense! But neither of my brothers has any sense!'

Dax watched with interest as Catherine said this. Her other brother had just stepped out from behind a tree.

'How's this for sense?' he said, and a red blur struck Catherine's head so hard she flew head-over-heels into the air.

26

Francine screamed and sank to the woodland floor as Catherine landed heavily several feet away from the grave, the cricket ball glancing off her forehead. The girl shot up immediately, staring wildly at Gideon and seething with rage, a livid red welt rising instantly on her forehead.

'You! *You!*'

'Yeah,' said Gideon. 'Me.'

'You tried to *kill* me!' she gasped, amazed and affronted.

'Yep.'

There were two sharp clicks and Owen and Tyrone emerged on either side of Gideon, bearing their rifles.

Catherine's face closed into a sneer. 'Oh no you don't,' she said and at once both guns twisted up and spun back over Owen's and Tyrone's shoulders. Owen cursed and ran to get his but Tyrone stood his ground and instead reached over to Gideon's shoulder. 'Keep looking at her,' he said.

Catherine walked towards them. 'Oh, forget it,' she sighed. 'You win. I've had enough of her anyway. Always whining on about her dead daughter.' Francine gave a sob, still on the ground. Dax watch from above and wondered how it could possibly be that easy. As it turned out, it couldn't. Catherine deftly leapt sideways, dropped to her knees, grabbed her half-dead brother and suddenly *threw* him upwards with her mind, as if he was as light as a cardboard box.

Gideon shouted in horror as Luke catapulted high into the trees and then dropped back down, slumping across a branch. The branch bowed down with the weight and Luke hung there, his legs and arms dangling and his eyes still closed, snagged precariously among the pine cones. Catherine pointed up to him and kept her arm steady. 'Don't worry, Giddy!' she smiled. 'I'm holding him there! He won't fall! Not while I'm holding him nice and safe. And don't think you can help! You do that and I'll *feel* it and I'll *make* him fall so hard he'll smash like china.'

She's bluffing, thought Dax. *She doesn't have enough power to do that.* But Gideon and Tyrone seemed frozen, staring from Catherine to Luke and back to Catherine again. Dax wanted to attack her—but what if distracting her made her drop Luke? What if Gideon and Tyrone couldn't catch him in time? And now, with the worst possible timing, his energy was draining out of him so fast it was all he could do to cling to his perch and stay upright.

There was another click and now Owen stepped back around the telekinetics, his retrieved gun aimed at Catherine's heart.

'Oh, Mr Hind, you wouldn't!' she giggled. 'I know you won't. Kill me and Luke dies. You'd better be ready to make a deal! Gideon can't save him—not even with his friend there. They care about him too much, you see! We're never so good with our powers when it's people we care about. He'll goof it up and Luke will be mush! He cares too much.'

'Yeah, well,' said Owen, '*I* don't.' And he shot her.

21

There was a crack and a rustle and Luke dropped from the tree like a stone—but his fall was broken by an invisible force as both Gideon and Tyrone caught him with their minds. Gideon's eyes were bulging with the effort and Dax realized what Catherine had said was true. It wasn't just Lisa and Mia who had problems with the Loved Ones Buffer. Then Tyrone leaped forward and caught Luke physically and Gideon let out a rasping breath and collapsed to his knees, white with shock. Dax found himself landing on his friend's shoulder before he even knew he'd flown. Gideon was shaking so badly he had to get off him to the ground, where he shifted back to a boy.

Owen walked across to Catherine and stared down at her, his face impassive; soldier-like. Mia walked across from where she had waited, a few feet back in the trees.

'Don't touch her,' said Owen, and overhead the chopping of a helicopter could be heard. A shadow flickered across the trees above them. 'That'll be Chambers,' said Owen. 'Well done, Mia.' Dax realized Mia was holding Owen's mobile phone; she had obviously called Chambers, who must have already been in the air, heading for the windmill.

Catherine lay on her back, her eyes closed. Her hand was clutched to a wound on her chest; her chest was not moving. Francine was sitting beside the shallow grave and rocking and crying hoarsely. '*Non, oh, non non non*,' she gasped, staring at the body of her replacement daughter. '*Elle est morte . . . Oh, non . . . Elle est morte . . .*'

Mia went to Luke, who Tyrone was holding. The boy's head lolled back and he looked as dead as his sister. Dax's heart clenched. What if all this had been for nothing? Gideon may have been thinking the same; he stared at his brother, still white and shocked.

Mia touched Luke's throat. 'He still has a pulse,' she said. 'Give him to me.' Tyrone transferred the limp body to Mia and she gathered Luke into her arms and closed her eyes, drawing a long, steady breath. Dax, Gideon, and Tyrone waited, the world around them suspended. Was it too late?

'So little left,' murmured Mia, her eyes still closed but her features awash with anger. 'She left you so little to live on.'

Dax stared intently at Luke's face and noticed a tiny bloom of pink below the boy's left eye. At first he thought it must be a bruise, but then the bloom spread and flowed across Luke's cheek like a tide of pink watercolour. Dax laughed out loud. 'You're doing it! Mia—you're doing it!'

Gideon clutched at his shoulder. 'We're not too late?' he asked. 'We've saved him?'

Luke's right hand twitched. His legs moved. He coughed.

'We're not too late!' cried out Gideon.

Luke opened his eyes and smiled at his brother.

A patrol of four men arrived within five minutes, running up through the trees from the lakeside where the helicopter had landed, bringing medical supplies. They were wearing weird all-in-one white suits and masks. They approached Catherine's body as if it were an unexploded bomb.

Her lifeless form was loaded onto a stretcher and strapped in place. Luke was also put onto a stretcher and strapped but he was far from lifeless. He hadn't spoken but he kept smiling and smiling and even weakly waving at them. His delight and relief were obvious. Then they were all taken back through the trees to the helicopter which crouched beside the water like a huge grey cricket, thrumming in the early evening sun. A few tourists were standing at a distance, staring and taking photos. On board, the stretchers were harnessed securely to the floor and they were all brought inside and strapped in along hard benches within the body of the aircraft.

Owen sat next to Dax and gave him a strange foil pouch. 'Energy gel,' he shouted, above the noise of the rotors as the chopper rose into the air. 'Get it down you *now*!' Dax broke the seal and gulped down the strange jelly-like drink, which tasted of slightly salty raspberries and rippled coolly down his throat. He felt the effect of it almost instantly and no longer feared that he might pass out at any time. Owen had picked him up and carried him back through the woods and Dax hadn't even had the strength to protest. Mia took an energy gel pack too, and gratefully drank it down.

Tyrone and Gideon were opposite, keeping an eye on Luke, whose stretcher was close by. Luke was still smiling, his eyes fluttering open and shut. Mia, sitting to Dax's right, finished her drink and glanced from time to time, shuddering, at Catherine's still body, at her feet on the stretcher. Francine slumped at the far end of the opposite bench, her eyes dull and her hair hanging like seaweed around her face. Dax felt desperately sorry for her and leaned across and shouted above the noise. 'It wasn't your fault, you know. She did the same with everyone. You weren't to know.' Francine said nothing. 'You saved my life!' added Dax and she looked at him and then at Catherine, and her eyes closed in misery.

Chambers was also on board and soon joined them, sitting between Dax and Owen, to be brought up to date with what had happened.

'You took your time,' said Owen. 'Where were you?'

'Well, after you all so kindly abandoned me at the airport I had to get the Ministry involved,' said Chambers. 'And then we had to strike a deal with the French and share some information. You may have noticed that we are in the company of the DST.'

Owen looked grim. 'Just what we needed! The French secret service all over our business.'

'Nothing else for it, not after Gideon and Tyrone's little show. You're lucky they didn't shoot you all on sight.'

The energy gel made Dax feel much, much better. So did Owen's voice. He sank back against the curved metal interior of the helicopter and allowed his eyes to close. How long since he had slept—if you didn't count the bit when he was nearly dead? Many, many hours.

Feeling safe at last, Dax drifted away into dreams of the tree house and the fells and le Mont-Saint-Michel and a particularly delicious Bakewell tart that Mrs P had made him. Catherine wanted some of the pudding but Dax was telling her that she couldn't taste it anyway. You couldn't eat stuff when you were dead. Catherine laughed and said 'Oh, that doesn't apply to me!' and dabbed at the tart with her fingers. Dax was annoyed with her, because he didn't want to eat it now.

'Get your fingers off!' he said. 'You're spoiling it. Get them *off*!'

He drifted awake, having slid sideways onto the bench a little, as far as he could in his harness. Mia had edged along a bit to make space for him. He drifted back down into sleep despite the thundering of the aircraft and still Catherine was digging into the white icing. He could see her fingers running along it and poking at it. He *could* see her fingers—running along Mia's white trainers. Dax's eyes shot wide in horror, as he realized he was no longer dreaming.

A second later the helicopter tipped violently sideways.

28

The aircraft dropped with a terrifying lurch that made Dax cry out in fear, but his eyes remained riveted on Catherine's hand clenched over Mia's right foot. In the sudden panic, nobody else seemed to notice, not even Mia. But as the helicopter tipped back upright and then lurched a second time, now tipping forward as if teased by some giant playful puppet master, Dax gripped his harness and stared at Catherine's ribcage where the neat red gunshot wound was beginning to reduce in size behind her torn yellow dress. Catherine's eyes were closed and her face unmoving, but her hand still clutched Mia's foot. Dax shouted out. 'MIA! Your foot! Get her off it!' But this was lost in the scared shouts as another jolt hit the aircraft.

'What the hell's going on?' yelled Chambers, but the pilots were urgently attending to their controls.

A fourth lurch sent the machine into a sickening spin and everyone grimly hung on to their harnesses, too scared to even shout. The French agents, in their white suits, clung to the walls and bellowed words he didn't understand, but Dax could see the flash of fear in their eyes, in spite of his mask.

'*A terre! A terre!*' Owen's French cut through the roar. '*Il faut descendre MAINTENANT!*'

Dax glanced through to the window ahead of him and saw they were back over the wide stretch of coast that was known as 'the polders'; the pilots set to getting the aircraft down onto the sand flats. Gideon, Mia, Luke, and Tyrone all had their eyes screwed shut, but Dax could not tear his own from the dead girl who was healing herself on the helicopter floor.

He shouted a warning again, and shook Mia, but she was too scared by their terrifying descent to unlock her eyelids. 'Hold on, Dax! Just hold on!' she cried out, but she couldn't see what he could see. Catherine's eyes were now open just a slit—just enough to watch the chaos—and a small smile was slithering along her lips. He shoved at Owen and then saw that Owen was already staring at Catherine in grim awareness. Dax reached to tear Catherine's hand away from Mia's foot, but Owen grabbed his arm and hauled him back.

'No!' he yelled, against the anguished metallic screams coming from the aircraft all around them. 'Not you!'

Of its own accord, Catherine's hand fell limply away from Mia, shaken by the chopper's violent descent through the sky, but the work was done. Mia was pale and hanging in her harness, but she was still conscious and breathing. Now Dax and Owen noticed something else. Catherine's foot had slipped out of its muddy leather sandal and was pressed hard against Gideon's leg. Gideon too, was oblivious. He gripped his hands tightly around his harness and screwed his eyes shut against the terror unfolding around him, and had no clue that his sister still lived and was even now drinking power out of him to seize control of the helicopter.

Owen lunged forward and hauled Catherine's foot off Gideon and almost immediately the aircraft stabilized. A few seconds later they had landed and Owen was shouting 'Out! Everybody get out!'

They were helped out of their harnesses and everyone stumbled outside, except Owen, Chambers, and one of the French agents. First they emerged carrying Luke, and a minute or two later, they brought out Catherine's stretcher. 'Don't touch her! Not even with gloves!' commanded Owen, and repeated it in French.

Francine stood a few feet away with one of the French agents, hugging her arms around herself and gasping with shock. Mia and Gideon were slumped on the sand. Dax knelt down by them. 'Didn't you see? Didn't you see?' he gasped and they looked at him, white and shocked. 'It was Catherine! Catherine! *Look!*'

Both stretchers had been laid on the sand. Luke was awake, looking rather sick, but OK. Catherine was simply gazing across at them, smiling. As they stared at her in horror, Catherine moved her head round and stared up imploringly at one of the white-suited agents.

'Please help me,' she gasped. 'I seek the protection of France.'

The agent took off his mask and head-covering and stared at her. She repeated her plea in French. *'Veuillez m'aider. Je cherche la protection de la France.'*

Her green eyes were dazzling and her plea so heart-wrenching. Dax knew she was using her strongest power of all.

The agent looked at Owen and his face set. 'We will provide alternative transport to take you back. But the girl stays in France.'

'She is in the *care* of the Cola project,' said Owen.

'She is not British—you have no rights over her. She is a French citizen.'

'She *is* British,' said Owen. 'Although an American on her passport. And she belongs with us.'

'Arguing will get you nowhere, Hind,' said the Frenchman. 'You know it. Take your charges home. Look after your own; we will look after our little Lazarus.'

Owen shook his head, but Dax could tell he knew he was beaten. It was a rare thing to see. 'Fine. Take her—but you will need to be briefed. She is nothing that she seems. She needs to be kept in the most secure unit you have—and *no physical contact. Vous comprenez?*'

The Frenchman smiled. 'We understand, Mr Hind, and we thank you for your co-operation.'

At his feet, Catherine whispered, *'Merci, oh—merci,'* and turned her eyes triumphantly towards the party of Colas on the sand.

'This is not right,' said Mia, her voice low and cold. 'It's wrong. She should not be alive. This is not right.'

Catherine locked her smile on Mia. 'Thanks, sweetie!' she said. 'You really helped me out back there!'

'This—is—not—*right*!' Mia's voice deepened to a growl

that made Dax gasp and suddenly the air around him seemed to shake and there was a scream from Catherine. Mia barked out a single hard laugh but Catherine kept on screaming.

Her hair was on fire.

29

'Did her scalp come off in big burnt chunks, by any chance?' asked Lisa, picking up a bit of toast and marmalade.

'No,' said Gideon. 'They scooped up sand and put it out really fast. All her hair was pretty much gone, but there wasn't any serious damage to her head.'

'Shame. I would've liked to have seen that.'

'You're a bit sick really, aren't you?' said Gideon and she shrugged.

'She had it coming. How did it happen?'

Dax and Gideon looked at each other. 'They reckon it was the helicopter fuel leaking out and a stray spark.'

Lisa looked at them. 'But you don't . . . ?'

'I don't know,' mumbled Dax. The alternative was too frightening.

Lisa read him and nodded. 'Let's just leave that bit for now,' she said. 'I still can't believe Catherine brought herself back from the dead; now that *is* scary.'

Dax shook his head. 'No—Owen reckons she never was dead. She just decided to play dead and she had enough power left and enough sense to slow her heartbeat right down to about a beat per minute. It's happened before—with ordinary people. It's very rare, but some people can control their pulse.'

'But she could heal herself,' said Lisa. 'I mean, she did that back at Tregarren College, didn't she? That time in the woods. She nicked a bit of healing power off Mia and then cut her arm and healed it, just for fun. And there's nobody else we know who can do that. I still say they should've shot her again. She's too dangerous. I wish Mia had *totally* torched her—after what she did.' She glanced at Dax's arms, where two ragged red scars were still vivid on his skin and then looked up at both of them, realizing she had said out loud what they had all been thinking.

'Who would ever have thought it?' murmured Gideon. 'Mia setting fire to someone. Even someone like Catherine! It's scary. I thought there was nothing but sweet and good stuff in Mia.'

'None of us are all sweet and good and nothing else,' said Lisa. Her eyes went to the window. Classes had been cancelled for the day and outside most of the other Colas were clambering about in the adventure playground, looking for all the world like normal children. 'But it is a bit of a shock, I admit. Is she still up with Janey?'

'Yeah,' said Dax. 'She's sleeping for a while, getting some of her strength back. She didn't say a word all the way back on the plane. She just closed up. I think she might be in shock at what she did.'

'I don't think so,' said Lisa, unexpectedly. Dax and Gideon looked at her curiously, across their breakfast, which had been laid on for them extra late so they could sleep in after flying back in to England in the early hours.

Lisa had waited to join them and hear the story of their adventures in France.

'It's about the black obsidian,' said Lisa. 'Wait here—I'll explain.' She ran out of the dining room, leaving Dax and Gideon shrugging at each other.

'You all right now, mate?' said Gideon, as they waited.

'Yup. They put some A-Positive in me on the plane,' said Dax. 'That was why I couldn't sit with you. Having my blood put back in. Well—*someone's* blood. I feel great now.'

Gideon also looked at his arms and did not seem convinced. 'What really happened to you at that place?' he said.

Dax tried to concentrate on his porridge and brown sugar. 'Oh—you know ...' The image of the world spinning sickeningly flared in his mind.

'Can't you tell me?' said Gideon.

'Yeah—I will. Just give me a while, OK? I need to not think about it for a while.'

Lisa returned at that point, carrying *The Crystal Directory*. She sat down at the table and laid the book open at a page with a black stone on it. 'Black obsidian,' she said. 'That's the stone Mia chose for her bracelet. She chose moonstone for me.' Lisa turned her wrist and the pale milky-blue stone glowed on it. 'And that's because she thought I needed to be a bit nicer to spirits. Moonstone is supposed to "encourage acceptance of psychic gifts"—it's also meant, as you *know*, to make me less stroppy.'

'Has it?' Gideon leaned forward, cautiously, and Lisa narrowed her eyes at him.

'I seriously doubt it,' she said. 'Anyway—Dax's is the stone of transformation. That's malachite. All good stuff, but apparently it can bring up some nasty home truths. And you've had a few of them, eh, Dax? After Gina and Alice arrived?' Dax nodded. 'Gideon's is serpentine— for warding off parasites. Mia chose that very carefully, I reckon. It also holds off psychic attack and it's a really comforting stone and, tell me if I'm wrong, Gideon, but aren't you actually quite all right? I mean—considering all the stuff that happened in France?'

Gideon thought for a moment, his eyebrows raised, and then bit into his third bacon sandwich. 'Yeah— weckon wor wight!' he agreed.

'And so we come to black obsidian,' said Lisa, rather theatrically. 'Mia's choice for herself. I read this while you were all gallivanting around France, leaving me out! Now, you would think, being a healer, that Mia would want rose quartz or amethyst or something. Those are the really nice, sweet, healer-y stones. All pretty and kind, like Mia. But no. Mia went for black obsidian instead. And I know why. Thing is—she doesn't *need* any more healing power. She's got tonnes of it. What she needed was a sort of balance.

'She was getting really fed up with being the soft and sweet one all the time. All that fainting and fluttering about, and having to get rescued and everyone always being careful not to overstretch her—she really hated it.'

Dax and Gideon glanced at each other. This had never occurred to either of them.

'Black obsidian,' went on Lisa, 'is all about toughening up. I mean—yeah, it's good for all the psychic blah and all that—*but* what it does to the person that's wearing it, is make them more forceful, more likely to stand up for themselves, maybe even more selfish. Lets them get some anger out without being ashamed of it. It's a Strop Stone. Unlike mine, of course, which is a Be Nice To People Stone. Mia wanted to be able to get stroppy, and after what you've just told me I'd say black obsidian worked.'

Dax and Gideon stared first at Lisa and then at each other. Mia *choosing* to be stroppy—to toughen up. It was a very odd thought.

'It's a good thing for her,' said Lisa, closing the book. 'I think. But the pyrokinesis is a *bit* worrying.'

'Pyro-what?' mumbled Gideon.

'Pyrokinesis. She's turned into a fire-starter. I really hope that doesn't get her into trouble.'

They absorbed what Lisa was saying in silence. Dax remembered the time in D3, when they had just returned from talking to Luke, and Mia had been filled with fury about Catherine pulling out his tongue. First Mia's eyes had turned black and then she had held Dax off from going to her and then the light had caught fire. It was starting even then, no matter what Mrs Sartre had said about the candles.

'I think she might have just joined the Dangerous Crew,' said Gideon. 'Better hope she hasn't got to walk around with fire extinguishers trained on her for the rest of her life.'

'It's all gone,' said Mia, curled into the armchair in the common room that afternoon. 'Whatever it was inside me that made that happen—it's all gone now. I couldn't do it again if I tried. It was a one-off.'

Dax and Gideon sat on the couch opposite her and Lisa perched on the arm of the chair. She patted Mia's head. 'Good. Can't have you scorching my nice T-shirts every time you get jealous,' she said. Mia smiled. She looked calm and rested after a long sleep, overseen by Janey in the medical room. They had kept Luke in a bed some distance from her, to be sure she didn't inadvertently send healing to him while she was needing to regain her strength. Dax had a feeling that this wouldn't have happened now. Not with Mia Mark Two.

As the day went on, the other Colas came and asked Dax or Gideon what had happened (except Spook, who kept his distance). They told them the jist of it all, without much detail. For all of them, thought Dax, it was just too big and too awful to get their heads around.

'Frankly, I'm amazed you all got out of France!' said Clive, as he and Dax strolled around the lake that afternoon. 'The DST can be fearsome. You don't mess with them.'

'Who's the DST?' asked Dax, remembering that Chambers had called the white-suited men by the same initials.

'*Direction de la Surveillance du Territoire*,' said Clive, with a surprisingly good French accent. 'The Directorate of Territorial Security. Their secret service—their SAS—their top-ranking military. The big boys. I'm not a bit surprised they wouldn't let Catherine go. I would've thought they'd try to bag all of you.'

'I'm not sure they knew much about the rest of us,' said Dax. 'I mean, they must have known *something*, but only Catherine—and Mia—showed any Cola powers in front of them. And I don't think they knew it *was* Mia who set her hair on fire. They thought it was helicopter fuel and a spark. And of course, it *was* only Catherine who was begging for sanctuary in fluent French.'

Clive took him to the library and showed him his family tree chart, which he'd completed and put up on the wall. 'Look,' he said, 'it starts in 1614 with Clara Mont-Richardson and goes all the way through to the last time there was a family in this house. That was at the turn of the nineteenth to the twentieth century with the Jermyns. After then it was just left derelict for a while. Then it was used by the army in World War Two. Then it was a hostel in the sixties and then it went to rack and ruin again for years until they found it for Cola Club.'

Dax ran his finger down the graph paper and looked at all the names of people, long gone, who had walked and slept and eaten and loved and argued and played—and a good number died—here in the house he now knew as home. His fingertip came to rest on Robert Jermyn and his wife, Mary, and two children, James and Matilda. Mary, James, and Matilda had all died in the same year—

October 1907. And then Robert had followed in January 1908.

'What did they all die of?' he said.

'Oh, diphtheria,' said Clive airily. 'Loads of people died of it back then. Actually, though, there's no record of how Robert died—just his wife and children. Sad.'

'Mmmm,' said Dax. Something was stirring at the back of his mind. Something relevant that he couldn't place.

'Come on, Dax,' said Gideon, striding up beside him. 'Let's go and see how Luke's doing. Janey said we could pop in. I bet he's well bored, waiting for us. Nice chart, Clive.'

Leaving Clive in the library, they ran up the stairs, two at a time. Dax was feeling remarkably well considering that only a day earlier he had been on the point of death. Seeing Luke made him better still. The boy was a normal colour and his eyes were bright green and free of fear. He was wearing pyjamas and was tucked up comfortably in the bed that Dax had spent time in the previous winter. The only sign that he needed more care than the rest of them was the fine tube that was running into his left wrist, drip-feeding him with essential nutrients. Dax had had something similar attached to him to replace some of his lost blood during the plane trip back from France. Janey was reading at her desk in the corner. She gave them a welcome smile and told them not to wear Luke out.

Dax and Gideon told him about their day—that

Owen had gone back to France with Paulina Sartre that morning, to brief the French about Catherine and how to deal with her. Dax suspected the French were keen to find out a lot more about the other children they had met, and that Owen and Mrs Sartre would do their best not to tell them anything. Gideon told Luke about the theory of Catherine slowing down her pulse and not really being dead—and then about Mia and the black obsidian thing that Lisa had spoken about.

Luke lay back on his pillow and smiled. He didn't say anything.

At length, Gideon dropped his eyes and said, 'Luke—can you . . . *can* you speak?' Luke dropped his eyes too. He shook his head. 'Have you tried?' asked Gideon, earnestly. Luke nodded and then smiled again, sadly.

'Give it time,' said Janey, getting up and walking past them to the door. 'He'll talk again one day. I'm sure of it.' She went out.

Dax shivered. Luke still being mute was a chilling reminder of Catherine. Then Luke tapped Dax's arm and pointed over his shoulder, a look of recognition on his face. Dax turned and saw the pointing boy. This time he was just standing at the end of the bed, looking from Luke to Dax. Dax sighed.

'I'm sorry,' he said. 'I just don't understand what you want—do you, Luke?' He looked back at Luke who shook his head ruefully and shrugged.

'What are you two on about?' said Gideon. Dax explained about Pointing Boy as Gideon stared wildly about the room, trying to get a glimpse of the ghost. But the boy had faded even from Dax's view.

'Haven't you asked Lisa?' said Gideon.

'Yeah—but she had a queue of other spirits and ghosts waiting and wasn't that interested.'

'So what's in the wall then?' Gideon got up and started poking across the wallpaper.

'Nothing that I could see. I mean—it could be something from another dimension, that Pointing Boy can see but we can't.'

'Or it might be buried in the brick,' said Gideon, tapping along the paper. 'What could it be? If I had some idea I could probably make it move and we'd work out where it was.'

Dax thought hard. Luke was staring at him and he concentrated, trying to remember yesterday, when they were both almost dead and the spirit world had allowed them a 'visit' to that other dimension. Pointing Boy had sat beside them in the tree house and said something . . . and he'd been holding something that glinted. Dax shut his eyes and focused on the memory . . . there had been something curved in between the boy's fingers . . . and a chain of some kind, looped around his small thumb.

'A pocket watch,' he said, looking at Luke. 'I think it's a gold pocket watch.'

Luke frowned, also remembering, and then nodded.

'OK,' said Gideon, and began to focus hard on the wall above Luke's head. After a few seconds there was a faint scraping noise. Then a peak was suddenly knocked out into the wallpaper. 'Brilliant!' said Gideon. He pulled his folding knife from his pocket and cut a rough cross over the peaked wallpaper and a small shower of sand and lime cascaded from it, hitting Luke's shoulder. Gideon put his hand below the wounded wall, gave another mental tug, and then whooped with delight when something dropped into his palm.

'Here you go,' he said, and turned around to show them.

It *was* a gold pocket watch. Heavy and attached to a chain. The face was white and elaborately scrolled with Roman numerals. The hour, minute, and second hands were fine arrows of black metal, each with a gold tip, and the glass casing rose from the clock face in a shallow dome. Gideon put it onto Dax's hand, and he turned it over, fascinated. On the back were engraved letters— *RWJ*.

Dax felt his skin prickle and looked around to see Pointing Boy was back again. The boy rested his eyes on the watch and a sad smile lifted his pale face. He looked directly at Dax and he spoke. There was no sound but Dax could read his lips and in any case, he knew what he was going to say. As he had in the tree house, Pointing Boy said, silently, 'He doesn't come.' And then he vanished.

'No,' said Dax. 'He doesn't.' Suddenly a surge of meaning rushed into his head like an incoming tide. He set off to find Lisa, Gideon trailing after him, trying to get him to explain, but it was hard to explain when he didn't know it all yet. The letters on the watch made some sense though. First Dax went to the library and scanned the lower end of Clive's family tree chart. Yes—there it was.

'Robert William Jermyn—RWJ,' said Dax, aloud. Gideon peered at the chart and then at the watch.

'So who's Pointing Boy, then?'

Dax rested his finger on the last family entry; a final, sad, spur of ink. Matilda and James. 'I'm guessing James,' he said.

They found Lisa coming back after a late afternoon swim. She was emerging, her hair damp and her face pink, as they marched up the steps to the pool house. Dax showed her the watch and she made a *So what?* kind of face.

'The spirit man who's been bothering you,' began Dax.

'Which one?' she huffed.

'Listen—the one you said thought I could help him. The one who was looking for James,' said Dax. 'Said I had something in common with James. Have you seen him again?'

'Oh—*him*.' Lisa stopped and took a quick, surprised breath. 'Well, *he's* quick off the mark, I must say! He's just popped back in now.' She looked past Gideon's shoulder to the step below him and Gideon jumped uneasily to one side, looking round.

'His name is Robert Jermyn, isn't it?' said Dax.

Lisa looked surprised and then seemed to be consulting. She nodded. 'Yeah—why?'

'Well, he was right. I do have something in common

with James. Will you please sit down and talk to him properly, so we can sort this out?'

'Robert William Jermyn was the last of the gentry to live here,' said Lisa. 'He was a good man; his servants liked him. Good to the people who lived in his cottages and farmed his land. He was married to Mary and had two children—Matilda and James. He really loved them, but he spent a lot of time away on business in London. He says James missed him a lot. Robert had some problems with his money and had to do a lot of legal stuff, I think. I'm seeing piles of documents and pens and stuff.

'He loved this place, but he wasn't around much here—he couldn't be because of all the money problems. He . . . oh . . . I see the watch now. The last time he saw his family, he gave it to James to keep safe. He said it was his job to look after it, as the man of the house, until he got back from London and James said he'd put it somewhere safe.

'It was a bad time in the country around here—lots of illness. The mother and the kids got ill . . . diphtheria. The mum and daughter died first, and James two days after them, just a day before his dad got back. That's why Robert's always trying to find him. He promised he'd come back and he did. But it was too late and he feels like he broke his promise to his son. Even after he died—and he really died of sadness—he went on feeling so bad. He really should have met up with James and sorted it out by now.'

Dax felt his throat close up and his eyes went blurry. 'Wait there,' he said, and walked swiftly across the grass towards the edge of the wood and the tree house. At the foot of the ladder he closed his eyes. 'Come on, now,' he said, out loud. When he opened them, to his surprise, Pointing Boy had obeyed. He stood in the soft green-gold light, making no indent on the leafy ground. 'I shouldn't have said that to you—last time,' said Dax. 'I shouldn't have said *they don't come*. Your dad *did* come. He's over there and he's waiting for you.' Pointing Boy turned, so very ghostlike in his white nightgown, and looked. 'See that girl? She's your way through to your dad.' Pointing Boy looked back at him and a radiant smile lit up his features.

'What do you want me to do with this watch?' said Dax, and the boy pointed once more, this time at *him*, and grinned. 'Thanks,' said Dax. 'I'll keep it to give to . . . to my dad. It's the same initials for him, see? Robert William Jones. I'll give it to him. When he comes.'

The boy simply slipped out of sight. Dax walked back to Lisa and Gideon, to find Lisa scrubbing hard at her face with the corner of her swimming towel. Gideon pulled a warning face.

Lisa sniffed sharply and got up. 'All sorted,' she said.

Dax stopped her walking away. 'Tell me!' he said.

She sighed and her voice wobbled as she explained: 'They found each other! It's kind of . . . you know . . . kind of sweet. James wanted his dad to know that he *had* taken care of his watch—he'd hidden it behind a loose brick in his bedroom. That's what *he* was worried about. Anyway, it's all sorted now. Big hug and then . . . gone.' She sniffed again and Dax realized he was beaming at her. 'Don't know why they had to keep bothering you, though,' said Lisa, clearly forgetting that she had largely ignored Robert Jermyn for several days. 'I don't know what made him think you'd understand James better than I would.'

'No,' said Dax. 'Can't imagine.'

30

Owen had made a fire in his room. Sticks and logs and a small hill of coal glowed red and gave off the occasional crackle, throwing shadows around the furniture and bookcase. The smell of roasting applewood was wonderful.

Owen sat back in the corner of one of the couches, cradling a mug of tea and looking tired. He had arrived back from France only two hours ago, too late to eat dinner with them.

'He will come, you know, Dax. I'm sure he will. Your dad loves you.'

Dax ran his finger across the malachite stone on his wrist and thought about transformation. It wasn't just a shapeshifting thing, he realized. He had changed in other ways. He had faced up to Gina and what she really felt about him and he had also had to accept the hard fact that although his dad loved him, he wouldn't dash from one end of the country to the other for him. Wouldn't even pick up the phone, in fact.

'Yeah, I know he loves me,' Dax said. 'For what it's worth.'

Owen said nothing. Perhaps he had picked up Dax's thoughts in one of his empathic flashes. At length, he

269

coughed and said, in a teacher-like voice, 'I called you up here to tell you that you are grounded, Dax Jones.' Dax sat back in his own corner of the couch in surprise.

'I had Gideon up earlier, and Spook. They're both grounded too. No trips outside the college for six weeks and no Cola allowance money for six weeks either.'

'But—'

'No buts! It's nothing less than you all deserve. Gideon totally disobeyed me and Spook helped him. Then you broke all the rules too. I can't allow this to continue . . . especially not now.'

Dax bit his lip. Owen put down his mug and leaned his elbows onto his knees, regarding his grounded student intently.

'It's *out* now, do you see, Dax? Catherine is being held by the French—at her own insistence. They have Francine too. *If* nobody touches Catherine—and that's a big *if*—she'll just go back to being ordinary. There are no other Colas around her now, so she's not likely to pick up anything too extraordinary. But the DST will study her and test her and I am sure she will tell them everything she can about the Colas. So—it's out now. We've struggled for two years to keep you all a secret from the big bad world, but we've failed.'

Dax felt a pang of guilt. He hadn't helped. He hung his head.

'Don't look so bleak, Dax,' sighed Owen, and the teacher tone had left his voice. 'It was only ever a matter of time. You're all too—too incredible to keep quiet for ever. But you see now, don't you, why it's so important to keep you all safe, *here*, under your own country's protection? People all over the planet are going to want you. And you wouldn't like what they'll want you *for*.

'Promise me you won't do anything like this again. Please. Promise me.'

Dax nodded. He realized that Owen was looking at him curiously and then dropped his eyes to his left arm. He had been rubbing the livid red wound on it, without knowing he was doing it.

'What *did* she do to you, Dax?'

Dax sank back further into the couch.

Owen took a sharp breath and spoke through a clenched fist across his mouth. 'It looked like she'd crucified you.'

'Well,' Dax tried to laugh, 'it wasn't *quite* like that . . . '

The man opposite him stood and walked to his window, where the sky was now dark velvet blue and bats swooped between the house and the trees. He rested one arm against the open sash and stared outside. 'If I get the chance, Dax, you have to know, I *will* kill her.'

A shiver ran up Dax's spine. Not because he was shocked by what Owen said, but because he knew he would do the same.

'Go on,' said Owen, turning back into the room. 'Get to bed. You've got lessons in the morning.'

Dax laughed out loud, it was so absurd.

'Come join the Cola Club,' he said. 'Visit the dead, lose most of your blood, fight with killer triplets, and do favours for ghosts—and then double maths in the morning.'

31

The girl kept her eyes closed; her bright green gaze shielded against the white light. She felt no pain, only anger that smouldered and lay twisted inside her, like the little remaining hair on her head.

'Come on, Catherine. Speak to me,' said the man in a dark suit, while the woman beside her bed wrote across a clipboard with a scratchy pen. 'Speak to me and I'll make everything better.'

The woman sighed, turned away and spoke to him in Spanish. They didn't want her to understand. But they hadn't noticed, when the girl moved in the hospital bed, that her hand trailed off to one side and brushed ever so gently against the woman's shoulder.

'Oh, I've had enough of this,' said the woman. 'She needs more rest. And so do I. I have such a headache.' She got up to go and then spun back when Catherine whispered: '¡Espere! Tengo cosas que decirle . . .'

'Wait! I have things to tell you . . .'

ACKNOWLEDGEMENTS

With huge thanks to David and Mary Kingston, Kelvin Woodage at the Allsorts Psychic Café, Southampton, Andy Hinton at the Hawk Conservancy, Weyhill, and David Adcock (*mon professeur*) for his help in France, and whoever—or whatever—planted all that mistletoe in Brittany.

ALI SPARKES

Ali Sparkes was a journalist and BBC broadcaster until she chucked in the safe job to go dangerously freelance and try her hand at writing comedy scripts. Her first venture was as a comedy columnist on *Woman's Hour* and later on *Home Truths*. Not long after, she discovered her real love was writing children's fiction.

Ali grew up adoring adventure stories about kids who mess about in the woods and still likes to mess about in the woods herself whenever possible. She lives with her husband and two sons in Southampton, England.

1

The snow glowed in the half-moon light, a glittering white quilt across the valley. It covered hedges, softened walls, delicately mantled the trees, and drifted across the frozen lake in tapering fingers.

Only one set of tracks could be seen marking the whiteness; tracing a path around the handsome stately house, skirting the frozen water, and then heading straight for the frosted woodland.

A fox, sending a flurry of fear through the winter wildlife, was trotting swiftly west.

Dax Jones reached the first few slender young oaks at the edge of the copse and lifted his snout. It was a fantastic night to be a fox. As soon as he'd smelt the snow coming, early that afternoon, the hair on the backs of his arms had stood up and he'd said to Gideon, 'It'll be here by four o'clock! You wait! And by midnight it will be thick all over the fells. We have to go out in it! We can be the first ones to walk in it!'

But when it came to rousing Gideon, the boy had hidden his messy blond head under the duvet and groaned. 'Can't . . . too tired . . . you go, Dax. Tell me what it's like when you get back.'

Dax had shoved him and muttered, 'You know your problem, Gid—you've got no sense of adventure!'

Gideon had snorted, 'Yeah right!' and Dax had grinned, shaken his head, and leaped nimbly onto the windowsill, pulling up the sash and surveying the wondrous scene below.

Now he was part of it. He could have been crunching heavy boot-shaped indents into the cold sugary crust over the grass—but the light touch of his paws on the snow was delightful to him. One of the best things about being a shapeshifter was that he could experience the world three different ways—as a boy, as a fox, and, if he felt like it, as a falcon. Tonight though, in this strange white world, nothing could beat being a fox. Dax streaked across the temporary tundra and deep into the woods, where the snow was lighter, blown in sideways by the wind and powdering down softly between the branches to pick out twig and leaf and berry in silveryblue highlights. The wildlife tensed, but he was not out to hunt tonight. There was no need. And the smaller creatures could smell this too. Voles and mice moved judiciously away into the undergrowth, but soon relaxed. Dax walked on, passing the badger sett and nodding at the snout of the chief badger boar, just emerging to check out the snow for himself. The badger regarded him for a moment, gave a small grunt of recognition and ambled on out into the moonlight, his striped head turning left and right, sniffing the chilled air.

Dax wished, for the hundredth time, that he was able to actually have a conversation with other animals. He could communicate with them, but it was mostly about body posture and scent and the occasional telepathic flash. He had worked out a few months ago that the badgers were quite relaxed around him. He had even gone down into their sett once and found them all staring at him in surprise, but without hostility. Rather like polite relatives who had been visited without warning by a distant cousin. They knew the fox was no threat to them; although Dax walked through his little wood as king—there was no predator higher than he—he'd never be idiot enough to take on a badger.

He was drawn back to the edges of the woodland by the promise of deeper, more luxurious snow to bound through. Leaping from a fallen log, he found himself engulfed up to his furry chin. He couldn't help laughing out loud—a light volley of happy barks. He rolled over onto his back, collecting white flakes on his thick winter coat. Then he was suddenly on his feet again, stock still. Scenting. Listening. Watching. Something was coming.

At the perimeter wall, a quarter of a mile away, a shaft of golden light opened up. The electric gate was moving. A black vehicle was coming in. Dax swiftly turned and jumped back on to the log, where he shifted instantly to a peregrine falcon; sharp round eyes glittering black in pools of yellow. In a blink his vision had improved tenfold. With no difficulty at all he made out a soldier at the booth leaning out towards the car, rifle held across his chest, nodding and in conversation with the driver. The driver's hand, gloveless and large, patted the sentry on the shoulder before withdrawing, and the black four-by-four moved on, following the wide gravel driveway up to the lodge, as the electric gate slid shut behind it.

Who was out this late? wondered Dax. It must be getting on for 1 a.m. Even the scientists were normally tucked up in bed by now. He shivered and felt a tickly sensation at the back of his neck. He'd felt that a few times recently and wondered if it was some kind of warning. But nothing in his life at the moment suggested any trouble coming. There'd been plenty of it over the last couple of years, but for nearly eight months he and all the other Children of Limitless Ability here at Fenton Lodge had simply got on with schoolwork and play and arguing and mucking around without interruption—unless you counted a rather heavy cold they'd all managed to get in the last couple of weeks. No—it had all been pretty normal. Well, as normal as it got when you were a Cola.

Dax thought about flying after the car to find out who it was, but it was too cold. Peregrines are not night fliers even in the summer, when a few leftover warm thermals from the day might still be creating a bit of uplift. Here in the deeply chilled Cumbrian hills of January, he could manage a swift wing up and down from his bedroom window, but more than that would be folly. He decided to leave the late night driver to his own business, and have a bit more snow play. The glazed lake was calling to him. They'd all been forbidden to go on it by Mrs Sartre, the college principal, even though for days the smooth sheet of ice had looked about a foot thick, and startled geese kept sleighing across it in confusion whenever they tried to land. As a fox, Dax didn't weigh a third as much as he did in boy form, so he was more than happy to take the risk. Grinning to himself, he made his way ungracefully through the snow, lurching this way and that in the drifts. He wished Gideon was out with him to see this, but at least he wouldn't have to feel guilty about not letting his mate follow him out on to the ice.

The glistening sheet sent prickles of shock into the pads of his paws, even though they'd already been numbed by the cold of the snow. Dax gasped and then he chuckled; a raspy, growly sort of noise, and put all four paws onto the ice, claws digging in to stop himself sliding. There was no crack—no noise at all. And later he was to wonder why he didn't hear the man coming, given that his fox ears were so incredibly sensitive. All he knew was that five seconds later a white shape descended upon him and seized him so fast and so silently that he had no time to even glance around. He heard his sharp teeth clack together as a hand efficiently snapped his shocked muzzle shut; felt himself lifted expertly and pinned to the chest of his assailant, and before he'd even had the chance to growl he was borne with great speed back towards the wood he had just left.

Panic would have had him screaming and snarling if he had not been able to call now—a little late—upon his senses. He knew who this was, and the knowledge stunned him into silence. Deep inside the wood he was at last deposited on the floor.

HAVE YOU READ THEM ALL?

THE SHAPESHIFTER